THE SECOND WAVE

Tom Reynolds

"But man is not made for defeat. A man can be destroyed but not defeated."
Ernest Hemingway, The Old Man and the Sea

ONE

Anyone who tells you that they'd choose invisibility over flying is an idiot, a liar, or a creep.

Seriously though, what good is invisibility? It sounds good in theory, but what are you really going to do with it? Sneak into the girls' locker room? Do you have any idea how many people have that exact idea now that there are literally thousands and thousands of people on Earth who have metabands? In the first week the metabands fell from the sky, there were so many "incidents" that most of the gyms around the country had to temporarily close to retrofit their locker rooms so they would be harder for the new Invisibles to sneak into.

The saddest part is that a lot of the incidents didn't just involve someone getting caught; people were actually hurting themselves. Being invisible sounds like a great idea until someone opens a door in your face, or walks into you from behind because they can't see you, and both of you go toppling onto a wet tile floor. Nothing's creepier than watching blood seemingly appear out of nowhere, pooling around a shower drain.

So what about the Invisibles who aren't huge pervs? Even they have very few legitimate reasons to use their powers for the greater good. Outside of being a creeper, the other popular use for invisibility is theft. The problem with that is, along with it being illegal, most Invisibles don't think ahead about what they're going to do with the loot once they've reached it. Unless you're not concerned about someone seeing expensive necklaces and rings floating themselves out of a jewelry store, you've got to find a way to hide them. You don't want to know where the best places to hide jewelry are if you're an Invisible who already has a mouth full of expensive watches.

1

In the first month alone, there were three separate cases of Invisibles locking themselves inside a bank vault, and being forced to call the police before the oxygen inside the locked safe ran out. Again, you really don't want to know where they were keeping their cell phones. The lucky ones had the foresight to bring a cell phone. Some Invisibles weren't discovered until someone tried to figure out why the bank vault suddenly had a pungent odor. Today, even the lowest budget banks have basic lasers set up to detect movement inside the vaults. They've had no choice but to install the lasers. Insurance premiums have gone up a lot because of the dummies who locked themselves in and weren't found until a bank employee tripped over their invisible body a week later.

On the opposite side of the power spectrum, there's flying, and let me tell you: flying is awesome. Correction: flying, plus super-speed, plus some level of invulnerability equals awesome. The invulnerability thing speaks for itself, I think. Obviously, flying isn't as much fun if you have to spend the entire time worrying about colliding with a pigeon at five hundred miles per hour. The speed thing isn't one that a lot of people think about, but if you don't have the ability to move quickly, flying becomes real boring, real fast. Aside from being able to snap some great pictures of the city, you're basically relegated to being a human blimp if you can't fly faster than you can walk. Not that there's any shame in that. There are quite a few lucky metaband finders who are actually making very good livings holding up huge advertising billboards high above the city.

I'm lucky because my metabands happened to give me all three of these abilities, along with a whole bunch of others. One of my abilities is enhanced vision, and it's the ability I'm currently using as I fly over Bay View City, looking for any kind of trouble being caused by the thousands of new metas attempting to use their new abilities to cash in somehow. It doesn't take long before I find some.

About a thousand feet below me, I can see what is clearly a bank heist taking place. It's probably the most cliché and obvious of all the moneymaking schemes that the more villainous metahumans have taken up. The bank itself is relatively small, but that actually makes it a better target considering most of the larger banks have installed an array of anti-meta measures beyond the laser-activated alarm systems. Most don't even keep cash on the premises any more.

Outside the bank, I can easily spot an eight-foot-tall Brute. Brutes are what the world has started calling metas whose abilities are mainly related to strength and invulnerability. Underneath his fire-engine-red, skin-tight suit is what looks less like muscle and more like poured concrete. His intensely mean-looking face appears as though it has been chiseled out of granite, and not by someone who was a particularly skilled sculptor. He stands, looking back and forth, cracking his knuckles over and over. He must be the lookout for whoever is inside, busy looting the minuscule bank of whatever tiny fortune is inside their vault. Regardless of the approach I take, I'm going to have to deal with this guy at some point, so I might as well get it out of the way.

"Hey, Handsome!" I yell to grab his attention. "Up here. The guy wearing the red tights. Name's Omni. What's yours?"

The Brute slowly turns his gaze skyward, taking a second or two to find me hovering against the backdrop of the city. By the time he has a fix on my position, it's too late for him as I'm already flying as fast I can with my fists out in front of me, ready to barrel into him. And I do barrel into him. The only problem is that it doesn't seem to really have much of an effect. Bouncing off his chest, I stumble about a hundred feet or so down the quiet commercial street, past stores that have long since closed for the night. The Brute grins at me, showing me a mouthful of mangled teeth.

"All right then. Let's try this another way," I yell down the street as I run toward him.I mean, I assume it's a him; if it's not, yikes.

I strike him square in the ribcage with the hardest punch I can muster. He just laughs and punches me in retaliation, not putting any of his weight behind it. Again, I find myself tumbling down the street. Even for a Brute, this guy is pretty strong and might require a little more tact.

He slowly marches toward me, and the city concrete trembles under the force of each step. My eyesight changes and a red haze comes over everything. It's not anger that clouds my vision, though; it's heat. Heat that I release with just a thought, aimed squarely at the Brute's chest. He stumbles backward, almost falling to his knees, before once again finding his footing and marching toward me. I intensify the heat I'm directing at him, and while it seems to be slowing him down, it is certainly not stopping him.

"You think your flashy powers can hurt Malfour?" the Brute asks in a voice that is so gravely and low that it'd be comical if he weren't trying his damnedest to kill me. But he's partially right. This guy doesn't seem like he has many powers beyond being incredibly strong and impervious to damage, but he's definitely stronger than me. I won't be able to beat him in a slugfest.

He's within twenty feet of me, still pushing against the heat vision I'm trying to bore through his chest, when I find a question to ask him.

"All right, 'Malfour,'" I begin, my voice dripping with sarcasm at the stupid name he's chosen for himself. "You're strong, I'll give you that. But let me ask you this: can you fly?"

"Fly? Ha!" Malfour laughs. "Why would I need to fly when—"

"That's all I needed to know," I say, cutting him off as I lunge for the lapels of his costume.

The look of confusion on his face is priceless as I bend my knees, gather my strength, and throw Malfour straight up into the air as hard as I possibly can. He's out of eyeshot before he even has a chance to scream. If I can't beat this guy up, I can at least throw him a few miles into the sky to keep him out of my hair for while I deal with whatever problem is waiting for me inside the bank. Maybe he'll use the time it takes to fall back to Earth to take a good hard look at the life decisions that have created his current predicament.

I take a moment to quickly grab a couple of nearby traffic cones and cordon off a roughly ten-foot area where I know he'll leave a crater when he lands. He'll be fine, but if someone is unlucky enough to be under him when he lands, they're going to be pancaked.

The bank itself is unusually quiet when I enter. The police scanner reported two Metas sighted at this location, so I know there's at least one other in here with me. I'm not sure how much he heard of the commotion outside, but on the off chance he didn't hear my little *skirmish*, I decide to play it as quiet as possible. My patience pays off when I find him.

He has his back to me, and he's intensely focused on the steel vault in front of him. It's no wonder he didn't hear me outside. Blue and white-hot flames shoot out in front of him from the palms of his outstretched hands. The flames cause loud, metallic screeches and scrapes as they slowly melt through the steel vault. Great. An Elemental. Elementals are annoying. They're a dime a dozen now that there's thousands of metas running all over the place, but I've yet to meet one that doesn't think they're special just because they can control fire or water. Great powers for showing off at a party, but in the real world, their powers tend to be fairly limited. The knucklehead in front of me is demonstrating this by trying to burn his way through a foot of steel with fire that isn't *nearly* hot enough, unless he has all day to sit here and wait. He'll catch the whole building on fire before he gets through three inches of that door.

"Ahem," I cough to get his attention.

The Elemental turns toward me, a little startled. As his gaze turns, so does the blue and white fire shooting out of his hands. Maybe all Elementals aren't all talk, though, because the flames coming out of this one's hands just threw me straight through a loan officer's cubicle, the nearest wall, and into the street outside.

Rising to my feet and trying to clear the cobwebs out of my head, I see the Elemental following me through the hole he, well I guess technically *I*, created. His face is expressionless as he walks toward me. I'm not too badly injured, but it's apparent that he sees me as little more than a temporary obstacle in his way to an easy fortune.

"Wait! Please!" I yell as I work to scramble away from him. "Don't come any closer."

He doesn't say a word. He just squints his eyes as though trying to figure out a calculus problem, or maybe it's algebra in his case. But he can't be *that* stupid. He knows I shouldn't be this scared of him considering I'm not visibly injured. Surely, he knows I must be trying to use reverse psychology in order to get him to come closer to me.

What he doesn't know is that I know that he knows what he *thinks* I'm doing. I'm using *reverse* reverse psychology, which I guess is a double negative, and maybe it's just "psychology?" I don't know. All I know is that he's exactly where I want him, and I only need him to stay there for a couple more seconds.

"Where's Malfour?" the fire Elemental asks, looking around the street.

"Oh, don't worry. He'll be back in ..."

There's only a hint of a scream before Malfour comes crashing out of the sky. He lands right inside the cones that I'd set up, and right on top of his would-be bank-robbing

6

accomplice. A huge plume of concrete, dust, and debris flies twenty-feet into the air, hitting a nearby traffic light and sending it into a nearby building.

Malfour's created a pretty large crater, and both of the metas are out cold.

"...no time flat," I finish. There's no response from the hole, and certainly not a laugh. "Dammit! I thought I had that timed out perfectly! 'He'll be back in *no time flat.*' Get it? He's huge, and he landed on you. Now you're squished flat ... like a pancake? Man, that would have been so perfect. Ugh. That's really going to bother me all night, guys. Thanks a lot," I say into the pit.

With a sigh, I concentrate and will part of my suit to retreat from around my pants pocket. I pull out a small metal and plastic electronic device with a numeric keypad. It looks more like an old school pager or calculator than a high tech security device, but I suppose that's partially the point. Tapping on the side of my cowl, I hear a beep, and I'm connected.

"Silver Island. Challenge code: 53252143," a voice on the other side of the connection says into my earpiece.

I tap the numbers into the electronic security cog I just pulled from my pocket and hit Enter. The display instantly updates with a new set of numbers.

"Omni. Response code: 93213532," I say.

"Access granted. Ready for incoming teleportation. Bay C, quadrant three, seven."

It might not seem very impressive, but the system works. There hasn't been one successful break-in to Silver Island since the second wave of metabands began appearing. Basically, once a "friendly" meta verifies his or her identity to security at Silver Island, a set of coordinates is given in return.

There are four bays located at each corner of the island's main security facility. Inside each bay is a grid of one hundred individual squares of solid steel columns. If a meta is cleared for access, one of the four hundred columns is lowered into the ground, and its coordinates are relayed to the meta. The meta teleports themselves and their arrest to the now-empty space. Once their identity is visually verified, additional columns are lowered to allow their entry into the receiving area of the facility.

Teleport yourself to a coordinate at random, and you've got a three hundred and ninety-nine in four hundred chance of finding yourself stuck inside a steel wall. Try to teleport yourself anywhere else inside the facility and the electromagnetic Faraday shield surrounding every building will bounce you right back out. For metas who can teleport, it's the quickest, easiest, and safest way inside Silver Island, and when you're transporting prisoners, those three things count for a lot.

Two

"Well, well, well. Look what the cat dragged in," Halpern says to me as the steel columns lower to offer a path to the receiving area. This is the place in Silver Island where all inmates go first. The room itself, if you can even call it that, is cavernous in size with a ceiling at least twenty feet high. Sounds echo endlessly against the unadorned steel walls. Hovering over the receiving area like a control tower is a glass-encased room full of computers and technicians. Their job is keeping an eye on the inmates already here and making sure new residents are "welcomed" without incident.

Halpern, or rather *Agent* Halpern, works for the M.O.N.I.T.O.R. What does M.O.N.I.T.O.R. stand for, you ask? Good question. Metahuman Observation and New Investigation Tactical and Operational Response. They're the multi-national government organization tasked with all things metahuman. Most people just refer to them as "The Agency" because for a long time, when the first metahumans arrived over a decade ago, they were so secret they didn't even have a name. If you ask me, nowadays, they keep the name "The Agency" around just because it lets every other government organization know exactly how important the world considers them in comparison.

Halpern is a white guy in his late forties who looks exactly like you would expect a government agent to look. While not especially tall, Halpern is in pretty good shape for a government agent. Must take advantage of the gym benefits. He might be in better shape than most guys his age, but a head full of graying hair shows the stress the job has put on him over the years.

The Agency is actually composed of many different organizations that all fall under its umbrella. Halpern works for Containment, the group in charge of confining rogue metas. Not an easy task by any means, but things have come a long way in a short time. Since the second wave of metabands began appearing, no prisoner has escaped from an Agency facility. Well, there hasn't been one that the rest of the world knows about, at least. That's the other thing about the Agency; they're very, very good at keeping secrets.

"Figured you were getting bored working these overnight shifts and you might want some new company," I say to Halpern as I drag Malfour and his Elemental partner behind me through the receiving area.

"Wow, two in one trip? Very nice work." Halpern gestures over to a dozen, heavily armored guards who move quickly to surround the metas I've dragged in.

"They've both had a pretty rough night. Metaband power levels should be down to stand-by mode," I tell Halpern. One of the few things known about metabands is that if a meta sustains enough damage while powered on, they'll be temporarily weakened until their bands have a chance to recharge. Then, the bands must be reactivated to fully bring them back online.

They charge using some form of energy we don't understand yet, or at least, that's what we all assume based on the fact that no one can figure out how they charge. Considering how no one had any idea how solar panels worked a hundred years ago, it's not too far-fetched to think there are other ways of gathering massive amounts of energy that we just haven't figured out yet.

"Good work, Omni," Halpern says to me. "Guess all there is to do now is read them their rights and ask them the question.

Gentlemen," Halpern begins before looking back at me. "They're both guys right?"

I shrug.

"Anyway, gentlemen, ladies, whichever you are. You have been detained by a government-authorized meta during an alleged attack on a federally-backed financial institution. You are hereby ordered to power down your metabands or face detainment," Halpern says to the barely conscious metas I've brought in.

The big one, Malfour, is the first to seem to process the question and reply. Fortunately for everyone, his reply is simple. He brings his fists up to his chest, connects his metabands, and deactivates them. Standing in front of us is no longer a hulking monster, but instead, a very scared looking young woman who appears to be barely out of college, if she's even that old.

"Drop your metabands! Drop them now!" one of the guards screams in her direction with the laser sight of his assault rifle aimed squarely at her forehead.

She reaches for the metaband on her right hand.

"Slowly!" another guard yells, his rifle also trained on her.

She jumps slightly at the order and slows down her movements. She slips the metaband off of her right wrist, and it hits the ground with a clang that reverberates throughout the steel and concrete structure.

"The other!" the first guard yells.

She nods and removes the metaband on her left hand. Before it has even hit the ground, a stun gun is fired, and she falls to the ground.

"Hey! She's complying! You didn't have to do that!" I yell at the guard.

He turns to me, and I see his eyes widen before I feel a blast of heat hit my back.

The Elemental's metabands have recharged enough to allow him to reactivate them. Alarms begin sounding throughout the facility as warning lights bathe the entire room in red. Stupid. I should have never turned my back on him. I need to incapacitate him before he hurts anyone here, or before they kill him.

I can hear the clicks of triggers being pulled fractions of a second before I react. I run toward the Elemental, driving him into the nearest wall. This accomplishes two things: First, it gets him out of the way of the hundreds of bullets, fired by the facility guards, about to rip him to shreds. Second, it knocks him out. Or at the very least, it disorientates him to the point where he can't use his powers.

This meta is a criminal, and there's no doubt about that. He tried to rob a bank that didn't belong to him, and he's done his best to hurt me in the process. Luckily for him, I decided not to carry a grudge and know that neither of those actions deserves execution by firing squad. He tried to hurt me, not the guards after all, and I can take it.

"Get him into the processing room, now!" Halpern yells at the guards who just put holes in the large, pristine white and stainless steel hall that we're in. "And get Rogers!"

The guards rush in and grab the nearly unconscious, would-be fire starter. They quickly lift him before running to a nearby room. The room is covered on all sides by glass with ceilings even higher than the hall we're currently in. I've heard stories about the processing room, but I've never seen it used.

A slender, middle-aged man enters the hall by himself, wearing a pair of khaki pants and a blue, oxford button-down shirt. He's skinny and bespectacled, wearing black, horn-rimmed eyeglasses. While he looks the part of a meek corporate drone, he walks with the kind of confidence and intent that suggests otherwise.

"What have we got?" Rogers asks Halpern without even glancing at me. As a guy wearing head-to-toe, red, skintight spandex and a mask, I'm not used to being so blatantly ignored. So whoever this guy is, he's either not impressed, or he's used to seeing metas in person.

"Maybe a level two Elemental. Fire equipped. Low-level invulnerability at best," Halpern replies.

"We'll try the soft touch first then," Rogers says as he

thrusts his arms out to summon a pair of metabands right before he brings them together to activate.

In an instant, he transforms into a monster. Literally. His face still bears a strong resemblance to his non-meta appearance, but his body is another story altogether. Muscles bulge across his body to the point where his pale white skin appears paper-thin. Muscles also bulge across the two new sets of arms that have sprouted from his torso. His skin writhes and pulsates across his new form, which now stands a good three feet taller than he did two seconds ago.

The guards clear a path, and Rogers enters the processing room. A solid glass door closes behind him as soon as he crosses the threshold. He moves slowly across the room to where the fire Elemental is lying on the ground, just beginning to regain consciousness and gather a sense of where he is.

Rogers moves slowly but deliberately toward him.

"You've never been here for one of these, have you?" Halpern turns to ask me. We're standing shoulder to shoulder on the other side of the glass that separates us from Rogers and the Elemental.

"No, I haven't."

"Let's get audio from that room," Halpern instructs one of the guards, who then hits a button inside a panel on the nearby wall.

"Under the Twenty-eighth Amendment to the Constitution of the United States of America, you are hereby ordered to remove your metabands. Failure to comply with this demand will result in the forfeiture of your Eighth Amendment rights with regard to cruel and unusual punishment for the purpose of securing your detention. Do you understand your rights as I have read them to you?" Rogers asks the fallen meta in a deep monotone growl that reverberates throughout the glass cage.

There's a long silence both inside the containment area

and in the hall where I'm standing. All that can be heard is the labored breathing of the fire Elemental, still lying in a heap in the far corner of the containment cell.

"Sir, do you understand your rights as I have read them to you?" Rogers asks again.

Without warning, the Elemental's breathing morphs into a scream as he turns to blast a wall of fire toward Rogers. I instinctively move toward the door, but a hand reaches out and grabs my arm, stopping me. The hand belongs to Halpern. He gives me a pensive look and shakes his head slowly, telling me with his eyes to not even think about it.

I turn back to the window of the cell where the fire is still raging, but slowly growing smaller as the Elemental depletes the last bit of energy in his metabands. The fire is still large enough to completely envelope Rogers to the point where he cannot even be seen from where I'm standing. And then suddenly, it stops. The Elemental collapses with a thud on the glass floor. Rogers emerges unscathed, and begins slowly walking toward him.

"I'll take that as a 'no' then," he growls. He's not amused. "Let's take the rest of the energy out of those bands, shall we?"

What follows is hard to watch. Rogers pummels the meta over and over again. The Elemental repeatedly tries to rise to his feet, only to then be bashed back to the ground by fists the size of basketballs.

"Stop resisting. Deactivate your metabands, immediately," Rogers barks, but the Elemental does not listen. He continues to try to get to his feet and return the attack.

Finally, when it seems as though I can't stand to watch this any longer, the Elemental's bands begin to glow red. They've been depleted and are in standby, or life support, mode. They will not allow the Elemental to use any of his powers until the bands have had time to recharge and are manually reactivated.

Rogers grabs both of the Elemental's wrists and pulls them as far apart as he can without ripping his arms out of their shoulder sockets. The doors to the glass cell fly open quickly, and the room is once again accessible to the outside world.

"Move! Move! Move!" an armed guard shouts from behind me. I step aside as a team sprints into the cell, holding various pieces of metallic hardware. Halpern casually follows them.

"It didn't have to be that way," he says with a sigh to the Elemental.

The Elemental's face is covered in blood. He doesn't even seem to have the strength to hold his head up and is only on his feet because Rogers is holding him there.

With the precision of a stock car pit crew, the guards quickly slip bulky cylindrical steel sleeves over the prisoner's forearms. The second they're in place, one set of guards moves out of the way as another set moves in, holding enormous drills that are already revving to make sure they're working and ready.

Without hesitation, the guards begin drilling screws through holes in the steel sleeves, directly into the Elemental's flesh. His head jerks up suddenly as he screams and writhes in pain. Rogers continues holding him by the arms, preventing him from moving, as the guards move their drills around the sleeves, driving screws through steel and into flesh. Once the screws are tightened, another guard moves forward with a blowtorch, which he uses to weld the screws in place, ensuring they can't be removed.

The Elemental is no longer screaming, but now softly weeping in pain. Twenty more seconds and it's done. There are two pools of blood on either side of the prisoner from where his arms were held out to his sides. Finally, Rogers releases his grasp and the Elemental crumples to the floor, cradling his newly steel-encased arms close to his body, crying.

THREE

"Drink?" Halpern asks as he unlocks a wooden cabinet in his office and pulls out a bottle of what I assume is whisky, along with two small rocks glasses.

"I'm all right, thanks," I reply.

"Oh, that's right. You're too young to drink. I always forget."

"How did you know that?"

"I didn't. Until just now, that is," Halpern says with a smirk as he places one of the glasses back in the cabinet. The other is put on his desk, and he pours himself a rather large glassful of the brown liquid.

Stupid. I sometimes forget to keep my guard up around Halpern. I forget that he's always after more information about me and about metas in general. Nothing about my appearance right now indicates that I'm only sixteen. Right now, I stand at six feet, three inches tall and look like I'm two hundred and fifty pounds of pure muscle barely contained within a skin-tight crimson suit covering me from head to toe. Only my jawline is exposed, and even that is different, stronger looking, than how I normally look. "Normally" refers to how I look when these metabands aren't turned on, making me into a superhuman that can throw a car through a building if I wanted to.

"Listen Omni, I'm a big fan of yours. A lot of the guys around here are. You consistently bring in troublemaking metas, and you do it cleanly. No civilian casualties, minimal property damage, hell, you even manage to grab these guys before the press gets involved most of the time. That's actually the most impressive feat of them all, to be honest. We want to start making sure you're compensated for all the good work you've been doing around here."

"I'm not doing it for compensation."

"Sure you are. We all are. Whether it's cash, fame, glory, or vengeance, it's still compensation. At least, if you take the monetary compensation, I'll sleep better at night knowing what your motivations are."

As Halpern says this, he reaches under his desk, and I hear the beeping of a code being entered on a safe's touchpad followed by the click of a heavy metal handle being turned. Halpern leans under the desk and reaches into the unseen safe. When he sits back up, he places a steel suitcase on the table. Without saying a word, he presses the latches and pulls the case open, turning it toward me. It's full of neatly stacked bundles of one hundred-dollar bills.

"You'd feel better knowing that my motivation for doing this is getting paid, rather than the kindness of my heart?" I ask, somewhat sarcastically.

"Look, I don't care what the reason is, but if I know what it is, it helps me understand. And it helps me make sure—"

"That I don't turn against you?"

There's a long, awkward silence.

"We just want to make sure you're happy and taken cared of, Omni. Money is one of the ways we do that."

"And what if someone else comes along and offers me more?"

"I feel relatively comfortable with the United States government's ability to match any competing offer, provided you tell us what you really want out of all *this*."

"I don't want anything. All I want is for people to be able to live their lives in this city without fear. You're able to contain rogue metas better than anyone else; that's why I bring them to you."

"Fair enough," Halpern says. He turns the case back toward himself and closes it before pushing his chair away from his desk. He leans down to return the suitcase to the safe where, presumably, it'll wait for the next meta that Halpern doesn't fully trust. Relatively sure that we're done, I turn my back to Halpern and begin walking out of his office.

"There's one more thing I want to ask you, Omni," Halpern calls to me as he takes another swig of whiskey from the rocks glass on his desk. I turn to give him my attention.

"We've got a takedown that I'd like you to help with," Halpern says.

"A takedown?"

"A metahuman takedown."

I walk back toward Halpern's desk. "Okay. Who?"

"Well that's classified right now," Halpern responds.

I can't help but laugh.

"So, you want me to take down another metahuman, but you can't tell me who because that's classified. Look, I know secrecy is everyone's favorite pastime around here, but if you want me to takedown a meta for you, I'll need to know who they are. I'm good, but I'm not that good," I respond with maybe just a touch of ego.

"We don't want you to take him down. We want our guys to take him down."

"What do you mean?"

"We've got a team. Not many know about them, but they specialize in this type of job," Halpern says before pausing. "This is all very classified. I'm afraid I'm going to have to gloss over some of the details."

"Still don't trust me?"

"Asks the guy wearing a mask?"

He has a good point, but still, I have a feeling that he needs me more than I need him right now.

"Do you want my help or not?" I ask. He thinks for a few more seconds before grabbing his whisky off the desk and finishing what's left in one huge gulp.

"The hell with it, fine," he relinquishes as he slams the empty glass on the table. "We've got a special operations team that specializes in taking out metas. These guys are good. Very good, but this particular job is ... delicate."

"What does that mean?" I ask.

"I can't get into the details until I know if you're onboard, but let's just say that this meta is somewhat high profile."

"Then why all the secrecy if I presumably already know who he is?"

"That's just it. You don't. No one knows he's a meta, except us."

I'm very confused, but decide to keep listening before I ask any more questions. The whisky seems to have loosened Halpern up a bit, and I'm not going to slow him down now.

"This is a big one," he says. "Once this meta is taken down, there's not going to be any hiding the operation from the media or general public. Everyone will know."

"All right ..." I say, attempting to prod him into telling me more. He picks up the empty glass from his desk and turns his back to me to prepare another drink.

"People well above my pay grade think this is a good *PR opportunity* for us to publicly announce the existence of this task force. They think if regular people know that the government can take down a meta without the help of another meta, it'd make them sleep better at night," Halpern says as he pours another glass of whisky. This one is a little bit bigger than the last.

"So, if they want non-metas to take this guy down, what do you need me for?" I ask.

"To go in with them, of course," he says like I've asked the stupidest question in the world.

I give him a blank look to express my lack of understanding. He sighs.

"We need you to go in with them. Not like this," he says as he gestures up and down with the hand holding his drink at the outfit I'm wearing. "We need you to go in with them looking normal. Still powered up, of course, but not wearing the unitard."

"It's not a uni ..."

"I'm joking with you. Relax."

"So what? I go in there with them, take this meta out, and then they get all the credit?" I ask.

"No. They still take the meta down. You're just there as ... insurance. We want the public to know we can handle these types of situations, but at the same time, we can't take any chances with one this big. That's why I'd like your help as a backup. You're only there in case you're needed."

I stand in Halpern's office, considering his offer. I'm not sure it even is an "offer" since it doesn't sound like I get much out of it, other than taking a presumably bad meta off the streets. That should be reward in and of itself, I guess. If I were doing this for the credit, I wouldn't be wearing a mask in the first place, would I? Halpern takes another sip.

"So what do you say? Help us out?"

FOUR

It's been a long night, and I desperately just want to go home, but I haven't heard from Midnight all day, so I decide that I should swing by his new hideout to at least check in. I've made the mistake of not checking in before and had to deal with being chewed out often enough this summer.

I arrive at Midnight's new base of operations to find it completely empty. Well, that's not entirely true. It's full of various machines, computers, gadgets, and pigeons. So. Many. Pigeons.

Pigeons literally come with the territory, though, when you decide to move your base of operations from abandoned subway tunnels to the water tower on top of an abandoned skyscraper. Midnight said the place makes a lot more sense with the new threats we're dealing with. Or rather, the threats *he's* dealing with, and I just occasionally "assist" with, according to him.

Now that there are countless new metas out there, the top of a building gives you a much better vantage point than a tunnel twenty feet underground, especially when you consider how many of the new metas can fly.

What we weren't expecting, or at least I wasn't expecting, was that there would be so many pigeons. Pigeons, literally everywhere. The water tower has been retrofitted and sealed off from the outside. The walls were replaced with floor to ceiling panels that relay images directly from cameras mounted outside, essentially making it feel like you're out in the open even though you're safely hidden from the outside world. Well, hidden from everyone except the pigeons. They know. Somehow, they know, and somehow, they always find a way in.

I open the hatch in the floor and start shooing the three pigeons I find toward the opening and out of the water tower. Just as I get the last pigeon to leave, something heavy slams up against the ten foot long rusty ladder leading up to the hatch. It's Midnight, and he's hurt.

I grab his left arm as he struggles up the rickety ladder. I pull him into the tower, and the interior momentarily darkens as a series of red lasers crisscross the room, landing on Midnight and scanning his entire body. This is part of the water tower's automated systems and serves two functions. The first is identifying that this is, in fact, Midnight or me, as it did upon my arrival earlier tonight. The second is assessing what injuries either of us may have sustained and the appropriate medical attention required.

"What happened to you?" I ask as he pushes my hands away, indicating that he doesn't want my help standing up. "Oh my God, what happened to your arm?" I almost yell.

The left sleeve of his black, armored suit has been ripped to shreds, exposing his bare arm. Aside from bruising and lacerations, the skin on his arm looks strange. It's slightly pinker and shinier than it should be, almost like a skin graft on a burn victim. Upon further inspection, it becomes clear that this injury wasn't recent. The skin is smooth, hair giving the arm an almost plastic-like appearance. I only get another second's worth of a glimpse before Midnight retreats to the medical bay and slams the door behind him.

I still don't even know what Midnight looks like without his mask on, but I know him well enough not to even bother knocking on the door.

"I'm going to be awhile," Midnight says in a voice barely above a whisper. From the other side of the door, I can already hear the various medical machines moving into place.

"Number one or number two?" I ask through the door, trying to lighten the mood.

No response.

"All right then. I'm gonna head home for the night."

Still no response.

"Okay, I'll see you tomorrow. Feel better. Light a match when you're done, okay?" I say as I open the floor hatch to descend the ladder.

Still nothing. If it were anyone else, I'd be worried, but I learned months ago that Midnight could more than take care of himself. He's survived this long as a non-meta, running around dressed like one. He doesn't need my help after a rough night out doing ... whatever it was that he was just doing.

Another thing I've learned about Midnight, if tonight's any kind of example, is the guy doesn't know a good joke when he hears one.

Five

It's late by the time I finally get home. I'm still not completely used to the idea that this new apartment is home now. Since record numbers of metas have been appearing again, my brother Derrick's knowledge of all things meta is in much higher demand. A guy who used to be seen as just some weirdo investigating conspiracy theories on the Internet has quickly become a very in-demand weirdo now that everyone wants to know what he knows.

His work covering the meta beat at the *Rogerson Post* took off in a big way a couple of months ago. Just about every single one of his articles went viral within minutes of publication. It only took a few weeks before Derrick's posts made up the majority of the *Rogerson Post*'s traffic for their entire website. And it only took a week after that for him to decide he'd be better off without them and begin running a site of his own. ConnollyReport.com was born shortly after.

Derrick works pretty much nonstop now, but the upside to all of that newfound work is that we just moved into an apartment that cost about ten times as much as the house we previously lived in. Between moving from a one-story ranch style house to a thirty-fourth story penthouse, as well as moving from an abandoned subway station to a water tower, things are literally looking up these days. Actually, I guess, technically, they're looking down? Or at least, I'm looking down since I'm always up so high? Look, I don't know. It's a saying, and the pun works so I'm sticking with it.

The other nice advantage to being in the penthouse is that it's very easy for me to slip in and out through the skylight. I don't have to worry about wasting energy teleporting or accidentally smashing something that I didn't expect to be there when I arrive. Derrick's still mad that I landed on his new XStation. He didn't have time to play it anyway, but trying to tell him that probably wasn't the best way to calm him down.

He's not home right now, but that's nothing new. I miss having him around, especially now that I don't have to worry about keeping how I spend my nights from him anymore. He has a team of his own to manage with ConnollyReport.com, and a lot of people that count on him. On top of all of that, he's quite literally the face of the website, which also means a lot of media appearances.

Crap! That's why he's not home tonight. I almost forgot. Derrick's supposed to be on MetaLine tonight, his biggest national TV appearance to date. I set an alarm on my phone to remind me, but that doesn't do much good when my phone is underneath a suit created out of matter generated from intergalactic wristbands using my own imagination. Those alarms tend to get muffled.

I power down the metabands and grab the monstrous touch screen remote control that controls the ridiculously huge wall-mounted TV situated in the living room. I'm sorry, the "main gathering area" as the real estate agent described it. The TV clicks on, and I plop down on our huge new leather couch as my suit becomes fluid and pulls back into the powered down silver bands on my wrists.

I'm just in time as the image of Ruby Kelly, the host of MetaLine, fills the screen. Ruby looks almost impossibly perfect. Impeccable makeup without a blond hair out of place, and trust me, I'd be able to tell since I'm watching her four-foot tall face on the giant screen in front of me. MetaLine is one of the most popular shows on MNN, which is the most popular of three twenty-four hour meta-devoted news networks.

While it'd be tough to classify her as "anti-meta," she's a huge proponent of the idea that metas no longer get to enjoy a large number of rights when they assume the powers the metabands grant them. Privacy, from both the public and the government, is just one basic right she believes metas should no longer get the right to. Ruby believes metas should be held to the highest standard of our laws, and that if a meta wants to take it upon him or herself to become a "crime fighter," then they must do so by the same avenues available to any normal citizen: by becoming an employee of a federal or state government. To say she doesn't care much for vigilantism is putting it lightly.

The image divides into split screen, with Derrick on the right, looking confident and relaxed, and Ruby on the left. Derrick's gotten much better at this since the first few times he went on live TV and needed a bucket next to him. Ruby begins to give Derrick his introduction.

"Joining me tonight on MetaLine is a name you might be familiar with, but a face that's new to us on the 'Line: editor-in-chief of the world's most popular meta *blog* ..." Derrick is already rolling his eyes at his website being referred to as simply a blog, especially considering about ten times as many people visit his website everyday as watch Ruby's show. "... Derrick Connolly. How are you tonight, Mr. Connolly?"

Derrick suddenly seems to realize he's on TV and sits up straight, plastering a smile on his face. "I'm good, Ruby. Thank you for having me tonight."

"Thank you for joining us. I know that you're a busy man, keeping all those ones and zeroes moving along the Internet," she says with a laugh in an attempt to demean what Derrick does for a living. "Tonight, we've been talking about the recently proposed bill that would require all metas operating within the United States to formally register themselves with the United States government for the safety and wellbeing of all of us quote-unquote, regular citizens."

"Right, the bill basically creates a virtual internment camp for U.S. citizens who just happen to be tied to metabands, metabands that they oftentimes didn't even choose to own, I might add."

"Well, invoking the idea that this would be tantamount to an 'internment camp' is certainly a very harsh way to put a law that is simply being proposed to make sure that we know who these people are. They have the ability to kill en masse, after all. What do you say to proponents of this bill who say that you're blowing this out of proportion?"

"That I'm blowing this out of proportion? Are you serious? We're talking about a bill that proposes metaband owners turn themselves into the government, reveal their identity, and submit to monitoring akin to being a parolee. The vast majority of metas have done absolutely nothing wrong. Many metas have decided to use their powers for neither good nor bad, but simply for their own personal use to the detriment of no one."

"But if they have nothing to hide, then why not allow the government to know exactly who they are and what they are up to?"

"Wouldn't you be concerned if the government wanted to keep tabs on you twenty-four hours a day?"

"No, I wouldn't, because I have absolutely nothing to hide, but let's move on to another point you brought up. A lot of new metas who are part of the second wave, as it's being called, have decided that being a superhero *or* supervillain is just not something that interests them. Instead, they've decided to do something that many think is much more nefarious, and that's using their newfound abilities to put thousands and thousands of hardworking Americans out of a job. Industries such as shipping have been particularly hard-hit by the proliferation of Speeders who have farmed out their abilities. They've turned things like overnight delivery into a quaint, old-fashioned notion from an era before metas could literally run your package across the ocean in only a few minutes. We have countless people in the construction and manufacturing sectors out of work now that a single metahuman can do the manual labor of hundreds."

"Well, that's an entirely different subject altogether, but I don't see how having the government keep metas under around-the-clock surveillance is going to help any of those issues."

"But the surveillance would be a fairly simple matter. The government has already made it clear that they are aware of the exact number of metabands present on Earth at this time, along with their approximate locations based on satellite—" Ruby can't even finish her sentence because she's interrupted by Derrick laughing heartily.

"You really believe that, Ruby?" Derrick asks between laughs.

Ruby is stunned by the question.

"Yes, of course I believe that. What on Earth would the U.S. government have to gain by lying about that?" Ruby asks as Derrick takes a deep breath, preparing to unleash one of his trademark tirades.

"What would they have to gain? Are you serious, Ruby? You're asking the wrong question. The right question is what would they have to lose by admitting to the fact that they honestly have absolutely no idea how many active metabands there are in the world today. They would lose not only the trust of their own citizens, but also the respect, and frankly, the fear of the rest of the world who believes they have this situation at least somewhat under control. If people knew the truth, or rather, chose to even question the facts being presented to them ..."

The image of Derrick's face freezes on the screen before becoming digitally distorted and pixilated. Ruby holds her hand up to her ear, implying that someone is talking to her through her earpiece.

"I apologize ladies and gentlemen, apparently we're having a problem with our satellite feed from Bay View City. We're going to go to commercial right now, but when we come back ... Should you be worried about your friendly neighborhood meta's X-ray vision? We'll be talking with Ronald Mason, the inventor of Lead-ware, the latest in lead-lined undergarments that just might help you keep your privates, private."

Ugh. I hit the power button on the remote control and the television shuts off. This happens to Derrick half the time he goes on a show and starts spouting his conspiracies about what the government really knows and what they don't. The network pretends like they're appalled by the insinuation that the government is lying, because they rely on the government for protection. Since all the new metas started popping up, every television station in the world has become a target for attention-seeking metas looking to get in front of a camera with a room full of hostages and a list of demands. The major networks came together to sue the government and demand literal protection under the First Amendment, and they got it. Now, government-employed metas are randomly stationed undercover in most major newsrooms on a rotating basis. They're the newsroom equivalent of an air marshal.

While the network wants to make sure they keep the higher-ups in the government happy so that their newsroom doesn't "accidentally" get skipped in the random rotation, they also know that having someone like Derrick on TV guarantees a spike in ratings. Derrick's not stupid either. Regardless of how frustrated he gets during these interviews, he benefits from the increased traffic to his website, as well as just the notion of getting his ideas out to a mainstream audience that might not otherwise hear them.

So the networks are happy to have him on, roll their eyes at him while they drive up the prices for commercial time, and cut him off when he says something too controversial. What the networks don't know is that Derrick's brother is a meta, so Derrick is way closer to these stories than they'd ever guess. They also don't know that he's absolutely right;

the government has no idea how many metabands are out there, and that scares the hell out of them.

Six

The alarm clock must have been going off for a while, because it isn't until Derrick comes into my bedroom and throws a shoe at me that I finally wake up. Sunday night vigilantism always seems like a good idea at the time, but the non-meta version of me that has to deal with the consequences on Monday morning always begs to differ. The metabands and suit manage to keep any kind of lasting physical harm to my body at a minimum, but I still have a morning-after headache from getting thrown into a brick wall last night, and the bands do absolutely nothing for sleep deprivation.

"Get up, idiot. You're late for school, and I've got to go to the office," Derrick says as he ducks out of my room and back into the hallway.

"Thanks," I grunt. My eyes struggle to adjust to the morning light streaking in through the floor to ceiling windows that surround my corner bedroom overlooking the city. I practically fall out of bed and drag myself into the bathroom to take the shower that I probably should have taken last night, and would have if I hadn't been so tired. The metabands can do a lot, but they don't keep me from smelling like garbage after a night of basically running around the entire city. And by running, I mean mostly flying of course, but you know what I mean.

It's a bit of a hike to get to school now that Derrick and I have moved downtown, but I refuse to go to another new school. It took me a full year to make the few friends that I have at this school, and I'm not about to start over just because Derrick wants to live in a nicer neighborhood. Derrick offered to buy me a car with his newfound wealth, but I declined. The last thing I need is to stick out, and showing up to the first day of class in a sports car would have made that hard, so the city bus it is.

It's really not bad. Plus, if I ever need to get somewhere in a hurry, I've always got the option to teleport or fly, which aren't bad backups at all. Oh, and I can run at the speed of sound. Probably faster, but I haven't actually tested it. All I know is that sonic booms are a hell of a lot louder on the ground than they are in the air, as the storefront windows on Talbert Street can attest to. That wasn't my fault, though. I mean, it was my fault, but I didn't mean it. Well, I meant to test how fast I could run, so that much is true, but I didn't mean to blow out all the windows with a sonic boom. That's one hundred percent the truth.

Junior year started a couple of weeks ago, and knock on wood, so far, so good. Classes have been going well, and luckily, I've been able to keep my night job to just that, night only. Everything has been exceedingly normal, whatever the new version normal happens to be.

I feel a kiss on my cheek, and a voice behind me whispers in my ear, "You're late."

Turning around, I find Sarah Miller's smiling face. Wait, I'm sorry. My *girlfriend,* Sarah Miller's smiling face. She's up on her tippy toes to reach me and throws her arms around me as I turn to face her. She looks beautiful. Her short, chin length, light blond hair catches the garish florescent lighting and still manages to shimmer. There's a sparkle in her hazel eyes that gets me every time.

"I feel like I haven't seen you in a week," she says as she gives me another quick kiss, this time on the lips.

"Sorry, just been busy helping Derrick with the new apartment and everything," I reply.

"I know. I'm exaggerating. It's only been a weekend, but still ..." she says as she kisses me again. I think I got used to being able to fly quicker than I've gotten used to being able to kiss Sarah Miller almost everyday.

"How about I make it up to you?" I ask.

"Yeah?" Sarah asks back, cocking her head and giving me that smile that melts me every single time.

"Yeah. There's a new place opening up around the corner from Derrick's and my place this week. I think Rad Eskimo is supposed to be playing there tomorrow night."

"I love them!"

"I know you love them, that's why I remembered. Wanna go?"

Sarah leans in and kisses me again.

"I'll take that as a 'yes' then?" I ask.

"Absolutely. See you later," Sarah says as she turns and heads down the hallway on her way to class.

I'm still staring at her walking away and asking myself how I ever ended up with a girl like her when I feel a punch on my left bicep from behind. I turn and find Jim Young, my best, and for the majority of my time at Bay View City South, only friend. I make a mental note to myself about how easy it apparently is to sneak up on me when I haven't had enough sleep.

He opens the locker next to mine and begins shuttling books between it and his bag. His actions remind me how we became friends in the first place. It was almost complete coincidence; the school just happened to assign me the empty locker next to his.

Jim's let his dark brown hair grow out since the summer, and now it's well past his ears. He brushes part of it out from in front of his face and tucks it behind his ear. Jim and I have always been about the same size, both height and weight-wise, but I notice that he seems almost a little skinnier than before. I probably wouldn't have even noticed if it weren't for the fact that I've barely seen Jim in the month since school started.

"Stop staring, Connor. You're creeping everyone out," Jim says, teasing me.

"Can you blame me?"

"No. If I were as big of a loser as you, I'd be dumbfounded too at how I managed to become Sarah Miller's boyfriend. Hell, I'm dumbfounded anyway."

"Thanks."

"Don't mention it."

"Well if you're done inflating my ego, I really should be getting to class," I say as I swing my backpack over my right shoulder and begin to turn.

"Hey," Jim says, stopping me, "what are you up to tomorrow night? Want to come over and play the new Super Giuseppe ch?"

"Ah, I can't. I promised Sarah I'd hang out with her. Sorry."

"Oh, okay. No problem." Jim turns to leave and says, "See you later."

There's something not quite right here. Jim never gives up that easily. At the very least, I expect to be given crap for hanging out with my girlfriend instead of "being one of the guys" and hanging out with him. Jim's just kidding around when he says it, but he always says it.

"ID, sonny," an extremely elderly man says to me.

I'm so lost in my own thoughts that I haven't realized we've moved all the way through the extremely long line and up to the door of the club. The club itself is non-descript from the outside; something I'm told is common for this type of place. Apparently, this place is "too cool" to have a sign above the door. The man asking for ID is hunched over, wearing a newsboy cap and thick bifocals. His skin is so pale and paper-thin that I can see the blue veins bunching up around his hands and cheeks. If he's a day under eighty years old, I'd be shocked.

"Oh, sorry. I didn't realize you were the bouncer," I say, almost phrasing it as a question since he's the last person I'd expect to be watching the door at a brand new venue. I fumble with my wallet while Sarah does the same with her purse. We present our IDs, and his shaky hand reaches out for them. He pulls them in close to his face for a thorough examination. I notice that his lips are moving, but no words are coming out of his mouth. I realize that he's doing the math in his head to figure out how old we are.

"Sorry, young man. It's only eighteen and over tonight. I won't be able to allow you in," he tells us.

Sarah sighs as she takes the IDs back, hands me mine, and begins to place hers back in her handbag. I feel embarrassed and humiliated. I can tell that Sarah is immensely disappointed, but too nice to say anything. I planned this whole night, and I've screwed up something as simple as making sure that we were even old enough to get in. I have to try something.

"Are you sure?" I ask.

The old man simply nods his head and motions for us to move to the side so the people behind us can get through. Nice smooth talking, idiot.

"Come on, Connor. It's all right. We can see them another time. It's not your fault," Sarah says to me as she puts her hand on my elbow and gently moves me aside to clear a path for the couple behind us. They hand their IDs to the, man and he quickly waves them in.

"Hold on," I say to Sarah before turning my attention back to the elderly man in desperation. "Isn't there something you can do? We're not looking to drink or anything, sir. I promise you. Her favorite band is playing tonight, and I already bought the tickets. We're not going to cause any trouble, I swear."

"Huh?" the man says to me, cupping his hand behind his ear. "I didn't hear a word of that. You're going to have to speak up, young man. You're mumbling."

I open my mouth to begin pleading my case again, even

though I can feel Sarah's grip on my arm tighten and begin pulling me away. Before I can say a word, there's a loud crackle from the walkie-talkie attached to the old bouncer's belt. He holds a finger up to my face, telling me to wait while his other trembling hand reaches down to retrieve the walkie-talkie.

"Mortimer, where are you? We've got trouble at the bar. We need you in here, now!" says the voice on the other end of the walkie-talkie.

It's only as the old man lifts the walkie-talkie to his ear, straining to hear the voice that is almost deafening to everyone else in line, that I notice his wrist and the bright silver metaband around it.

Without another word, the man I now know as Mortimer, because of course a guy this old has a name like "Mortimer," heads inside the club. As the door swings open, the sound of men arguing escapes out into the street. The door closes behind the old man, and it's quiet once again. No one in the line moves since they all seem to be just as confused as me, including Sarah, who has stopped trying to pull me away. She's as interested as I am at seeing where this thing with Mortimer goes.

In an instant, the metal door to the club slams open and into the brick wall it's attached to. The crowd lined up against the outside wall of the club gasps as a blur flies past, missing Sarah and me by maybe six inches. The blur crashes into the street and tumbles down the road. The tumbling slows down, and it becomes apparent that the blur is a man. Not just any man, but a man at least twice as wide as me. He's covered up to his face in tattoos and looks like he could be an MMA fighter, if he isn't one already.

The door swings open once again, and Mortimer emerges, slowly shuffling out into the street and toward the man who was just literally thrown out of the club. He feebly reaches down, grabs the man by the throat, and lifts him into the air over his head, where he holds the man while looking straight into his eyes.

"Now, I'm going to ask again, you son of a gun. Do we have a problem here?"

The man's face is turning purple from the lack of blood and oxygen, but he manages to quickly shake his head "no." Mortimer releases his grip, and the man falls flat onto the pavement.

"That's what I thought. Now, run along, you hear. Get!" The tattooed man doesn't wait to be asked twice and tears off down the street.

I'm still stunned by what I've seen when Sarah shakes me out of my stupor by telling me she thinks she's going to head home.

"Are you sure?" I ask.

"Yeah, I'm tired. It's a school night anyway."

"I'm so sorry. I wanted this to be a fun night. Let me walk you home at least?"

"Don't be ridiculous. We're around the corner from your place, and I've got to head all the way across town," she says as she raises her arm, causing a passing taxi to pull over to the sidewalk. Grabbing the door handle, she turns to me and says, "Seriously, it's okay. We'll try this some other night. That place looked a little insane anyway."

"What gave you that impression? It wasn't the ancient doorman who just threw a meathead ten times his size clear across the street, was it?"

"Heh? What did you say?" Mortimer asks behind me, again cupping his hand behind his ear in a vain attempt to improve his hearing.

Sarah giggles and quickly pecks me on the cheek before sliding into the back of the cab.

"See you tomorrow, tough guy."

41

SEVEN

"It's a night off kid, take it," Midnight says to me over the communicator in my cowl.

Five minutes after putting Sarah in a cab, I decided to activate my metabands and see what, if anything, I could salvage out of the now wasted night. The nice part about being a superhero is that you make your own hours. Sure, the pay sucks, but you only work when you want to. The sucky part is that you're always on call, obviously. The really sucky part, which a lot of people don't think about, is that when you've got a night completely and totally to yourself, you often have no idea what to actually do with the time.

That's me right now as I'm arguing with Midnight while hovering about two thousand feet above the city.

"Come on, there has to be something going on right now," I whine over the communicator.

"Nope. Quiet night," Midnight says back to me.

I swear in the background I can hear him fire a grappling gun followed by the sound of Kevlar rope being reeled in through a gas-powered pulley. Midnight's out on patrols and lying to me about it.

"I just heard your grappling gun," I say to him.

"My what-ling gun? Sorry, I think you're breaking up," he lies to me again.

"Come on. I've got nothing to do tonight, and I'm bored. Throw me a bone here."

"Listen, you've got a night off. Enjoy it. Go home. Relax. You can't keep going at the rate you are You're going to burn yourself out."

"Don't worry about me."

"I'm not worried about you. I'm worried about the people who'll need you when you haven't slept for more than four hours a night in weeks. Rest is important. You're no good to

43

anyone if you're not sharp."

"Fine," I say with a sigh and tap the side of my cowl to deactivate my connection with Midnight.

Maybe I shouldn't, but I take it as an insult. Midnight barely sleeps from what I can tell. He doesn't take "nights off," but he thinks I need to. After months of him drilling into my head the idea that this isn't just a job, but a life that I'll lead full-time from now on, I'm more than slightly perturbed that he's telling me to just turn all of that off and head in for the night.

I'm trying to keep a balanced life. I'm trying to make time for Sarah, Derrick, and even Jim, not to mention school, but none of them need my attention tonight. None of them need me there to keep up appearances. Is that all I'm doing, "keeping up appearances?" Spending time with the people I care about shouldn't be a chore. It shouldn't be what I do just to fill the space between my work as a meta. Maybe Midnight's right. Maybe I do need some time to myself, my real self, Connor, not Omni. Maybe I am starting to lose the connection with my day-to-day reality.

My communicator beeps into my ear, and I give it a quick tap, assuming it's Midnight.

"Well, well, well, look who's calling back. I assume you changed your mind about needing a hand tonight?" I say.

"Connor, it's me," Derrick replies back. Whoops. There's only two people that have this number, and Derrick's the other one. Although, I did get an annoying telemarketing call the other night. You can keep a number unlisted, but that doesn't mean a robo-caller won't randomly dial it.

"I told you to call me Omni when you use this number. You never know who could be listening in," I quickly shoot back, somewhat annoyed.

"Omni," Derrick sighs, "where are you? Are you home?"

"You mean *my headquarters*?"

"Knock it off, Connor. Where are you?" He's not playing

along.

"I'm ... around," I reply, gliding over to the nearest gargoyle perched on the roof of MorganTech Tower to give myself a break from hovering. "Where are you?"

"I'm on a date at—"

"Wait! You're on a *what?* For a second there, I almost thought I heard you say you were on a date for the first time in like two years!"

"Would you shut up for a minute, Connor! Are you watching the news?"

"No, why?"

"I'm sending the link to your phone," he says a few seconds before I hear another beep indicating that the message has arrived.

I concentrate on my suit and force part of it open to allow me to reach into the pocket of the jeans I'm wearing underneath this crimson-colored suit, and retrieve my phone.

Tapping the link brings up a ViewNow page, showing a live stream of a close-up of a terrified man's face. The camera tilts down, and the image reveals that the man is dangling high above the city. On the right side of the video is a heading with the question, "Does this man deserve to die?" Underneath is a running tally: over five hundred thousand votes for "Yes" and less than ten thousand for "No." I also notice there's a timer counting down from less than three minutes.

"What am I looking at, Derrick?"

"He's calling himself Sentencer. He claims the man he's holding above the city is a registered sex offender who got a reduced sentence for turning on his cellmate in prison and providing information about terrorist activity. He's live streaming video and letting the Internet decide what should happen to this guy. Connor, he's going to drop him."

"Where is he?" I ask without a moment's hesitation.

Regardless of what this person has done, it's not up to an

anonymous mob on the Internet to decide his fate. History has shown that usually doesn't turn out well.

"I can't tell. He turned off geotagging on the live stream, but from the background, it looks like he's somewhere near downtown. He's at least a few hundred feet above any of the skyscrapers."

"Good, that ought to make him easy to find. He should stick out like a sore thumb."

"In this fog?" Derrick asks.

He's right. It is unusually foggy tonight and finding anything in the sky won't be easy, especially when it's someone who doesn't want to be found.

"All right, I'm going to see if I can find this guy," I begin to say as I will my suit back open and return the cell phone into the pocket of my jeans. "Let me know if anything—"

Before I can finish, I hear screams in the background on Derrick's end of the line. Before he even says it, I know that Sentencer has dropped the man he was holding.

I don't have time to think, only to react. Everything slows to a crawl as I fly into the center of downtown as fast as I can, concentrating on trying to see through the fog. My ability to see through objects does little good at this distance, and I decide to change tactics. Instead, I focus on what I can hear. It's faint, but the screams of a man falling through the sky finally pierces through the cool night air and reaches my ears. He's far away, but not far enough that I can't get to him.

The speed the sound travels to my ears is much faster than the speed at which he is falling, but I'm still far enough away that I need to compensate if I'm going to catch him.

The windows of a nearby skyscraper are accidentally blown out as I fly by at high speed. Whoops. Oh well. The city will just have to put it on my tab.

I'm flying down 4th Avenue when I finally see him. He's reached terminal velocity and is only hundreds of feet from the ground. I have four seconds, if I'm lucky. Catching him at the speed he's falling won't be much different from him hitting the concrete below, especially when you factor in how fast I'm flying. I need to think fast if I'm going to save the doomed felon from being killed by blunt force trauma.

My timing is perfect. That's not bragging. It has to be perfect or else he's dead. Just as I wrap my arms around him, I stop flying and let myself drop too. Only fifty feet, but it's enough to concentrate on the sky above and teleport both of us there. We're still falling when we arrive an instant later, and the man is still screaming in my ear, but within a few seconds, I've slowed our descent and carefully placed both of us back on solid ground.

Before the man has a chance to catch his breath and say anything to me, three police cars come sliding in from around the corner with their lights flashing and sirens blaring. They'll take care of this from here. I need to go take care of the thing they can't: the metahuman flying thousands of feet above the city, letting the Internet decide who should be executed on live video. The ground beneath me rumbles, and I hear a faint "thank you" in between gasps and uncontrollable sobbing before I leap into the air.

Flying straight up into the air, spinning as I rise, I pass the roofs of skyscrapers and scan the horizon for any sign of Sentencer. I reach what looks to be the height he was hovering at when he dropped the man I just saved, but there's no sign of him. This isn't entirely surprising, considering he likely saw what just happened and didn't think it would be a good idea to wait around for me to find him. This is the first time I've heard of Sentencer, and it's impossible to know what powers he possesses beyond flight. Even if he does possess other powers, it isn't the smartest idea to pick a fight when you're a new meta. Even though I'm hardly what you could consider a "veteran," I've still got a few months experience on him and that'll ensure he gets a one-way trip to Silver Island.

"Lose something?" a voice behind me asks. A voice I recognize but haven't heard in what feels like a very long time.

"Iris," I say before I even turn to confirm that I'm right.

Iris floats twenty feet from me, holding what looks like a pair of glasses. Her eyes glow a pupil-less white behind her black domino mask, which is partially obscured by the curly, platinum blond, shoulder-length hair whipping around her face thanks to the air currents up here. Her black and dark purple suit covers her from neck to toe and hasn't changed except for one notable addition.

"Nice cape," I tell her, referring to the short, almost waist-length cape flapping in the wind behind her. The cape is black with a purple lining. It actually does look pretty good on her, and for a moment, I'm jealous that she can pull off a cape and I can't. Granted, she's good looking enough that she could probably wear an oversized black plastic garbage bag for a suit and no one would question it.

"Thanks. I thought it added a nice touch," she replies.

"Where have you been?" I ask.

I haven't seen her in months. It seems like no one has, although it's hard to keep track of individual metas now that there are thousands all over the world. Unless they're doing something deadly or ridiculous, it's pretty easy to fly under the radar, no pun intended.

"I assume you're looking for this guy?" she asks as she holds up the glasses so I can get a better look, not answering my question.

Upon further inspection, they're not really glasses at all; they're ViewNow Specs, Internet-connected cameras mounted to eyeglass-like frames that I now realize were what Sentencer was using to broadcast his little show.

"Did you take them off him?" I ask her.

"Kinda."

"Kinda?"

"They came right off when I punched him in the face while flying at a few hundred miles per hour."

"I imagine they would," I say with a smirk.

"Seriously, they, like, hung in the air right where he was floating, even though he'd already been knocked about a quarter mile away. He took the smartest option available and kept flying after that."

"Probably would have been a better idea to have hung onto him instead of the glasses."

"He teleported out of here a split-second later."

"And you couldn't stop him before that?" I almost yell at her.

"Take a look around, Omni," Iris tells me.

I begin to argue back for her to stop changing the subject, but I realize it's no use. I can't force her to listen to me, and I can't force her to answer questions that she doesn't want to. Sighing in agreement, I do what she asks and take in my surroundings.

It's hard to notice at first, like missing the forest for the trees, or ignoring a starry night sky because you don't take a few seconds to look up and let your eyes adjust. What I see when I look out into the night sky are metas. Metas are everywhere, darting in and out of the city, flying in-between city blocks, and still others fly high above the cloud line. Metas are appearing and disappearing through teleportation or just because they're moving so fast.

I'm not stupid, and I'm not ignorant to the fact that there are exponentially more metas around now than there were before. What I hadn't noticed until this very moment was how many of them have begun fully harnessing their powers. The city sky is buzzing with activity, and it has happened so quickly that I didn't even notice.

"We're not the only ones up here anymore," Iris begins. "You have to start picking and choosing your battles. You saved a life tonight, and that's what's most important. Would you have rather a man died just so you could collar a rogue meta?"

"Somehow, I doubt the city is going to throw a parade for me because I saved a sex offender."

"Is that all that matters? Recognition?"

"Of course not. I'm just saying ..."

"The man you saved tonight wasn't a registered sex offender. He just had the misfortune to move into an apartment formally occupied by one. The database Sentencer used to find the address was out of date."

"What? Why didn't this guy tell Sentencer he wasn't who he was looking for?"

"You think he didn't? I wasn't there, but I'm pretty sure at some point he probably brought that up as he was being dangled over the city. Sentencer either didn't believe him or didn't care. I'm inclined to believe the latter. Mob rule can be a dangerously powerful motivator."

Eight

I decide to call it a night somewhat early, figuring that saving an innocent man's life should earn me at least one full night's sleep. Iris's words keep echoing in my head, though. The number of metas learning to control their powers is off the charts. What does a world with thousands of super-beings look like? There aren't enough bank robberies to foil or cats to rescue out of trees to keep all of us busy, and that worries me. Most people never intend to be evil or become a "villain," but opportunity and desperation can combine to make that happen. One of those two factors has dramatically changed in the lives of thousands of random people who just happened upon a set of metabands.

The next morning, I actually make it to school on time for a change. With all the late nights, I've been tardy often enough to be put on probation. This wouldn't be such a huge problem, except it's only September, and I can't imagine I'll be getting more sleep any time soon. It's a shame that I'd probably raise a few too many red flags if I started using my speed or teleportation to actually get here on time. By a few, I literally mean *all* the red flags, so the unreliable city bus it is.

Bay View City High School South is pretty much what you'd expect from a large public high school on the border of an affluent suburb. There're kids from rich families, kids from poor families, and just about everything in between. It's a large enough school, with over five thousand students, that there's really a clique for everybody, but it's also easy enough to get lost in the crowd. Getting lost in the crowd was something that bothered me a few months ago when I was the new kid who found just about every social group intimidating and impenetrable. Now, I thrive on the fact that it's easy to just go with the flow and blend into the background. Omni can stick out and be a symbol for people;

Connor can't. Not if Omni needs to keep his secrets. Why am I talking about myself in the third person? Is this a side effect that no one told me about? I should keep an eye on this.

I find my locker and fiddle with the combination. I'm here so infrequently that it's hard to keep these three stupid numbers in my head. On my fourth attempt, I'm finally able to get it open, and I begin swapping books from my backpack for the various books I'll need for the day. Again, it takes me a minute or two to remember A: what day of the week it is and, B: what classes I have today.

"Wow, you actually showed up for school on time for once," a voice says next to me. I turn my head and see that it's Jim.

"Yeah, don't worry. I'm sure it won't become a habit," I respond jokingly.

"I'm sure it won't, considering you've been M.I.A for the last couple of months," Jim says.

"Ha, yeah. Just really busy, ya know."

"I'm sure. You've got that fancy new downtown apartment now that Derrick's raking in the big bucks gushing about how much he loves metas to any idiot who'll listen."

The tone of Jim's voice is harsh and biting. He's mad. I can understand him being pissed at my not being around that much. He was the only person here who offered to be my friend when no one else would give me the time of day, and now, in his eyes, I've hung him out to dry because I've got a girlfriend and a nice place to call home. There's something else, though; it's not just that.

Before I'm able to ask what exactly is wrong, a silence falls over what was a very noisy, bustling hallway. Turning to see what has caused the silence, I see the face of the person walking down the hallway that everyone is looking at, but trying to pretend that they aren't. It's Brad Turner, a former bully and all-around jerk who suffered a brutal attack by a meta called The Controller over the summer.

Brad is walking with a slight, but perceivable, limp that he's trying very hard to hide. He's still tall and good looking with short, blondish hair and broad shoulders, but the months he's spent in the hospital have taken their toll. He's lost a significant amount of the formidable muscle and definition that contributed to his nasty nature. There's something else about Brad that he can't hide: the black eye-patch covering his left eye. We all heard that Brad was in very bad shape after the attack, but the extent to which he'd been injured was mostly speculation. The fact that his sister was killed should have been an indication to all of us that he was in worse shape than we ever could have guessed.

The crowd that had parted to make way for Brad quickly begins murmuring amongst itself after he passes. Some look frightened by the sight of him, but the worst looks are those full of pity. The most popular kid in school is now a social outcast simply because no one has the courage to talk to him.

"Look at that," Jim says to me. "Everyone's gawking and staring."

"You're staring too, Jim."

Jim's head snaps back to face me, and I don't think I've ever seen him so angry. He looks as though he's about to punch me, but is holding himself back.

"Right. It's my fault for staring at what a damn meta did to him," he says through gritted teeth.

"Whoa. Relax."

"Don't tell me to relax!"

Now the crowded hallway has turned its full attention to us, or rather to Jim, who just screamed in my face. I can hear little giggles of laughter that are most likely aimed at me, frozen in place in front of Jim's beet red face.

"Is there a problem here, gentlemen?" asks Mr. Reed, our social studies teacher from last school year.

"No. No problem here, Mr. Reed. Just kidding around.

Sorry," I lie.

Mr. Reed's head disappears back into his classroom. Jim turns back to his locker, slamming it shut with all of his might before swinging his backpack over his shoulder and storming off down the hallway.

"What was that about?" I turn to see a concerned looking Sarah emerging from the stream of students heading to class.

"I'm not really sure. I don't think I've ever seen Jim so pissed off before. He's mad that I haven't been around that much ..."

"What do you mean? You told me you hung out with him last week," Sarah interrupts.

Crap. It's hard keeping track of who I'm telling what to cover up that I'm not around as much as I used to be. I should probably start keeping notes. Nah, I think it would probably cause even more suspicion if I started writing down everything I say in a notebook.

"Uh, yeah, but I didn't hang out that long because I wasn't feeling too hot. Anyway, I don't think that's even really why he's so mad. He really flipped out when he saw Brad."

"Oh, yeah. Poor Brad. I can't imagine seeing him today helps, especially after what happened to Jim's dad last week."

"Huh?"

"Jim's dad? I thought you said you hung out with him last week? Didn't he tell you?"

Yeah, I'm definitely going to need to start keeping notes on all my lies.

"No, he didn't mention anything. He was kinda quiet to be honest," I say, finding myself becoming a better liar by the minute.

"I'm not surprised. He was pretty upset about it. His dad lost his job. The whole company was basically laid off."

"Oh man, that's horrible."

Even if I had hung out with Jim, it would make sense that he wouldn't have mentioned this to me. His family lives in

The Banks, which is not a great area to be sure, and although he would never talk about it, I've always gotten the impression that money is tight. Living paycheck to paycheck becomes a lot harder when the paychecks stop.

"Why would seeing Brad make him mad, though?" I ask.

"They all lost their jobs to a meta. The construction company fired everyone and replaced them with this one guy who has strength and flight. They aren't even using cranes anymore, just having this guy fly whatever they need up to the building roofs by hand. The construction company said they had to 'please the stockholders' by saving money and building faster. They didn't even give the workers any notice. They came to the worksite one morning and all the locks had been changed."

"Wow, I can't believe that. I'll talk to him."

"I think it might be better if you give him a little breathing room right now," she says.

"Yeah, but if anyone would understand how he feels ..."

"I know, and I'm sure Jim knows that too. He hasn't forgotten what you had to go through as a kid, but a lot has changed. I think he sees you more as the guy who was saved by the first meta seen in ten years than as his friend whose parents were murdered by metas. It's stupid, but he's upset. I'm sure when he's ready to talk, you'll be the first person he comes to."

"I hope so."

"Well, in more exciting news, guess what?"

"What?"

"My dad wants to meet you!"

My stomach drops, immediately. Her dad wants to meet me? Why? Is this some elaborate trap where he's going to threaten me with a shotgun and tell me to stay the hell away from his daughter? Is it a test? Is he going to ask me "what my intentions are?" My mind is racing a million miles a minute, and the hallway feels like it's spinning. Since getting my metabands, and even before, actually, I've almost gotten killed more times than I can remember, but the idea of meeting Sarah's dad, a man who is virtually a stranger, is more terrifying right now than anything else I could ever imagine.

Not that I have any reason to fear him. Sarah's only had nice things to say about him. If anything, he sounds boring. An accountant or something, I think? I don't really remember, that's how boring his job is, but he's raised Sarah, who by all accounts is pretty awesome. So, he can't be that bad of a person, right? Still, there's one thing I know for sure: he's the father of the girl I am dating. If I were in his shoes, I'd do everything I could to put the fear of God into someone like me.

"You okay?" Sarah asks.

I've almost completely zoned out. "Huh. Me? Yeah. Of course."

"Soooo, is that a yes?"

"To what?"

"To dinner at my house tonight. My dad really wants to meet you."

"Yeeeesss," I say, drawing out the word way too long because my brain is doing battle with my mouth for agreeing to something that I absolutely *have* to do when I would literally rather do anything else in the world. Not even a rogue meta deciding to demolish downtown is going to get me out of this, though. Tonight's a Connor night, not an Omni night, good or bad. Hopefully good, or at least, hopefully not bad.

"Yay!" Sarah cheers. "I'm so excited! He's going to love you. I just know it. Come over around six-thirty?"

"Yes," I say, again finding my mouth struggling to form the monosyllabic word.

As soon as it escapes my mouth, the class bell rings, and a cacophony of slamming lockers follows. Saved by the bell, except I'm not saved by the bell at all. Not in the tiniest bit.

"See you later," Sarah says with a smile and a quick kiss.

I'm still not sure how I got lucky enough to have someone like her like me. We'll see if that's still the case after tonight.

NINE

6:32 PM. I can't believe this. Tonight was supposed to be very, very simple. No training from Midnight, no searching the streets or sky for trouble, hell, I even got my homework done early. Yet here I am, already two minutes late for dinner with Sarah and her dad, and still at least ten minutes away from their house.

By the time I arrive, over fifteen minutes late, I'm out of breath, and I've managed to sweat clean through the dress shirt I borrowed from Derrick. Jogging up to the doorstep, I try to tuck my shirt back into my pants while also desperately tugging at the front of my shirt over and over again in an effort to get some kind of air circulation going. Taking my phone out of my pocket, I use its front-facing camera to take a quick look at myself. I look like a freaking mess. My hair is wet with sweat and sticking up all over the place. The armpits of my shirt are also noticeably wetter than the rest of my shirt. I give myself about thirty seconds of wasted time to try to fix these issues, but it's no use. At this point, I'm already so late that all I'll accomplish is making myself later. Maybe it's good that I look like this. Maybe Sarah's dad won't be as upset that I'm late if it's obvious I was in a hurry to get here? Sure, keep telling yourself that, Connor.

I haven't been to Sarah's house before, and it isn't exactly easy to find among the winding roads of Hillside, which is mostly why I'm late. Hillside is one of the nicer communities in Bay View City. It's not country clubs and personal butlers nice, but it's definitely "doing okay for yourself" nice. I double check the address Sarah gave me one last time, take a deep breath, and ring the door bell.

Inside, I can hear footsteps galloping down a set of stairs. I'm happy to hear that they're quick and light, meaning it's more likely Sarah rather than her dad. Midnight's been trying to get me to be more observant about things like this, saying it's necessary to be aware of my surroundings at all times. This is by far the most it has ever come in handy. I breathe a little bit easier knowing it'll be a friendly face that opens the door.

The face is more than friendly; it's beautiful. Sarah is wearing a floral dress, all pink and blue pastels, that falls just below her knees. For a moment, I'm so struck by how good she looks that I completely forget how terrible I look.

"You look like shit," she says to me with a smile.

"Glad you noticed," I say back as I wipe a river of sweat off my forehead with the back of my sleeve.

Sarah laughs and waves me inside. "My dad's in his office on a call. I'll show you where the bathroom is, and you can take a minute to clean up a little."

"Thanks. I'm sorry I'm late, and I'm sorry I'm drenched in sweat like this. It's just that the bus was late, and then I couldn't find a taxi, and then once I found a taxi I couldn't find the house—" I say before Sarah quickly turns around and shuts me up with a kiss.

"I'm just messing around with you. You look great. Just a little ... wet. And don't worry about being late, my dad's been on a conference call for an hour. He wouldn't have even realized if you had gotten here on time."

"Okay. That's a big relief. I'll be right out, all right?"

"Take all the time you need to dry off there, champ," she says with another quick kiss and closes the door to the bathroom to give me some privacy.

I take another deep breath as I look at myself in the mirror and assess the damage. It's actually not as bad as I thought. I splash some cold water on my face and already feel a hundred times better. There's a hairdryer next to the sink, and I grab it to at least try to remove the pit stains under my arms.

"Sarah, are you doing your hair again?" the muffled voice

of a man I assume is Sarah's father yells down the hallway.

Okay, that should be my cue that I'm overdoing it with the hair dryer. I'm not exactly sure how I'm going to explain that one to Mr. Miller.

I put the hair dryer back where I found it and open the door to the main hallway. I stop for a moment and look at the pictures hanging on the wall. Most of them are of Sarah when she was younger. There are no pictures of her father or her mother, for that matter. I know she's an only child, and her parents are divorced, but she's never gone into detail about what happened.

"I'm in here," Sarah calls from down the hallway.

I follow her voice to the dining room. The table is already set, and Sarah is hurriedly running between the dining room and kitchen through a swinging door. Each time she appears, carrying another plate or casserole dish full of food. We're talking about a notch or two below a full-on Thanksgiving dinner here.

"Holy cow, this is a ton of food," I say as she comes hustling back through the kitchen door with the last bowl of mashed potatoes.

"Yeah, I think I might have overdone it a little," she says with a look of concern that indicates she's coming to this realization herself.

"No, it's great. Everything looks delicious," I say, trying to reassure her.

"My dad and I don't get to sit down to dinner together too often, as you can probably guess since he's still on the phone, working. I just wanted tonight to be really special."

"It is really special. Thank you. It's been a while since I've had a nice home-cooked meal that Derrick hasn't burned to a crisp. I really appreciate you doing all this work to trick your dad into liking me by feeding him delicious food."

Sarah smiles and kisses me on the cheek. As if on cue, I hear the door open down the hallway and instinctively jump away from Sarah, which makes her giggle.

"Just relax. Be yourself. I'm sure Dad's gonna like you."

Sarah's dad walks into the room, and I can't believe my eyes. My mouth drops, and a single word comes out. A "hello" that winds up sounding more like "ha...llo" as I catch myself from uttering what I was about to say.

Halpern.

"You must be Connor?" Halpern says as he extends his hand to meet mine. "I've heard so much about you. It's nice to finally meet the guy my little girl won't shut up about."

"Daddy!" Sarah protests, embarrassed.

"Nice to meet you, sir," I say, almost on autopilot.

"Sir? Please, call me Mr. Miller," he says with a smile that makes it difficult to tell whether he's joking or not. I know because it's a smile I've seen plenty of times lately. "Sorry that took longer than I thought it would. Work never seems to end nowadays. I won't bore you with all that accounting talk, though. Let's sit and dig in!"

Halpern is Sarah's dad!!!! I feel stupid that it never even occurred to me that people who work for The Agency would have secret identities too. Of course they would. If anything, they're more at risk for retaliation than metas, especially considering they don't wear masks or have super powers. I suppose the fact that it never even occurred to me that someone like Halpern wasn't who he claimed to be is exactly what they want. A man wearing a mask is someone who obviously has something to hide, but a man wearing a suit and name badge doesn't invite any questions as to whether he is who he says he is.

"Everything looks so great, Sarah. You did an excellent job," Halpern/Mr. Miller tells his daughter. I realize I've been almost completely silent for a full minute. Halpern doesn't seem to recognize me, not that he would since I'm not covered from head to toe in crimson spandex right now, but I need to say something before he stops chalking up my silence to anything other than just nervousness.

"Yeah," I agree.

Great job, idiot. Well, at least I'm selling the nervous bit really well, I think.

"So, Sarah tells me you worked with her at the lakefront over the summer," Halpern says, trying to break the awkward tension.

"Oh, yeah."

"You were a lifeguard there too?"

"Um, no. I was a beach cleaner."

"Oh. Well, that's nice too. At least you were outside, right?" he says with a smile.

"Well, not when I was on toilet duty," I answer back, giving him information he has no interest in knowing, and putting thoughts into his head he'd probably rather not have while pouring himself more gravy.

"Connor was at the lakefront when the meta attack happened, Daddy. He was the one who called 911," Sarah tells him.

"Well now, I didn't know we had a real-life hero sitting with us tonight," Halpern says. I nearly choke on a forkful of roast beef and quickly grab my glass of water for cover as my face turns red before finally catching my breath and swallowing my food.

Halpern's cell phone, which is sitting face down on the dining room table, goes off. He picks it up, looks at the screen, and sighs.

"You'll have to excuse me for a moment, guys. It's work. Sorry about this," he says as he pushes his chair back and begins walking back down the hallway toward his office. The door is almost completely closed before he picks up, and the ringing stops. I wonder if I would have been suspicious of a business call being so private that he couldn't even pick up the phone and say "hello" before being completely out of earshot if I didn't already know who Mr. Miller really is.

Midnight definitely would have.

"So, what do you think?" Sarah asks me, as though my opinion of her father has equal weight as his opinion of me.

"Oh, he's really nice," I say, meaning it.

Halpern might not always be nice, but Mr. Miller certainly is, so far. My mind is still reeling with the revelation that Sarah's dad works for The Agency, and that he oversees almost all the meta prisoners on Silver Island. I guess in my head, I never thought of Halpern as a real person. I couldn't imagine him going home every night to a family and having a regular life.

"I wish he didn't have to work so much. I can't imagine how there can be so many 'emergencies' when Dad has the most boring job you could ever imagine. Seriously. If I can't fall asleep at night, I come downstairs to his office and ask him about his day. Within five minutes, I'm snoring. Every. Time," Sarah says. She either has no clue about what her dad really does, or she's just as good at lying as her father. Considering the level of secrecy The Agency operates at, I'm going to guess the former. "It's horrible to say it, but nights like tonight, I start to understand why Mom didn't stick around. I'm sorry. I shouldn't have said that. That's horrible of me."

"It's okay. No judgment here," I say, allowing her the opportunity to talk about her family if she wants to, but making sure not to push or pry.

"He just works all the time. I wanted tonight to be really nice for both of you, so you could get to know each other. Now he's locked back up in his office not even five minutes after meeting you. I'm sorry. I'm just really embarrassed."

"Don't be. Work's work. Trust me, I understand. I don't think I've seen Derrick for more than fifteen minutes at a time since he started his new company. The joys of being an adult, I guess."

"I guess."

The office door down the hallway squeaks quietly as it opens, and I can hear Sarah's father's footsteps coming closer and closer.

"Hi, Sweetie. I'm really sorry about this, but I have to go into the office. Something big has come up, and they need me there," Mr. Miller says to her.

Sarah's eyes begin to water ever so slightly as she quickly nods in his direction. She doesn't even protest his leaving, probably because she knows that those protests will fall on deaf ears. Or at least, ears that are unwilling to compromise the security of who knows what just to meet and spend time with his daughter's boyfriend.

The question of why Halpern is being called away has just entered my mind when I feel my phone vibrate inside my pants pocket. It's not a normal vibration, though, but rather a subtle Morse code-like pattern that indicates the alert isn't coming from a text message or an email. The alert is directly from The Agency. They're sending the coded message that allows them to contact me, directly, in case of emergencies. Midnight spent the better part of a week dissecting the app to ensure it contained absolutely no way for The Agency to track or otherwise spy on me before allowing me to put it on my phone. This is the first time it has ever gone off, and it can't be a coincidence that Sarah's dad is being called away at the exact same time.

"Uhhh," Sarah's dad begins, "I hate to do this to you, Connor, but I'm gonna have to walk you to the door, son."

"Daddy! What are you doing?" Sarah asks, dabbing her eyes to prevent tears from rolling down her cheeks.

"I'm sorry, honey. It's nothing personal, but you know the house rules: no boys allowed in the house if I'm not here."

"So, not only are you embarrassing me by leaving in the middle of dinner after you promised to meet my boyfriend, but you're kicking him out too? We didn't even eat yet!"

"Why don't you make him a plate to go while I get my bag

together for the office? You understand, don't you, Connor?"

"Yeah, of course, Mr. Miller. To be honest, I really have to get going too."

"You were going to leave anyway?!" Sarah snaps.

That was definitely the way wrong thing to say.

"Wait, what? No. I mean, yes. I mean, it's just that ..." I begin to stutter out before I'm interrupted.

"Fine. It's fine. I don't care. Both of you can leave. I'll take care of everything just like I always do. Don't worry about me. Like I even have to tell either of you that," Sarah rants as she bursts through the swinging door back into the kitchen.

I'm not sure what to do. I would follow her, but this isn't my house. If anyone should do anything, I assume it should be Mr. Miller and that I should let him take the lead. I glance in his direction to see if his face offers any clues as to what I should or shouldn't be doing in this situation.

"She'll be okay. She just gets worked up sometimes. She'll get over it. She's tough as nails, but she can be a little dramatic sometimes. Gets that from her mother," Mr. Miller tells me.

There's silence for a few seconds before Sarah's dad clears his throat and looks at his watch. Right. He wants me to leave.

"Well, I really should be going," I say. He jumps at the opportunity to begin ushering me out the door.

"Sorry about all of this. It genuinely was nice meeting you tonight, Connor. Sarah talks about you all the time, and I'm glad I got to see for myself that you're not some kinda weirdo or creep," he says.

"Uhh, thanks?" I say, not sure whether or not to take that as a compliment. Mr. Miller picks up on my confusion.

"I mean that in the best possible way."

I laugh nervously.

"All right then," he says. "I'll show you to the door before I have to jet out of here myself. I hope to see you again soon."

"Yeah, me too."

Ten

Upon my arrival at Silver Island, it is immediately obvious that there is a lot more going on here than normal. The normally empty hallways that lead out in every direction from the receiving area are full of men and women hurrying between rooms. Some carry folders full of papers and photographs while others are clutching assault rifles and wearing combat helmets. Every one of them stops for a moment when I pass. Six-foot-three inches tall and over two hundred and fifty pounds of muscle. In reality, I actually weigh much more or less, depending on the powers I'm using at any given moment, just another side effect of the metabands that no one quite understands. It makes perfect sense to me, but then again, I'm the one who can fly.

They all stop to look at me because everyone who works here is never one hundred percent comfortable with a meta walking the halls. It's hard to blame them. The majority of the metas they encounter are the worst scum on Earth. They mostly see Metas who are mass murderers, genocidal maniacs, and criminals who only care about making others afraid of them. They deal with the worst of the worst, especially the ones who refuse to relinquish their metabands once they're caught.

The processes for detaining metas who have been weakened to the point of metaband power failure but still refuse to remove them are often cruel, but they have proven very successful. There's never been an escape, at least not one that anyone has ever found out about. Still, it's hard to ever feel completely at ease knowing that hundreds of feet below this facility are some of the worst criminals in history. They're in their concrete and steel bunkers with no possibility of release or parole. There's no rehabilitation for these men and women. The risk of removing their restraints and allowing them to power down their metabands is just too great. They had their chance to take off their metabands, and they refused. There are no second chances.

I'm one of the "good ones," but there have been "good ones" who haven't been what they appeared to be. In the last few months, I've done a lot to prove myself to everyone at this facility, but some will never be one hundred percent comfortable seeing someone walk down these corridors wearing silver wristbands.

Halfway to Halpern's office, I feel a slap on my back and turn to find Halpern's grinning face. He must drive like a maniac to have gotten here before me, but I did have to make sure that I went all the way back to my apartment just in case I was being followed. Maybe it's Midnight's paranoia rubbing off on me, but the coincidence that Halpern is Sarah's father just seems way more than coincidental to me. On the off chance this is all some plan to expose my secret identity, I need to be sure.

"You finally made it," Halpern says.

"I made it Mr ... Halpern."

Great. All that trouble to make sure he doesn't find out my secret identity on the one in a million chance he's onto me, and I almost call him Mr. Miller directly to his face. That would have been a fun way to blow both our covers with one big stupid slip of the tongue.

"Please, call me Agent Halpern," he says with a quizzical look on his face.

I can tell he's curious as to why I've just referred to him as "mister." Luckily, there's too much going on for him to give it as much thought as he might like.

"Follow me. We're not going to my office. We're going to the Briefing Room."

I follow Halpern down a series of winding hallways that all the look the same. Door after identical door holding who knows what behind a series of biometric locks. Halpern is tapping away at a tablet that is just out of my line of sight. The little that I can see is almost completely unintelligible to me anyway.

"Soooo, are you going to tell me what this is about?" I ask Halpern, who hasn't looked up at me since I called him mister.

"In a minute. Need to make sure we're in a secure area."

"Secure area? Isn't this whole place a secure area?"

"There's secure, and then there's 'what I need to tell you' secure. This way," Halpern says as he takes a sharp right down another identical hallway.

The hallways are all sterile-looking, a lot of white and steel. If you make a wrong turn somewhere, it'd be almost impossible to remember where since everything looks so uniform. This place has "maze" written all over it. We pass almost a dozen doors before we arrive at the one that must be deemed "secure" by Halpern's standards. He presses his palm to a glass plate and bends down for a retinal scan. At the same time, he announces his name and identification number for voice recognition. The badge clipped to the lapel of his suit jacket emits a soft beep, and an unseen light inside of it glows green.

"I guess you can never be too secure," I joke.

"It's not perfect, but it's the best we can do."

"I was kidding."

"I wasn't. After you," Halpern says as the door hisses softly and rolls inside a pocket in the wall. The room itself is bare, brushed aluminum walls and little else. After Halpern enters, the door closes behind him, and we're now in complete darkness.

"Computer, load case file eight nine three five seven. Authorization code tango, bravo, zebra, eight, nine, nine, alpha. Agent Halpern," he announces into the darkness.

An instant later we're both temporarily blinded by the light of the wall in front of us as the entire surface becomes a display.

"I've told them a million times, they've got to install a dimmer on this thing," Halpern says as he rubs his eyes and blinks to adjust to the sudden change in lighting. "You sure you're ready for this, kid?"

"I'm not even sure what *this* is."

"Well, you're about to find out."

The ten-foot tall screen in front of us displays what looks like the type of photograph you see in private detective movies, a candid shot where the subject isn't aware he's being photographed. The man in the photo has dark, coffee-colored skin, with a cleanly shaven, bald head. He's tall with broad shoulders and wearing what I assume to be a very nice suit. I mean, it fits him better than the old ones I borrow from Derrick fit me whenever I need a suit. He's talking on a mobile phone while ducking into a limousine that's waiting for him on the street outside of an office building. He looks as though he's in his late forties but takes good care of himself.

"Do you know this man?" Halpern asks.

"No. Should I?"

"You really are just a kid, aren't you?"

I don't respond. The image slides over to make room for a cover from *Finance* magazine, where the same man is pictured alongside the caption: "The Baron of Bay View City."

"His name is Desmond Keane. He's one of the richest men in Bay View City and has been for a very long time."

"Okay ... so since when is that a crime?"

"Within the past few months, Mr. Keane has become one of the richest men in the world through a series of seemingly one-sided business dealings."

"I'm still not following how this has anything to do with us."

Halpern clears his throat. "If by *us* you mean myself and The Agency, we have reason to believe that his recent business deals are a result of telepathic powers Mr. Keane has garnered from a set of metabands believed to have been acquired on the black market. It's our belief that Mr. Keane has used his meta powers to coerce his business rivals and others into signing over assets and deals worth several billion dollars over the past month."

"There's a black market for metabands?"

"If you're as rich as Mr. Keane is, there's a black market for everything."

"But telepathy isn't a meta ability."

"No, it's not a *known* meta ability. There's still a lot about metabands we don't know. More active metabands are present on our planet than ever before. Just because we haven't seen an ability yet, doesn't mean it's not out there, especially with an ability like telepathy. If you're potentially able to control the mind of anyone on Earth, that's not something you're likely to start advertising. Especially if said ability came from illegally acquired metabands."

"Illegally? Since when did legality extend to metaband ownership?"

"Since the number of metas started passing into quadruple digits, kid."

"How do you know he has these powers since you don't even know if they exist?"

"Besides the circumstantial evidence like his main competitor just up and handing over the majority stake in his company for a hundredth of what it's worth on the open market? We have our methods."

"Which are?"

"Which are classified."

"Great. Of course they are. Does he have any other abilities, or is that classified too?"

"To the best of our intelligence, no. Telepathy seems to be the only meta power he possesses. However, we can almost never be sure of that, but you have experience with that from your buddy Iris's little shape shifting routine, don't you?"

"How do you know about that?"

"It's easy to get The Controller talking when you've got potato chips to trade after a month of eating nothing but slop."

"So what? You want me there just in case he's got powers you don't know about yet?"

"Partially, but there's another scenario we're more concerned about. Desmond Keane seems to have the ability to control the minds of his victims to some extent, even when his metabands are powered down. Or at least, we assume that, since there's no way he's been able to keep them powered on for an entire month without needing to recharge them. While we believe he cannot telepathically issue new orders to his victims while his bands are powered down, the orders he has issued seem to remain in the victim's mind as long as the metabands are attached to his body, even if they are dormant."

"So you need someone to remove his metabands before he has a chance to reactivate them."

"Exactly. If he's able to reactivate the bands before our tactical team takes him into custody, then we run the risk of him gaining telepathic control over the team."

"Why don't you just assassinate him?"

Halpern gives me a look of concern meant to convey the idea that they would never do such a thing.

"Don't give me that look. I know The Agency isn't above executions if the situation calls for it. Trust me, I'm glad that option's not on the table, but since I haven't heard a good reason why it's not, that makes me suspicious it secretly is, and you're just not telling me."

Halpern sighs and drops the mask of false concern. "The truth? Because we're not one hundred percent sure about any of this. We're close. Ninety-nine point nine, nine, nine percent. But, if we're wrong, we'll have assassinated one of the most powerful men in the world without any indisputable proof of wrongdoing on his part. The Agency can't afford that type of mistake."

"So, what do you need from me?"

"First," Halpern says, "we need to get you a uniform."

ELEVEN

A few short minutes later, I'm inside a small locker room where I've been given a military tactical uniform to wear. The suit I wear as Omni is controlled by my mind and powered by my metabands, but unfortunately, I have limited control over it. I'm fairly certain I can't shape shift beyond creating my somewhat simple suit and exaggerated physique, unlike some other metas, including Iris.

As a result, I need to wear the tactical uniform over my Omni suit since removing that would also remove the additional height and body mass the metabands afford me. I'm already extremely paranoid about The Agency finding out my actual identity, a desire they've made no attempt to hide. So, the last thing I want is for them to figure out what my real body looks like. It might be paranoia, but even something as simple as my height, weight, and approximate build could help them narrow down whatever potential list they undoubtedly have for identifying potential metas.

The tactical outfit isn't quite as form fitting as my Omni suit, but it also covers me head to toe. In fact, this uniform completely obscures my face thanks to a full-face shield. The shield isn't there to protect me, though; it's there to protect my identity. My fake identity as Omni, and I'm not the only one whose identity is concealed.

As I leave the locker room to meet up with Halpern in the hallway, he explains the working logistics of the team. Their identities are top secret, even to many members within The Agency. This is done for the same reason so many metas keep their identities a secret too: fear of retaliation. The team's job is to take down suspected metahuman criminals, many of whom were connected to crime even before acquiring their powers. A crime boss or terrorist can be just as dangerous in jail as he is out of it if he knows the names and faces of those who put him behind bars and wants to hurt their families.

The identities of the team members are unknown, even to each other. It's this level of caution and paranoia that allows me to join the group on this mission without raising any red flags, Halpern tells me. They're somewhat used to members joining and leaving based on the needs and priorities of the current mission. This time around, they've been told that I'm simply "in training." No other qualifier is needed regarding my background since it's assumed that if I'm a part of this team, it's because I'm a former Navy SEAL, Special Forces, etc. Halpern tells me to not even bother coming up with a background story since none of them will ask. In fact, he says the less talking I can do in general, the better.

"There's one other thing, kid," Halpern begins. "These guys, they aren't the biggest fans of metas. You have to understand, they see the worst of the absolute worst. They've had to go up against metas who have completely eviscerated innocent people, including children. You're going to have to keep who you are and what you can do under wraps unless we hit a worst case scenario situation."

"And what's considered a worst case scenario situation?"

"That Keane is, in fact, a meta and has abilities beyond mind control."

"So the worst case scenario is also the most likely scenario?"

"Pretty much."

Great.

"You aren't afraid that if he does have mind control abilities, that he could use them on the team to turn them against one another?" I ask.

"No. Keane hasn't shown any violent tendencies. He's a businessman. Corrupt, but not a killer," Halpern says.

"There's a pretty big difference between killing for money versus killing in order to avoid capture. You might be surprised what people are capable of when they're cornered."

Halpern stops in the hallway and looks directly into my eyes despite the fact that I'm wearing a tactical visor attached to a helmet that is completely obscuring them.

"Midnight's teaching you quite a bit, isn't he?" Halpern asks with a smile.

I've never discussed Midnight with him, but that doesn't mean Halpern's forgotten that we're connected to one another. I don't answer Halpern's question, and instead, ask one of my own. "What if Keane has a change of morals and decides he'd rather take over your team's brains than spend the rest of his life buried under a cement block?"

"They're mentally prepared against that," Halpern says.

"How? No one's ever seen a meta capable of telepathic powers before."

"That you know of. We've got to keep a few things to ourselves, kid. This is us," Halpern says as he stops at another unmarked, stainless steel door and submits his palm, retina, and voice for biometric scanning.

The door slides into the adjacent wall and reveals six soldiers dressed in identical uniforms to mine.

"Beta, Charlie, Delta, Echo, Foxtrot, meet Golf," Halpern says as a way of introducing me to the team I'm now a part of.

Why do I have to be "Golf?" Man, I always get stuck with the lamest names, but right now, I've got to keep that to myself, considering I'm sixteen and covertly infiltrating a highly trained tactical team.

"Welcome to Alpha Team," Beta says, extending his hand to shake mine.

I say "he," but I honestly, have no idea if Beta is male or female. Beta could be a damn robot for all I know since his voice is modulated through his mask to the point where it's barely recognizable as even human. But that's the point, I assume, since everything about the group and mission is more covert than I ever could have imagined.

"Thanks. Happy to be here," I say, not recognizing the sound of my voice as it goes through the modulation process to hide my true identity.

"All right, Golf. This is where I leave you. Remember the briefing I gave you. Beta is your commanding officer now. Good luck," Halpern says to me.

He walks out the same door we entered through. It slides behind him with a hiss, leaving me completely alone with the six soldiers.

"All right, Golf. Let's see what you've got," Charlie says with a slap to my right shoulder.

There's no turning back now.

TWELVE

"All right, surveillance indicates that the building is clear. Keane is en-route to his office to work late, as usual. Security is at its lowest since all non-maintenance staff are gone for the night. Keane might be one of the richest men in the world right now, but that doesn't mean he's not trying to save a few bucks by keeping a light security detail on at night. Not much to steal inside an office building where the most valuable asset is encrypted data that's worthless without the keys," Beta says.

He is giving us a detailed briefing as we ride inside a plain white van on the way to Keane Tower, where we hope to be only minutes behind Keane. The road is bumpy, and there are no windows inside the van, but I can tell we're driving fast to make sure we don't miss the opportunity the team has been waiting on for weeks. No one outside of Beta is talking, which makes me feel slightly more at ease since I'm terrified of blowing my cover. I keep trying to tell myself that all I need to do is keep my head down, stay behind everyone else, and this will all be over before I know it, but the rock in my stomach won't stop reminding me that I already regret this decision. The AK-47 in my hands isn't helping either.

It would seem that Midnight's aversion to guns has rubbed off on me, but I've never liked guns anyway. The fact that this one is full of blanks and has the safety on helps, but not much. Probably because I know that everyone else in the van has the same gun, but theirs is filled with live rounds.

There's a dip in the road, and I'm jostled out of my seat for a moment. Although I can't see it, I can feel that we've just driven down a ramp and have likely reached our target: the underground garage at Keane Tower.

There's a ton of maintenance happening in the building, most of which revolves around upgrading the existing automated security systems to a much more robust solution. Keane has just become very, very wealthy, and if he isn't already the target of both rival businesses and metas, he will be soon. That's one of the reasons this mission has to happen tonight. Next week, the new surveillance systems will be fully online, and any attempt to break into the building with any level of stealth will be exponentially harder, if not impossible.

The van we're in is disguised to look like it belongs to one of the many security contractors working on the security upgrades. The fake credentials the driver presents to security allows us to gain entry without much more than a glance, and why not? The building is empty. There's not much to protect. They have no idea that Desmond Keane is on his way to the office at this very moment.

"Placing garage security cameras on loop now," a voice from a technician at Silver Island says through our earpieces.

Apparently, it was very easy to hack the current security system and simply replace the live feeds with pre-taped feeds from earlier today. The guards watching the security monitors will never even see us if all goes according to plan, but that feels like a very big "if" to me. I still haven't been fully briefed on the exact plan, other than we're supposed to neutralize Keane and bring him back to Silver Island for further questioning without raising any alarms at the Keane Tower.

The van pulls to a stop, and the doors are opened by Beta as he utters a single word: "Move." I follow the others as they pile out of the van. The driver has joined us now and is once again masked. No one has seen his face since he only removed the mask after we were all safely locked inside the back of the darkened van.

Jogging behind the others, I find it hard to keep quiet. There're too many things attached to my "stealth" uniform that jingle and jangle with each step I take. The group stops and turns toward me. Even though they're all wearing lead-lined black tactical masks to prevent metas from learning their identities, I can tell that they're not happy with me.

"Sorry," I whisper as I quickly search my uniform to find the flashlight on my belt that has come unfastened and is the source of the noise I'm making.

"Just keep up, rookie," one of the others says to me with a sigh.

We collectively slip into an elevator. Once inside, Charlie slips a keycard attached to a wrist-top computer into the card slot beneath the floor buttons. A few taps on the device's screen and access is granted to the top floor, which is almost entirely taken up by Keane's office.

"There's a problem," a voice says into my ear as the elevator's doors close, and we begin to rise.

"What do you mean, there's a problem?" Beta asks.

Even with the voice modulation, I can practically hear him clenching his teeth. He strikes me as someone who doesn't like it when a plan doesn't go the way he expects, which reminds me how nervous I am about potentially exposing exactly what I am to this team.

"Keane is already in the building. I repeat, Keane is already in the building," the voice says over the communications channel.

"How can he already be in the building?" Delta asks.

"Our intelligence was wrong about his route to the building, and he's arrived ahead of schedule. He's entered the building through a new entrance that is already equipped with the upgraded surveillance system, which we do not have access to."

"Dammit," Echo says through his communicator. "Where is he now?"

"We have a team on the rooftop across from the building that confirmed he is in his office."

"We don't have much time," Beta says as I feel my heart begin to beat out of my chest. "So much for the element of surprise. This is about to get a little more complicated."

The original plan was fairly simple: wait on the top floor for Keane, the only person who would have access this time of night, and disarm him. The team had planned to wait on either side of the elevator doors, prepared to grab his arms as he exited the elevator. The strategy would have prevented him from activating his metabands and potentially taking control of our minds, as well as using any other powers he might possess that we do not know about. Once immobilized, he would be shackled with titanium arm restraints attached to a waist collar, and he would be ordered to summon his metabands for removal by the team. If he refused, which was expected, he was to be transported back to Silver Island for further interrogation.

The team has conducted many missions similar to this one, but never with such a high profile individual. If they're wrong and there's collateral damage, the consequences for the entire agency would be severe as Keane is a very powerful man, meta or not. There isn't room for mistakes, and we just lost the element of surprise.

"What's the new plan?" Delta asks, but there isn't time for a Plan B.

The elevator we're in opens directly into Keane's office. We'd be lucky if he doesn't already know we're on our way. Once those doors open, all bets are off. The elevator is already at floor twenty with sixty-eight floors to go.

"Weapons ready. We take this one the hard way. Lethal force is authorized," Beta says.

"But what about taking him alive? We don't know for sure that he's even a meta," I say, unable to help myself.

Beta turns his masked face slowly toward me.

"Excuse me?" he asks in a tone that does not convey politeness.

"We don't even know that he's definitely a meta. If we kill him, we might never know," I say.

"I can live with that," Beta shoots back.

Great. A cowboy. I'm starting to get the feeling that coming here was a bad idea. There's a long silence and the only sound in the elevator is the dinging as we pass each floor, an urgent reminder that we're running out of time for a solution.

"The primary objective is taking the meta alive, but if there are any complications, or if the target attempts to activate his bands, take him out. That's an order," Beta says as he flicks the safety off his AK-47.

Ding.

THIRTEEN

The elevator doors open, and the team rushes out past me. Even with my heightened abilities, everything moves so quickly I can barely keep my focus. The floor is dark and expansive. Most of the office is open concept or divided by floor-to-ceiling windows, allowing you to see across the entire top floor into the darkened outside world.

I follow who I think is Charlie as the rest of the team sprints across the floor toward the glass office where I can already see Keane at his desk. He hasn't noticed us thanks to the lights being off throughout the rest of the floor, but it's only a matter of seconds before he's bound to look up from his computer, see a group on soldiers running toward him with assault rifles, and react.

If he is a meta, he'll do what I would do in this situation and activate his bands at the first sight of us. After a while with them, activation becomes an instinct at signs of danger. We might be the good guys, but he doesn't know that. We could be any one of the numerous anti-meta terrorist groups that have sprung up in recent months. They don't negotiate.

We make it most of the way to the glass wall of his office before he notices us. His reaction is to reach under the desk and hit a panic button. In an instant, alarms sound and a steel gate descends from the ceiling to encapsulate Keane's office.

"Looks like our man's got something to hide," Delta yells without breaking his stride as he runs toward the now metal-encased office.

Yeah, he's got something to hide, or he's just a terrified billionaire who just saw a group of armed militants running at him in an empty office building in the middle of the night. In either case, the fact that he didn't use meta powers to stop the attack leads me to believe that he is not, in fact, a meta.

Either that, or he's determined not to expose himself as one unless it's absolutely necessary.

"Breach charge mounted. Detonation in five, four, three ..." Charlie says.

Before I have a chance to ask, "Detonation?" there's a flash of light followed closely by the sound of an explosion. Shards of metal hit the office's Italian marble floors, and a person-sized hole appears in the metal casing around Keane's office. No one waits for the smoke to clear before running through it and into Keane's office.

Between the flash of light, smoke, and sound from the explosion, everything becomes a blur. I follow the rest of the group into the office where I can barely make out muted yelling from the ringing in my ears. It's like the soldiers are all underwater until my metabands do their job and begin to clear up my vision and hearing. I see the five soldiers with their guns trained on Keane. Five identical red laser dots all rest on his forehead. The soldiers yell for Keane to raise his hands slowly and hold them out to his side. They specifically tell him not to raise his hands above his head since he might be able to activate his metabands before any of them would even have time to react.

Suddenly, there are new noises directly outside the steel-encased office, the sounds of boots and the metallic clicks of safeties being disengaged fills the office. In another instant, another team of men enters Keane's office through the hole in the wall. It's Keane's personal security team, ten men even more heavily armed than we are. They're wearing expensive looking black suits and yelling at us to drop our weapons. Us, the militants who have just blasted our way into the office of one of the world's richest men and who are not wearing any type of identifiable insignia or flag. There're absolutely no symbols indicating who we are on our uniforms. All of this is by design, of course. Plausible deniability if Keane turns out not to be a meta after all, and The Agency needs to do damage control. If Keane's not a meta, we were never here. It would be a great plan if it weren't for the ten men with rifles pointed at our heads.

Half of my team, if I can even refer to them as that, turn in an instant and train their rifles on the security guards. They're screaming just as intensely for Keane's men to drop their weapons, or they'll shoot Keane. My heart drops into my stomach at the thought that they're probably not bluffing. Keane's security does not relent, though. They have us outnumbered, and while they might not know who we are, it's safe to assume that if we were here to kill Keane, it would have already been done.

My gun is trained on no one. I stand in between the guards and the soldiers. Just my luck for being the last guy in the room. I'm terrified out of my mind and unable to utter a single word, even if I could find one I thought might help diffuse the situation.

Suddenly, there's another figure in the room, entering through the smoke from our explosion: a woman, unarmed and wearing a cocktail dress. The look on her face is one of complete and total confusion. Her eyes find Keane's, and she cries out his name. Before she can even finish the last syllable, one of the soldiers is screaming at her to stop and moves his laser sight to her chest.

"No!" Keane yells as he reaches out his hands toward her, motioning for her to stop where she is and not come any closer.

Before his arms have even come close to the front of his body, Beta yells, "Take him!"

Bullets fire from three of the soldiers' guns simultaneously. They stop in mid-air as I rush to jump between them and Keane. Everything is moving in slow motion as I move faster than anyone in the room can even register. With each step I take, I notice something else; metabands begin appearing on Keane's wrists. He's summoning them, maybe even unconsciously, but they're appearing. He is a meta.

The bullets hit my back. Just three at first, but three more an instant later as the automatic weapons continue firing. Keane's metabands have now fully materialized, and my hands are reaching for them, trying to ignore the pain of the bullets ricocheting off my back.

More gunfire comes from all around the room. Even moving at this speed, I don't dare chance the time it might cost me to look back. Judging by where the sounds are coming from, it's safe to assume that Keane's security has also opened fire.

I reach both hands toward Keane's wrists and feel the cold metal of his bands. They're straight out in front of his chest, inches away from touching. I pull on them, sliding them off his wrists before they can touch. They come off easily, just as they did when Midnight disarmed me the first night we met, and he couldn't be sure if I was friend or foe.

Time resumes its normal speed, and Keane's bare wrists slam into each other before he's even had a chance to realize that his metabands are gone. There's a look of contorted confusion and horror spreading across his face when I stop moving and time catches up again. His powers are gone, and he already knows that he'll never get them back. The slow, low rumbling booms of each gunshot turn into a seemingly endless barrage of noise.

"We've been infiltrated! Fire!" Beta yells as I begin to feel heavier caliber ammunition, like grenades, hit my back.

There's hardly any pain, but even still, getting hit by a grenade isn't exactly pleasant. My tactical uniform has been mostly torn away at this point, exposing the deep red Omni suit underneath.

"Hold your fire!" I scream at the top of my lungs as I turn to face my now former teammates. I'm careful to stay in front of Keane in order to block any errant bullets in case they don't listen. "I'm with you!"

"The hell you are!" Charlie yells back, his gun still trained on me, and his finger itching for a reason to pull the trigger.

"Halpern assigned me. I swear."

"Drop Keane's metabands and kick them over. Now!" Beta barks at me.

I do as he says.

"Fine. Fine. Here. Take them. I'm on your side. I just don't want anyone to get hurt," I say, trying my best to defuse the situation.

"It's too late for that," Delta growls.

It's then that I notice what's happened. The ten security guards are all lying on the ground, motionless. Echo and Foxtrot are down too, along with the woman who came running into the room and started all the confusion. They're lying in a puddle of blood.

"No!" Keane screams, his voice cracking. "What have you done?"

Keane runs toward the woman, but only makes it a few steps before an electrical charge is fired at him, dropping him to the floor in a fit of convulsions.

"Not so fast," Delta says to him, holding the stun gun responsible for the hit.

Keane lies on the ground in a heap, writhing in both physical and emotional pain as Beta pulls his arms behind his back and handcuffs them. Charlie places the metabands into a titanium case and seals it shut.

After Keane and the office are secured, I assume they looked back toward me, still trying to figure out if I'm a liar, and if I am, what to do with me. But it's too late; I'm already gone.

Fourteen

When I teleported out of Keane Tower, I go to the first place that literally pops into my head: Midnight's water tower. I'd hoped that Midnight wouldn't be there so I could have some time to just be alone and think. My hope is misguided.

Midnight is across the room when I materialize, sitting at his computer and analyzing whatever it is that he spends all night analyzing when he's not busy breaking noses, but within seconds of my arrival, he's across the room.

"What is this? What happened?" he yells, pulling at the shreds of the military uniform that's been ripped to pieces by the bullets.

"I got shot at."

"I can see that. By who, and why are you wearing this?"

"Security guards."

My mind is still in a daze over what happened. All those guards. All dead. They weren't bad guys. They weren't killers. They were just men who were paid to do a job: protect Desmond Keane. They had no idea who he really was or who we were. All they saw was a group of soldiers opening fire on their boss, and they reacted. They didn't deserve to die. I should have protected them.

Midnight steps back, and his concern turns to unnerving quietness. "Were you at Keane Tower?"

"Yes. How did you know?"

Midnight stares at me for what feels like an eternity. Without saying a word, he turns, picks up a remote control from the nearest stainless steel workbench, and hits a button. All of the monitors in the water tower, including the massive north-side wall, which unbeknownst to me was a video monitor this entire time, change to one of the news channels.

The news channel is showing the view from a helicopter hovering outside Keane Tower, next to the eighty-eighth story windows that were shattered by gunfire only minutes ago.

"We're looking at Keane Tower, which just moments ago became the scene of what sources are telling us was a siege enacted by rogue militant forces. The unknown assailants have taken billionaire Desmond Keane into their custody and have killed a number of security personnel here at Keane Tower. Their motivation is unknown at this time, but considering the wealth of Mr. Keane, it can only be assumed that their target was chosen based on his significant financial holdings. Currently, the whereabouts of Mr. Keane and his alleged captors are unknown. The city has issued a full-scale search and an all-points bulletin on the white van seen entering the Tower's garage earlier tonight. City officials ask that any meta-powered individuals stay back at this time to avoid risking contamination of the crime scene," the anchor says over video footage of bodies laying on the ground as seen through the veritable hole the gunfight put through the building's exterior.

"What the hell were you doing there?" Midnight growls at me through gritted teeth.

I hadn't even noticed that he'd moved within inches of my face. I was in a complete daze watching the newscast, trying to wrap my head around the events that just transpired.

"They asked me to help," I say.

"Who? Who asked you to help?" Midnight screams back.

"The Agency."

Midnight stares into my eyes, seething with rage he can barely contain.

"Get out."

"What?"

"You heard me. Get out. Now."

"This wasn't my fault. None of this was supposed to happen this way ..."

"I'm not going to tell you again," Midnight says as he turns his back on me.

I decide not to test Midnight's threat that he won't ask me again, and teleport to the second place that pops into my mind: home.

FIFTEEN

It isn't until about three a.m. when Derrick comes home. I'm sitting on the couch, still wearing the tattered tactical uniform over my Omni suit. I've pulled back the parts of both suits that cover my face. Even though the Omni suit feels like a second skin when it's on, the mask feels like it's suffocating me tonight.

"What are you doing, Connor? You can't just be sitting in here like that! What if I was with someone?" Derrick whisper yells as he opens the door, steps inside, and quickly shuts it behind him.

"Ha. That's the first funny thing I've heard all night," I reply.

"What's your problem?" Derrick asks.

"Rough night. Very rough night," I say.

"Another one of those 'rough nights' that you can't talk about because Midnight doesn't trust me?" Derrick asks with a sigh.

"Midnight does trust you. Ish. Kinda. But no, Midnight wasn't even with me tonight. I was working for The Agency."

There's silence before he asks, "You were at Keane Tower tonight, weren't you?"

"Yeah."

More silence. I'm not surprised. He hasn't mentioned it yet, but I'm positive the reason why he was working so late has everything to do with what happened at the tower tonight.

"What happened there?" he asks.

"Confusion. It was an accident. I couldn't stop it in time."

"There weren't any reports of a meta other than Keane at the tower tonight."

"I was undercover. The Agency didn't want anyone to know that they needed a meta to take down Keane. The other guys on the squad didn't even know I'm a meta. When they found out, they weren't happy."

Derrick slowly slides down onto the leather couch next to the armchair I'm hunched over in.

"Connor, this is some serious stuff. People died tonight. You're telling me there was a cover-up about what happened?"

"Yes, that's what I'm telling you. Off the record, of course."

"You have to tell me something is off the record *before* you say it. That's how it works."

"Well, I'm trusting that you probably can't print that your source is your sixteen year-old brother since I doubt many people would buy that."

"Look, I know I'm just your brother, and even though I'm bigger than you, I can't make you do anything you don't want to ..."

"And I have super strength," I interject.

"I'm trying to be serious here. I don't think you should be working with The Agency anymore. I'm worried about them getting you into trouble, especially since they'll lie and say anything to protect themselves."

"I know, but if I'm not on their side, then they're going to start asking a lot of questions about whose side I'm on."

"You're on your own side."

"Ha. The only thing they like less than people who aren't on their side are people who are independent. Makes it harder for them to put you in a box and figure out what exactly it is you want."

SIXTEEN

The next day at school, I'm even more tired than usual, which is saying something. I couldn't sleep at all the night before. I just kept replaying the same images through my mind over and over again, trying desperately to think of some way I could have prevented what happened. I can't see how, though. If I had let them execute Keane, those security guards still would have shown up. There still would have been a fight, and they still would have lost. Even with my speed, there were just too many of them to take out all at once.

"Mr. Connolly?" I hear a voice ask through the haze my mind is currently neck deep in.

It's Mr. Morrison, my chemistry teacher, and by the tone of his voice, I'm guessing this isn't the first time he's had to say my name to get my attention.

"Sorry. What?" I ask, trying to shake the cobwebs out of my brain.

"I was asking just what it is outside the window that you find so interesting?" Mr. Morrison asks, presumably for at least the second time.

There's a chorus of giggles from my classmates.

"Nothing. Sorry, Mr. Morrison. I didn't get much sleep last night."

"Maybe you can see the future, Mr. Connolly, and were up late studying because you knew we were going to have a pop quiz today?" he says.

The class' giggling changes to groans, and a handful of insults are hurled at me.

Mr. Morrison hands a stack of papers to the first person in each row, who then takes one and hands the rest back until I get the last quiz since I'm seated at the end of the row. I stare at the paper, completely dumbfounded, realizing I know absolutely none of the material. How could I? I've slept through about eighty percent of the class this year.

After class, Mr. Morrison holds me back to "have a talk." The talk is pretty one-sided, with him telling me how close I am to failing and me listening to something that I'm already pretty much aware of. I wait until he's finished, and then explain that I understand, and I promise to make an effort to do better. This is true, I am going to make an effort; the problem is that it probably isn't going to have that much of an effect.

My grades are in the toilet for one reason and one reason only, and that's the metabands that are around my wrists right now in standby mode so they're invisible to the rest of the world. Lately, with everything going on, something's had to give, and that something wound up being school. I can't be out all night bashing bad guys' heads in and still be expected to have read half of *Pride and Prejudice* by Monday.

If something is going to get lost in the shuffle, I don't want that something to be Omni. With all that's going on, with thousands of new metas all over the world and new metabands being found every week, I need to be Omni right now. The world is becoming a very dangerous place. Everyone is remembering the metas who use their power to kill innocent people and steal, or the maniacs who quickly lose all sense of their own humanity once they think they've become gods. For every meta who gets recognition for doing a good deed, there're ten times as many who become infamous for being bad. It's the names of the bad metas that kids remember and think about at night, worried that they're under their beds.

And for all the bad metas who are out there, there are even more with dubious morals. Those who do good when it's convenient for them, or when there's some kind of financial gain involved; men who have become indestructible and choose a career performing movie stunts instead of becoming a firefighter; or those who kill when they think it's necessary, knowing that the courts have little or no recourse when trying to convict a meta, other than issuing a warrant through The Agency, despite knowing that it will go to the bottom of a very long pile for the overworked department. There aren't enough metas like me out there right now, and the world needs more.

Plus, I like being Omni. Being Omni is cool.

There's another priority I don't want to give up right now either, and that's Sarah. It might have taken me awhile to get a girlfriend, but now that I finally have one, I really hit a home run, if I do say so myself. She's perfect in every way. No matter how rough a day I've had, she always makes me laugh and smile. She doesn't even know the most interesting thing about me, but she makes me feel like I'm the coolest guy on Earth just because she cares about me.

I'm lost in thought for about a minute, thinking about how lucky I am to have Sarah, when I finally snap out of it and realize that she's standing right in front of me. Okay, so maybe I was actually literally asleep on my feet.

"You all right?" Sarah asks.

"Me? Yeah. Of course. Why?"

"It looked like you fell asleep standing up."

"Asleep standing up? Me? Nah. I was just resting my eyes."

"And swaying."

"I was thinking about a song I heard earlier."

"Uh huh," Sarah says in a voice that lets me know she doesn't believe me, but is going to let it slide because she's already asked me why I'm always so tired about a million times. "Are you walking this way?" she asks.

"Yup."

"Great, I'll walk with you." We start walking and there's a few seconds of silence before she says what I knew she would, "Sorry about my dad last night."

"Oh, that? No, don't worry about it."

"He's always like that."

"Bring a lot of boys home, do you?" I joke.

"No, stupid," Sarah says, playfully hitting me. "He's just always wrapped up in his work. Ever since Mom left, it's like he just replaced that hole in his life with work."

"And when was that?" I ask. She turns her head to look at me, as though the answer to whether or not she wants to have this conversation is written on my face. "It's okay if you don't want to—"

"No," she stops me, "it's fine. I wanted to tell you, in fact. I just wasn't sure how to bring it up. It's not really something I ever talk about. I barely remember her, and Dad hasn't mentioned her name once since she left."

"It was that long ago?"

"Yeah. I must have been about three or four years old."

"Oh, wow. I had no idea."

I have more questions, but I'm careful to tread lightly. She'll let me know what she wants me to know on her schedule. There's no need for me to rush her just because I'm nosy.

"It was bad," she continues. "Dad used to drink a lot. Trying to forget about my mom, I guess. When I got older, it hurt me to see how badly he hurt. He really loved her, and she just left him ... and me." There's another long, pregnant pause, and I can tell Sarah is trying to figure out whether or not to share another piece of herself. She finally decides. "He was a meta, you know."

"What?" I ask.

"The guy. The man my mom left my dad for."

That was the last thing I was expecting to hear. Now I've got a lot more questions, but most of them are related to how this revelation fits in with her dad working for The Agency, which is something I assume she doesn't even know.

"Why didn't you tell me before?" I ask.

"Because ..." She goes quiet. "Because of what happened with your parents. You must already hate metas so much. I didn't want to remind you of that with my own story. It's way different with me. My mom was her own person. She didn't have to leave us for him. It doesn't matter what he was."

"I don't hate metas," I say.

"How could you not?" she asks.

"Because having a pair of fancy snap bracelets doesn't make a person good or bad. They are what they've always been. A meta is still just a person."

"Well, those fancy snap bracelets can change a person when they're suddenly able to knock a building off its foundation. Anyway, it all hit Dad pretty hard. He never really bounced back after that."

"And what about your mom?" I ask.

"She stayed in touch for a little while, but then it became too hard for my dad to deal with. He filed for sole custody, and she didn't challenge him. I haven't seen her since."

"Wow. That's gotta be really hard."

"Not really. I never really knew her, and my dad has more than made up for her in the overprotection department, as you saw last night."

"Ha, yeah. Well, that's just how dads are, I guess. Not like I'd really know much about it."

"You've got Derrick. I know he's not your dad, of course, but I have a feeling he'd do just about anything for you and that he does his fair share of keeping you out of trouble."

"You'd be surprised," I say with a smirk, thinking about how she has no idea how I spend my nights.

"Well, if you don't have a problem with metas, I was wondering if I could make last night up to you, and see if you'd be interested in going to the Metahuman Circus with me tonight? I got tickets a while ago, and it's supposed to be absolutely amazing. Metas providing a little entertainment instead of destroying buildings and lives," Sarah says with sarcastic cheer in her voice.

The Metahuman Circus. A throwback to one that existed during the first wave, except much more elaborate now that there's a wealth of metahumans looking for a way to earn an honest living without having to hide the fact that they have powers. While it might be a somewhat honest way to make a living as a meta, it's not without its detractors. A lot of questions have been raised over the speed at which the Metahuman Circus kicked back into production after being quiet for over a decade, not to mention the human circus performers who are lucky to get a job cleaning up elephant poop now that metas are back. No one wants to see a man be shot out of a cannon when they can see one who can fly.

I'm definitely more than a little curious to see metas up close without them trying to bash my head in. I might not make any new friends tonight, but it's a good idea to observe others with powers as much as possible to see if there's anything new I can learn. Plus, I'm still due a real night off. I can always catch up on my sleep in Mr. Morrison's class tomorrow.

"Sure, I'd love to."

Seventeen

The word "circus" is not an apt description for the absolute frenzy that is happening in front of us, and we're not even inside the arena yet. The crowd is immense, with thousands lined up to get in, and seemingly even more outside the gates, desperately searching for a ticket for sale. Alongside them are a plethora of anti-meta groups staging protests. While anti-meta sentiment is high, it's rare to see a public display of it, mostly because it's not always a great idea to protest a group of people who could potentially vaporize you with their eyes. At the Metahuman Circus, there's a feeling of safety for the protesters as the metas performing are all on their best behavior, lest they lose their jobs. There's also media all over the place, covering the event, so any attack on the anti-meta groups in front of this many cameras would only further their cause.

"Hey buddy, you got tickets? Look, I'll buy 'em off you for a thousand dollars!" a man says, grabbing my arm before I can find the line to the arena's entrance.

"A thousand dollars?" I practically yell.

"Only a thousand? I'll give you two thousand!" another man yells from farther down the line where it looks like he was haggling over the price of a ticket from another attendee, only to interrupt it when he heard what he thought was a bargain.

"Two thousand dollars?" I yell again, not learning my lesson the first time and attracting even more people in search of tickets who think I'm holding some type of impromptu auction.

"No, no, no," Sarah says, waving her arms in the air. "Sorry everyone. Big misunderstanding. We're not looking to sell our tickets."

"Yeah, sorry everybody," I say. "My mistake. Good luck,

though."

The crowd slowly disperses, muttering and grumbling about us wasting their time before they head out to look for scalpers who are more than willing to part with their tickets for the right price.

"Sorry about that," I say to Sarah. "I just couldn't believe people are willing to pay that much money for a circus."

"Not just any circus, a Metahuman Circus! I wouldn't miss this for any amount of money."

"Right, me either," I say and then pause. "Still, I mean, two thousand dollars is a lot of money. I bet you could go to all kinds of other shows with that much money—"

"Connor," Sarah interrupts me, "they're my tickets. We're not selling them. We're going to see the Metahuman Circus."

"Right, right, of course. I was just thinking out loud."

"Uh huh," she says, not believing me, but looking to change the subject.

"How did you get these anyway? They must have cost you a fortune"

"Nope, they were free actually. My dad got them from some guy at work, apparently he couldn't make it."

Yeah, I'm sure it was something like that. Man, she really has no idea, or she's even better at lying than her dad is. We find our way through the crowd to the actual line to enter the arena. Even the line takes a good thirty minutes or so to get through before we're able to get inside.

The setup of the circus looks just like any other circus you would expect to see. There are three rings in the center for the entertainers to perform inside of; some of the rings already have caged animals or various contraptions ready and waiting, having been loaded by the crew in advance of the show. We find our seats right as the lights go down, signaling that it's time for the show to begin.

Once the audience is seated and quiet, a single spotlight hits the middle of the center ring. There's applause as a red-suited ringmaster takes a bow and announces the night's first act just as she's entering the spotlight in the ring to his right.

Before the performance begins, the audience is asked to reach under their seats and find a small bag of reflective confetti and have it ready. Sarah and I exchange looks of confusion, but there's certainly an element of excitement around the arena about how these bags will fit into the performance. Part of reason for the excitement is that the meta who has stepped into the ring doesn't look much like any of the metas you see flying or running around the city. She's in her late fifties, overweight, and tired looking. She's been stuffed into a sequined spandex suit, but there hasn't been much additional effort put into her clothing or taming her frizzy black and gray, shoulder length hair.

The ringmaster introduces her as "Elaine, The Human Tornado," who has the ability to control the weather and the wind using her powers. I sit up in my chair since this is an ability no other meta has demonstrated yet, as far as I know. I'm even tempted to text Derrick to see if he's ever heard of such a meta, but I decide to wait to see what the actual performance is before potentially embarrassing myself. Within a few seconds, I'm glad I made that decision.

The Human Tornado doesn't have the ability to control the air, weather, or anything even remotely like that. She's a Speeder, with the ability to move quickly. Very quickly. I haven't had to track down many, and I'm glad. Based on the few encounters I've had with them and the videos I've seen online, there are some Speeders that I don't think even I'd be able to chase down. It's not just running that metabands enhance; it's pretty much everything, as Elaine, The Human Tornado, is demonstrating. She begins spinning around and around in a circle. Soon, she's a blur, and you can hear the air around her starting to whip. Dust from the dirty circus floor begins to rise and slowly circle her feet.

"I'm gonna go run to the bathroom," I whisper to Sarah.

"What? The show just started!"

"I know, but I have to go. I figure I better do it now, during Amateur Hour, than wait and have to duck out during one of the good parts."

"Shhhh!" someone at least three rows back hisses.

Sarah looks back and mouths the word, "Sorry." She rolls her eyes and motions for me to just go.

As I bound up the steps, I look back at the ring when the audience begins to gasp and applaud. People have begun throwing their confetti into the air toward the ring, watching as most of it gets swirled into the previously invisible tornado that has formed around Elaine.

All right, I'll admit that it looks pretty neat, but considering the face value of these tickets, I really hope the rest of the show is a little more impressive.

Eighteen

"You believe this crap cost over a hundred dollars a ticket?" the college-age guy with a backward baseball cap standing in line in front of me at the concession stand asks.

I've made a slight detour after hitting the bathroom to grab some snacks. All right, so maybe it was a major detour, because I walked halfway around the arena just to find the Burger Shack stand, but A: It's going to be totally worth it because their burgers are amazing, and B: I'm feeling slightly anxious watching metas with Sarah.

I'm an idiot for not realizing that, of course, I would feel this way. I'm juggling not only my secret, but also her dad's secret in my head. I have to constantly remind myself not to seem to have too much knowledge about metas, how their bands and powers work, etc. At the same time, I also have to constantly remind myself not to act like a total idiot who has never even heard of metas since that would probably seem even more suspicious. The entire world is obsessed with them, and I constantly catch myself acting like I've been living under a rock for the past six months.

I really need to just relax. My brother runs one of the biggest meta sites on the Internet; it would totally make sense for me to have a lot of knowledge about metas. Hell, I had way too much knowledge about them even before I got my bands, simply because Derrick likes to hear himself talk.

"Yeah, not that great, so far," I finally reply to the guy in front of me after what was probably way too much time staring off in the distance, thinking about whether or not I'm pretending to have the right amount of knowledge about metas.

"I'm just waiting for The Multiplier. He's who I'm really here to see," he says.

"The Multiplier?"

"Really? You spent this much money on tickets to this lame fest, and you don't even know who The Multiplier is?"

"I got the tickets for free. Didn't really look into it too much beforehand."

"Still, have you been living under a rock or something?" he asks.

Even when I'm being truthful about my meta knowledge, I come off looking like an idiot.

"I just haven't heard of him before."

"He's the only reason to come to these shows, in my opinion."

"What's his power?" That's better. Act interested, like a real human being.

"He can multiply!"

Ask a stupid question; get a stupid answer.

"What does that mean, though? Like, he knows all of his timetables up to infinity?" I awkwardly joke.

At the very least this guy thinks I'm just a garden-variety weirdo, rather than a person trying to hide something.

"He can multiply himself. Split himself in two, and then split those two into two, and then split those two into—"

"I think I get it," I interrupt to make sure I'm not standing here all night with this guy. "So, what? Is he a Manipulator?"

Manipulators are metas who have some type of control of matter outside of their own bodies. It's not quite telekinesis, but the ability to create complex objects out of what looks like mid-air. Scientists have since verified in a lab that it's not actually "thin air," since there's matter and dark matter around us at all times. As best as they can tell, Manipulators have the ability to rearrange these basic building blocks of existence and change them into something more complicated.

Some Manipulators are only able to create the most basic of objects. A plain item with no moving parts, for example. Others are able to create basic machinery, vehicles, weapons, etc. The most talented are able to create actual complex living organisms, creatures that they can control just through thought. The Controller was a Manipulator, although he was probably the most advanced one the world has seen. He could not only create seemingly living creatures, but he did so from a great distance. Most Manipulators are limited to only being able to create and control objects that they are close enough to see with their own eyes.

"What's a Manipulator?" the guy in front of me asks.

Whoops. Maybe that was too much information. Hard to keep straight the information I get from TV or Derrick from what I hear from Halpern or Midnight. Each source needs to be somewhat carefully compartmentalized in my brain so that I don't reveal anything I hear from Midnight or Halpern to anyone else or to each other.

"I think I read about it online somewhere. You know, just a meta that can make things out of thin air," I say.

"Nah, I don't think so. He *splits* himself. Like he's made out of Play-Doh or something. Do you know what time it is?"

"Uhh," I say while pulling my hand out of my pocket to glance down at my watch, "it's ten minutes to nine."

"Crap! I'm gonna miss it. This is his first performance with the circus, and he's going to try to multiply himself a hundred times. It's never been done before! Here, you can take my spot. I've got to make sure I'm back before he starts," he says as he leaves the line and starts a light jog, presumably toward the direction of his seat.

I briefly think about leaving the line too since this guy was so excited about the act, and because the ability he described isn't one that I've heard about before. All known Manipulators, even the most powerful ones, are only able to create and control a single projection at a time. If they try to create more, the first one begins to decay and break down. The idea of someone being able to create not only a projection as complex as a human being, but also multiple ones, just doesn't sound believable. My guess is he's just some run-of-the-mill Manipulator who has figured out a clever illusion to make it look like he's got an ability that no one else has. It makes sense after all. Why come to the Metahuman Circus if you're not going to see anything you haven't already seen before? They've got to do something to draw people watching the news and ViewNow videos of metas out of their homes and down to the circus.

The line for Burger Shack is still wrapped around the corner, but enough people are starting to leave the line that I'm able to round the counter and at least catch a glimpse of the act on the large screen television perched over the Burger Shack stand. Sarah is going to kill me for missing this, but my stomach will never forgive me if I give up on Burger Shack when I'm this close. Priorities.

The lights in the entire arena dim, and the spotlight appears once again in the center ring where the ringmaster is already standing and waiting.

"And now, ladies and gentlemen, boys and girls, we have a very special treat for you tonight," the ringmaster announces as a hush falls over the entire arena. Even the line I'm standing in for Burger Shack has gone silent, and everyone's eyes are glued to the TV in front of us.

"Ladies and gentlemen, we live in a fantastical world where humans are now capable of doing things that we have never been able to do before, feats and abilities that were previously thought to be impossible or limited to the world of science fiction. I don't have to tell you about the amazing events we see unfolding on television everyday, but I can tell you that tonight, you will have a chance to see an entirely new type of meta. One that has never before been seen in the world. A meta with an ability so mind boggling that even our nation's top scientists and metaologists refuse to believe he's real. They refuse, only because they have not seen him with their own eyes. Well tonight, ladies and gentlemen of

Bay View City, you are going to walk out of here with undeniable proof that you have witnessed meta history within the walls of this arena!"

The roar of the audience is deafening, even from the hallway outside the arena. More of the people waiting in line are now deciding that this is something they just can't miss and start rushing back to their seats. As the line thins out, I'm able to keep moving closer and closer to my date with destiny: a Burger Shack burger with cheddar and bacon. When I die, I won't regret that I didn't get to see a new type of meta displaying his abilities for the first time, but I will probably regret not eating more Burger Shack burgers when I had the chance, even if they're just as likely to kill me as another meta, if I ate them as often as I'd like.

"Please welcome to the world's stage for the very first time: The Multiplier!"

The crowd roars again, louder than before, which I didn't think was possible. A man walks out from the darkness before another spotlight catches him on his way to center ring. He's a tall white man, probably in his early thirties, with a thick mop of black hair that's been parted to the side, and is so long, he has to brush it out of his eyes. He's wearing an outfit not unlike the ringmaster's, but in black instead of red. It's an elaborate tuxedo that probably looks ridiculous up close, but it works when most of the people looking at you are hundreds of feet away. The Multiplier meets the ringmaster in the center ring and stands there, expressionless.

"I ask for total silence now as The Multiplier attempts his first multiplication."

The crowd obliges, and you could hear a pin drop as he closes his eyes and concentrates. For the first few seconds, nothing is happening at all. I begin to feel nervous for him, being in front of all these people, trying to demonstrate your new superhuman ability. It's enough to give anyone a bit of stage fright.

Just as I'm starting to really feel sorry for him, his entire body starts shaking from side to side. His posture remains completely upright, but he's moving faster and faster, sliding from side to side within a three-foot radius. The vibrations are happening so fast that he becomes a complete blur, and gasps can be heard throughout the crowd. Slowly, the blur grows more distinguished. There are now two identical versions of the man standing side by side in the same position. The vibrations slow down, and the blur becomes clearer, until it stops completely. Two separate, identical men stand in the center ring.

He really did it. He's a new type of meta. Wow. I guess this circus really is all it's cracked up to be. The cheer of the crowd breaks my concentration, and I stop staring at the television and turn back to the Burger Shack line, except there is no line. The entire line has disappeared since everyone ran back to his or her seat but me. The Burger Shack employees are all watching the same TV monitor and have their mouths hanging open in disbelief. They're used to watching basketball games in this arena, not men violating the laws of physics. So, it's understandable that no one called out to let me know I was next.

"Hi, sorry about that. Welcome to Burger Shack. Wasn't that incredible?" the young female employee asks me when I finally snake my way through the now empty, zig-zagging rope lanes.

"Yeah, it really was," I reply.

"Yeah. Wow," she says, still staring at the television monitor, even though all it's showing is The Multipliers, plural, taking their synchronized bows.

"Umm ..." I say.

"Sorry," the employee says, shaking her head. "I've just never seen anything like that. What can I get for ..." Her eyes slowly drift back to the monitor.

I turn around and see that The Multipliers have walked to

opposite ends of the arena and are entering the audience, much to the delight of the many screaming and applauding fans. Each Multiplier stands in front of an audience member in the first row and begins shaking again before once again splitting in two.

"Holy cow!" the Burger Shack employee exclaims.

"Yeah, that's really something. So can I have a ..."

"I mean, that is just incredible!" she says, completely ignoring me again

At this point, I decide to just let it go and join her in watching the show. Hey, at least I got to basically cut the entire line, right? After ravenous applause, the four Multipliers split again, now becoming eight. The crowd applauds even louder. The audience members in the front rows are now all grabbing at The Multipliers in front of them, wanting to touch a part of them. I'm not sure if it's to make sure that they're real, or if it's a rock star type thing. Before I have time to figure it out, The Multipliers split again.

And again.

And again.

He's splitting faster and faster now, only taking occasional pauses for a handful of his clones to step up to the next row to begin the process all over again. In mere seconds, there are enough Multipliers that there is one of him standing in front of every single audience member in the arena, thousands and thousands of copies.

"Wow, that is nuts!" I say over my shoulder before turning to look at the Burger Shack employee.

She's gone, though; there's just a headset on the counter. I catch a glimpse of her out the side door as she runs toward the main area of the arena.

She looks back and says, "Sorry! I've just got to see this! Wait right there. Your burger's on the house when I come back!"

* * *

I begin walking back to my seat, having given up any hope of a Burger Shack burger, but find myself slowing my pace as I struggle to pull my eyes off the TV monitor.

"And now, ladies and gentlemen," the thousands of copies of The Multiplier say in unison, much to the delight of the audience, "don't move."

All at once, The Multipliers reach into the waistband of their costumes and pull out large, identical, curved knives. In one fluid movement, every copy yanks the audience member in front of him to their feet and puts the knife up against their throat. Screams ripple through the audience, but no one moves. Everyone is frozen in place, the steel of the knives pressing into their flesh hard enough to make an indent, but not hard enough to draw blood.

Yet.

My heart and mind are racing, and I feel a lump in my throat as my mouth begins to dry out. This can't be real, can it? It must be part of the show. The look of terror on the faces of the people in the audience indicates that it isn't part of the show, though. This is very real.

I look around the empty corridor and consider my options. There aren't many. Security cameras record every inch of the arena. If I light up my metabands, I'll show up in the security footage for sure. My identity will be exposed, and people like Sarah and Derrick will never be safe again.

"This will all be over shortly. Which camera should I speak into?" The Multiplier in the center ring asks, looking around at the various live cameras covering the event for pay-per-view.

Those who couldn't get a ticket are paying exorbitant fees just for the privilege of watching the circus on TV and the Internet. Now, they're getting a show that they weren't counting on.

From the hallway entrance leading into the main arena, I

see one of the cameramen raise his shaking hand to indicate that he's controlling the camera that is currently live. A copy of The Multiplier has a knife to his throat as well.

"Good," the original Multiplier says as he walks closer to the camera. "Hi there everybody at home. I hope you're enjoying the show so far. No doubt you're certainly getting your money's worth now, getting to watch all of us metahumans dance around and entertain you. I guess we're not so scary when we're safely behind your TV screen, but here's the problem. The people here aren't so safe, especially not right now. Luckily for them and their loved ones at home, there's a way to save them."

The Multiplier reaches into his pocket and pulls out a smartphone and a piece of paper, which he unfolds and holds up in front of the camera. Glancing up at the monitor in the hallway, I can see that it is a long string of seemingly random letters and numbers.

"This is a ByteCoin address. My ByteCoin address, coincidentally enough. Now we're going to do a little experiment. I'm going to demand one hundred million dollars be deposited into this account in the next five minutes, or I'll begin slitting throats. One at a time."

There's a gasp throughout the arena, and various audience members begin squirming. All are held back by the copy of The Multiplier in front of them as the steel blades press more firmly against their throats.

"Now, here's the really fun part. I don't care who pays the ransom. There's over twenty thousand people here tonight, so let's do some quick math," he says as he pauses and looks upward, presumably doing the necessary division in his head. "Wow, that's only five thousand dollars per hostage. Really not that bad when you think about it. Here's the problem, though. I don't want to deal with all the logistics of accepting payment for and releasing individual hostages; so it's all or nothing. If you know someone who's here tonight and you think they're worth saving, start sending your money, and maybe between the twenty thousand of you, there're enough people out there who think you're worth five grand each. But don't wait, because the executions will be randomized to try to make sure this goes as quickly as possible. I've got places to be, and I'm sure you don't want this little diversion interrupting the rest of tonight's scheduled programming.

"Oh, and if there's some disgraced billionaire out there looking to win back some of the public's popular opinion, I think you could do a lot worse than putting up the entire ransom and saving twenty thousand people tonight. Even the most popular metas would have a hard time beating that number for saves in a day," The Multiplier says into the camera in front of him.

The corridor is still empty since I'm the only person who thought to try to get food during the biggest act of the night, but the security cameras rule out any possibility of activating my metabands, unless I want to unmask myself. If it comes to that, I'll have no choice, but in the meantime, I have five minutes to think of something else.

My phone vibrates in my pocket. I pull it out and see the name "Martin Northcott" on the caller ID. I don't know anyone named Martin Northcott, but I didn't even have to look at the phone's display to know who would be calling. I tap the answer button and put the receiver up to my ear.

"I'm working on it," Midnight's voice says through the telephone.

"Good, because I'm all out of ideas, as long as these cameras are on," I reply.

There's a commotion in the arena, and I glance up at the monitor suspended in the hallway to see what's happening inside. A man is being brought down the stairs of the arena's seating area by four copies of the Multiplier, each holding one of his limbs. The man is thrashing and struggling to break free from them, but it's no use. As soon as one limb breaks free from a copy, that copy splits in two and uses the new copy to help regain control of the freed limb.

"Well, well, well, what do we have here? The night's first hero," The Multiplier says. "There's always one, right? Bring him down here."

The camera, presumably being controlled by either a cameraman with a knife to his throat or directly by one of The Multiplier's copies, zooms in on the man. He's at least a few years older than me, muscular, and with a fresh crew cut.

"So, you thought it was a good idea to disarm one of my copies and slit its throat before it could do the same to you, huh?" The Multiplier asks rhetorically.

I can see now that the man's hands and white t-shirt are covered in blood.

"And what exactly did you think taking out one of my copies would accomplish in an arena full of thousands more?"

"We're not going to be terrorized by monsters like you," the man defiantly states, still struggling against the copies holding him.

"Well, you aren't any longer," The Multiplier says before slitting the man's throat in one fluid movement.

There are cries of horror throughout the stadium that are only broken a second later by all twenty thousand copies of The Multiplier, in perfect unison, commanding the audience to be quiet.

"Anything?" I plead into my phone at Midnight.

"I'm still working. Five minutes."

"Five minutes? Sarah's in there! Someone's already dead. He's going to kill more in five minutes!"

There's nothing but silence on the other end. I don't have to explain the situation to Midnight. It's not like my whining will make him work any faster, so I decide to just shut up and wait.

"All right, I have a better question," I begin, receiving a

grunt on the other end of the line, indicating that it's okay for me to continue, but the rapid fire keyboard taps in the background are a reminder that I don't have his full attention. "Once you disable the cameras, then what?"

The brief hiccup in the sound of Midnight's typing doesn't reassure me that he has a real plan either. "Right now, we have to work on getting those cameras down. With them online, there's nothing you can do," he says.

"But what can I do when he's got a knife to the throat of every person in here? I'm not fast enough to take them all out."

Midnight pauses before answering, like he's accessing some type of database inside his head and searching for the answer. "He's a replicator. His power is entirely dependent on the health of the original. Cut off the head and the rest wither away. Take him out, and the rest are vapor."

"How can you be sure? And how can I be sure that I can take him out quickly enough that he doesn't have a chance to use the clones to hurt anyone? He might have super strength, but I just don't know it."

"He doesn't. If he did, that man wouldn't have been able to take out one of the copies so easily. If we don't do anything, these people are dead."

He's right, but there has to be another way. A safer way. As I stare down the corridor leading back to the Burger Shack, trying to figure out what exactly this better way could possibly be, I suddenly hear more commotion inside the arena. I peer up at the TV monitor and see what looks like a meta, covered in a tight yellow and purple suit and bug-like eyes bulging from his masked face, wrapping his arms around The Multiplier. In an instant, the nearby copies of The Multiplier spring into action and pull him off of the original, restraining him a few feet away.

"What's the matter?" The Multiplier asks. "You were able to teleport in here, but you couldn't teleport out while taking me along for the ride, could you?"

The new meta struggles to break free from the grip of the doppelgangers holding him down, but it's no use. There are too many of them. No doubt this meta has seen what happened to the last would-be hero and is now terrified of suffering the same fate.

"That's not going to work, you see. There's just too many of me. They're my anchors. Let me reiterate that to any other Teleporters who might be watching and thinking this is a great chance to play hero. It's not going to work," The Multiplier says into the nearest camera, almost as though he's looking straight at me through the monitor suspended above my head.

"That's it," Midnight says through my phone's earpiece.

"What's it?" I ask. "He just said that he's anchored to his clones. How does that possibly help the situation?"

"If he's anchored to his clones, that means they're also anchored to him."

"Right. Still not seeing how this is a good thing ..."

"You get him far enough away from those copies, and they won't work."

"Are you not watching the same thing I am? That Teleporter just tried to get him out of here; it didn't work."

"That's why you're not going to teleport. You're going to use two powers the other meta didn't have: your speed and your strength."

"Huh?"

"All you need to do is get him away from those copies before he has the opportunity to react. You're strong enough to break those bonds. If you run at him at full speed you, might be able to carry him far enough away from there that by the time he's able to react, he'll be too far from the copies to keep them stable."

"Whoa, whoa, whoa. Right, *might* be able. How do you know for sure that I'll be able to do that?"

"I don't."

"Then why the hell would I even try? It's just money. Who cares? Give it to him."

"There're two minutes left until the next execution, and he's only got a quarter of the ransom he's demanding. Are you willing to watch another person get executed when there's a chance you could do something about it?"

"I don't want anyone to be killed, but how can I risk the lives of all of these people just to possibly save a few?"

"By taking the risk out of the equation. You can't just *try* to break the connection; you *have* to break it."

Midnight's right. Of course he's right. He's been doing this a lot longer than I have. This is an arena full of completely innocent people. People with friends and families who care about them. Not one of them deserves to be killed, let alone on live television. No one deserves that, but especially when the reason is money.

"There's something else," Midnight begins. "I'm running a background analysis on The Multiplier. Apparently, he's not who he told the circus he is. His real name is Charles Bennington. He's a war criminal and profiteer accused of killing thousands of innocent civilians during the Kurdistan civil war during the first wave of metas."

"Well, I was already convinced he needed to be taken down, but that just cements it."

"I'm not telling you this to convince you of what you need to do. I'm telling you because he started a war based on the rumors that a pair of metabands was being hidden in the northern part of that region. He's been looking for powers for a long time, and he's not afraid to kill. Connor, everything I'm reading in his profile and seeing on television leads me to believe that he's going to kill those people, even if he does receive his ransom."

Midnight's words are just starting to sink in when I notice the monitor feed has switched to one of the other cameras in the auditorium. The image is sweeping across the crowd. The faces of terrified people with knives held to their throats fill the screen before the camera abruptly stops, right on Sarah's face.

"Aww, what a pretty young thing. Bring her down. If she doesn't bring in the big bucks, no one will, and I'll just cut my losses. Get it? *Cut* my losses?" The Multiplier says to a completely silent arena full of terrified people. "It's a joke about slashing all of your throats! Jeez, tough crowd."

"Midnight ..." I say into my phone, my voice trembling with fear and anger.

"I'm in. Thirty seconds and I'll have power cut to the entire building. You'll have only a few seconds before the backup generators kick in, but it should be enough time."

"I don't care if it's enough time or not. In thirty-one seconds I'm launching in there whether the cameras are down or not."

"Connor ..."

"No. I don't care. What good is keeping my identity a secret if I can't save one of the few people I care about?" I say into my phone's receiver, trying not to yell but failing.

On the screen, I see one of the copies dragging Sarah by her arm down the coliseum stairs. She's not moving quickly, but she's also not struggling in an obvious way. She saw what happened to the last person who put up a fight, and she's smarter than that, but the fear on her face is real.

The feed switches to a different camera, and I can see her eyes. I see them scanning the arena, panicked, looking for someone to help her. Looking for me. There's no doubt in my mind that I'm going to save her. Not because I'm confident in this plan, but because I cannot imagine anything other than saving her. I cannot fathom a world where I fail at this. She may be looking for Connor to help, but Connor can't. Omni is her only hope now.

"Ten seconds," Midnight's voice says in my ear.

My eyes are still glued to the monitor, watching Sarah slowly being dragged to what she must think is an almost certain death. For a moment, the idea of grabbing her instead of The Multiplier crosses my mind. I don't know whether or not I can save everyone in this arena, but I do know I could grab her and be miles away from here before anyone even noticed.

I can't though. Once I go down that path, there's no coming back. I can't sacrifice an arena full of innocent people just to save the one person I care about most. It's all or nothing, and I know that from the second the idea pops into my mind.

"Five seconds."

Sarah trips on one of the stairs, and the copy holding her splits in two, each grabbing one of her arms and holding her up so they can bring her down the stairs faster. They can't wait get her in front of the cameras and use her as leverage to try to get what they want. Money. Or notoriety. Or outrage. At this point, I'm not sure what it is he's actually after. I'm starting to learn that it's a waste of time to even speculate about the motives of monsters like him.

"Now, Connor!" Midnight shouts into my ear.

The lights in the arena all flicker out a mere second later. There's a slow, dull sound of the equipment around the massive complex grinding to a halt, but I barely notice because I'm already running before the last light has even gone out.

The television monitors turn black, and the last light flickers off. This is it. Without breaking my stride, I flick both fists out to my sides. Before my metabands can even fully materialize, I'm already bringing them up to crash into each other across my chest. There's an explosion of energy as my body is enveloped in crimson. Still running, the suit pours down my body and reaches my legs and feet. As it finishes its job and covers the last bits of my body, I push off on my right leg and everything stops. Everything but me, that is.

At first, I can barely see more than a foot in front of me, and I run toward where I think the floor of the arena is based on memory. My left foot misses a step, and now I'm falling. Time seems to slow down even more to allow me to correct this misstep. Now, even I'm moving in what feels like slow motion. As I fall through the air, about to face plant right onto the concrete steps, my vision finally adjusts. Still flailing in the air, I can immediately see everything in the pitch-dark arena as though it were bright as day. Including and most especially, The Multiplier standing in the center ring, waiting for Sarah to be brought to him.

I catch my footing, and time begins to retain its normal speed for me, but the rest of the crowd is still perfectly frozen in place. They're frozen in time like statues, with no idea that the next seconds of their lives are either going to be their last or when they're saved from almost certain death.

Pushing these thoughts and self-doubt out of my head, I focus on my target. He's frozen with the rest of the crowd, a relief considering I couldn't have known for sure if he possessed super speed too. It was a concern I didn't have time to share with Midnight, but one I'm sure he had as well.

I weave in and out of bystanders and Multiplier replicas, finding a central path to the original version. There's nothing between me and the original Multiplier, standing in the center of the ring, completely alone. If I have any hope of breaking his bond with these clones, I have to dig down deep and run faster and harder than I ever have before.

A few feet from him, I begin to see the air ripple in front of me, a sonic boom just beginning to form. I put my head down and aim for The Multiplier's abdomen. It's a strange feeling to actually *hope* that someone has super strength, but I really, really don't want to run into this guy so hard that he's cut in two. I won't be responsible for another death, even when others' lives are in danger. And doing it now, when so many of these children have already witnessed unimaginable horror, is not what I want my legacy to be. No, if all goes according to plan, the only thing the audience will see is The Multiplier and his clones suddenly disappear. I'm moving so fast at this point that I won't even be a blur to them.

Contact. I hit The Multiplier hard and wrap my arms around him to make sure he stays with me and isn't thrown to the side by the sudden wave of momentum. My focus changes from him to the emergency doors behind him. That's where we're going.

We reach the outside, and I see dozens of police and emergency vehicles surrounding the building. Police tape has been rolled out in front of them, creating a perimeter to keep back morbidly curious pedestrians, but also the family and friends of those inside, desperately hoping for some positive sign, some hope, that their loved ones will be okay. I'm hoping to be that positive sign, even if they can't see me.

While the intentions of most of these people are good, they've created a problem that I hadn't anticipated: how am I going to get around them? They're packed so closely together that I don't have room to weave in-between them, especially not with a passenger along for the ride. My mind is working as quickly as my legs are, but still, I'm running out of ideas, fast. Teleporting is out of the question; I'm not far enough away from the copies yet for it to work. Flying is an option, but I can't fly as fast as I can run. Not yet, at least. I've been running my whole life. All right, maybe not my whole life, but you get the idea. Flying is still relatively new to me. Drastically changing directions isn't an option either. I can't chance even a slight reduction in speed. A quarter of a second might be all he needs to send a message to all of his copies to kill.

Even with time slowed down around me, I'm approaching the crowd fast, and I don't have the luxury of calling Midnight to ask if he has any ideas. There's only one thing I can think of, something I haven't tried yet, but I hope will work. I take three more running steps before I jump as hard as I can. My hunch was right. Before my feet leave the ground, I can see the cracks in the concrete begin to spider web out from the impact point. I launch into the air without slowing down at all.

My ascent continues above the arena itself, and then above even the nearby skyscrapers. The feeling is very different from flying. I can feel the weight and momentum behind my leap and the lack of control. The city shrinks below me as I pass through the motionless clouds above.

Ever so slightly, the positioning of The Multiplier's body begins to change. I was moving so quickly when I grabbed him that his body hasn't had time to catch up with the momentum hitting it. Now, his body slowly begins to crumple and drape over my shoulder. He still can't have had the time needed to register what's happened to him, but I don't know how strong his powers are. It may not take very much thought at all, little more than instinct, for him to command his copies to carry out their deed before he's too far away to control them.

I reach the apex of my jump and begin the descent back to the ground below. Breaking through the cloud cover, I see that the city is starting to fade away behind me in the distance, but there's something else too. A pulling. The arc of my fall back to solid ground doesn't feel right. Something is pulling me back toward the city.

It's the copies. It's their link to The Multiplier. They still exist, and if they're still strong enough to pull The Multiplier back toward them, then they're powerful enough to follow his commands.

Less than a second has passed from when I grabbed him. The Multiplier's brain has to have realized that something has happened, but is still temporarily shocked and confused, no doubt. I struggle to keep moving forward, but it's impossible as the only elements controlling my fall right now are gravity and the pull of the copies. I still can't risk flying since it might slow me down just enough to give The Multiplier the split second he needs.

The ground is coming up fast. I steady myself and prepare for the impact. There isn't time to trip again. No time to screw this up or have it slow me down. Past the tree line, I can see the ocean. That's my chance. The one place nearby where I'm sure there won't be anything to stop me.

I lean forward and prepare to, literally, hit the ground running; there's no room for error. A winding road comes into view below me, and I decide to make it my target as best as I can during this controlled fall. I'm almost there when I can feel slight movements on my right shoulder. It's The Multiplier. He's beginning to stir now that I've slowed down. This is my last chance.

My feet are already moving when I hit the pavement. They're moving so quickly that they barely even touch the ground. I bear down and push myself down the winding road toward the ocean. Even the sand on the beach doesn't slow me down. My legs and feet are moving so quickly that they're becoming a blur even to me. Just because I have this speed and strength doesn't mean I'm completely immune to pain, however. My legs hurt more than I've ever felt them hurt before. Lactic acid fills my thighs and burns, and my muscles cramp and spasm. There's no time for that, though.

Hitting the water does not feel any different than hitting the sand at this speed. At a certain point, every surface feels the same, even water. I'm running too quickly to create splashes, but I can still feel the pull of The Multiplier's copies at my back. The pull is stronger than ever, and I hope that means that I'm near the breaking point. I have to be, because I can't bear to think of what will happen if I'm not, and my legs feel like they're close to giving out no matter how insistently I command them not to.

A rogue wave appears in front of me. I must already be hundreds, if not thousands, of miles out to sea when it begins to loom in the distance, at least a hundred feet tall. For a moment, I consider plowing straight through it, but I have serious doubts about my ability to make it all the way through to the other side with time already beginning to slip away from me and my body screaming in pain at being pushed so hard. The wave is too wide to go around, though, so there's just one other option.

The first few steps up the face of the wave are difficult; I can feel the water beginning to give way beneath my feet as I struggle to scale an object made purely of liquid. The fifth step is where I gain my footing, and before I know it, I'm at the crest of the wave. The pull of the copies back at the circus is stronger than ever. I hit the top of the wave and push off with my left foot as hard as I can manage, hoping to propel myself past any other waves that may be hiding behind it.

Only a few feet into the air and I feel it, like a rubber band reaching its limit and snapping. The pull isn't there anymore, and the momentum carrying me forward is let free. Suddenly, I'm flying through the air many times faster than I was before. Time catches up with me, and everything is moving at its normal speed now, except for The Multiplier and me. We're both moving at many times the speed of sound.

I struggle to hold onto him as we both hit the surface of the water, immediately skipping off of it like a well-thrown stone, hundreds of feet into the air. Then, we hit the water again. This happens over and over and over. Water enters my lungs, and it feels like this is never going to stop.

When it does finally stop, the new situation isn't that much better. I'm God only knows how far away from land, and I've lost sight of The Multiplier. I begin to panic as I wonder if maybe I underestimated his abilities after all, and he just teleported out of here once he got a grip of what was actually going on. Maybe he simply teleported himself back to the arena. If he did, he'd have to work quickly to replicate himself enough times to regain control of the crowd, now that I've broken the link between his copies and they've undoubtedly disappeared, but it's still possible. He would have to know the arena would be the first place I would check for him, though, and he wouldn't be that stupid, would he?

There's another possibility, which is that he's hurt or maybe even worse. I hit him at top speed, maybe even as fast as anyone could. His metabands should have provided him with enough protection against the impact based on the invulnerability he demonstrated previously, but there's just no way to know for sure.

This monster may be a murderer, but if I'm going to be different from him, I need to do whatever I can to save him. Let a jury decide his fate, or at least, The Agency. I don't need another life on my conscience; I've got enough already. He doesn't deserve to die out here in the ocean; he deserves to die of old age after being locked in a cell for decades.

The best plan to find him seems to be getting above the water and using my enhanced vision to try to see where he is. Once I've found him, it should be easy to apprehend him and bring him into Silver Island now that his metabands are presumably weakened. Speaking of weakened metabands, mine have to be somewhat low on energy now that I've run halfway across the world with them, but I should be able to take in The Multiplier, assuming he's even more wounded than I am after being ripped away from his clones.

This all seems like a really good plan in my head, but that's the thing about plans: no matter how good they sound in your head, they don't mean anything when you're not expecting what happens next. In this case, the unexpected element thrown my way happens to be the fact that not only is The Multiplier not dead and very much alive, but he's also not nearly as weakened as I hoped. I find this out by being pulled back underwater just as I'm inches from the surface and about to take my first breath.

Normally, it wouldn't be easy to pull me underwater when I've got my metabands activated. After all, I'm pretty strong when they're powered up, as evidenced by my ability to run across the globe in less than a few seconds. I find out pretty quickly though, that it's easy to pull me underwater when my metabands are low. I'm exhausted, and there are hundreds of hands doing the work.

The Multiplier's copies didn't simply disappear when I *thought* I broke their connection in the middle of the ocean. They got dragged along with him, and now they're dragging me under the water. I kick at the hands as hard as I can, trying desperately to shake free of their grasp, but there's too many of them. I can't teleport with this much luggage either. If I'm going to beat him, or *them*, I need to get out of the ocean and back into the sky.

Turning my head up, I can see the sun shining through the placid surface of the water. Fingers are now reaching for my shoulders and arms, scraping at my suit as though they're trying to rip it right off my body, like that would mean getting a firmer grip to bring me down to a watery death. They're not going to get that satisfaction, though.

The water around me begins to vibrate and bubble as I summon up the last reserves of my energy. I've got to give this my all if I have any hope of breaking free of what now feels like thousands of bodies dragging me deeper and deeper. The clones seem to realize what's happening, and their grips tighten even further. They're not going to let me go that easily.

The bubbling around me intensifies as if it were boiling, and I know it's time. At first, the water feels like it's fighting against me as I rush toward the surface, but soon, it feels as though there's no resistance at all. The space around me is getting brighter and brighter as I reach for where the water meets the sky. The surface tension of the water explodes as I reach the air and now travel even faster into the early afternoon sky of whatever time zone I'm currently in. I take a deep breath and fill my lungs with air once again. It feels like I haven't taken a single, full breath since I began running at the circus. I realize that it's probably true.

The clones are gripping tight, but they feel lighter and lighter the higher up into the sky I go. Looking down, I can see a cascade of them falling off, losing their grip on the mirrored copy above them and falling into the sea. Even with super strength, it would be hard for anyone to maintain a grip when they've got dozens of bodies clinging to them. They continue to drop. Dozens and dozens of them splash down into the sea until there's just one left, desperately gripping my ankle.

"Help!" he gasps, choking and coughing water out of his lungs.

It's The Multiplier, or the original, I should say. There's a look of terror in his eyes that I know is real. Even a psychopath like him couldn't act this well. One of his hands slips loose and the other tightens around my ankle as he lets out a desperate scream.

My metabands begin beeping and displaying a red flashing light bar. Reserve power. Time to be careful. I come to an abrupt and sudden halt. The change in momentum causes The Multiplier to lose his grip and continue flying upwards, even though I've stopped completely. Luckily for him, I reach out and grab his throat as he zooms past me. I stop him from continuing his trajectory into the afternoon sky.

His breathing is labored, and his eyes are wild. He's gasping for air and clinging to my outstretched arm even though I've got a tight enough grip on his neck to ensure that he's not going anywhere.

"I can't swim!" he finally manages to scream out in between breaths.

"What?" I ask.

"I can't swim! I almost drowned!" he yells after taking a few more deep breaths.

Looking down at the endless ocean below, I can see his copies thrashing in the otherwise completely placid water. One by one, they disappear below the waves and sink. Before they are completely out of view, they seem to slowly fade away and disappear from reality completely.

"Are you freakin' serious?" I scream back.

"Please. Please! I'm begging you. I can't swim. Don't let me go, please!" he sobs.

I grab him tighter around the throat and shake him.

"You killed an innocent man tonight and would have killed more if I hadn't stopped you, and for what? Money?" I yell into his face, causing his sobbing to intensify.

"I'm sorry, I'm sorry! Okay?" he yells back, terrified.

"Why shouldn't I just let you go?" I ask.

"If you let me go, you're no better than me," he replies.

I think about this for a long while. I think about that man whose throat he slit. About his family. His friends. All of them watching that happen. I think about Sarah and what he was about to do to her. I don't realize it, but my grip has tightened even further around his neck. The Multiplier's face is beginning to lose color as my hand restricts the flow of oxygen and blood to his head.

I can see a few remaining copies still flailing in the water. They're panicking, pulling each other under, desperately trying to breathe. I've never felt so angry in my entire life. I think about my parents and how no one was there to save them. How a monster, like the one I'm holding by the throat, killed them.

"Can you feel that?" I ask, gesturing down to the copies of

The Multiplier that are drowning and disappearing below us.

"Yes. Yes. Please, just stop. I'll power down my bands," he says and raises his shaking arms to bring his metabands together and deactivate them.

I put my free hand in-between them and stop them from hitting each other.

What am I doing? This isn't me. I move my hand out of the way and allow The Multiplier to power down. An instant later, we're both teleporting.

For a minute there, I almost left my soul out in the ocean.

Nineteen

The booking process at Silver Island is quick and easy. Halpern is there, but has to be physically restrained by his co-workers from trying to kill The Multiplier after what he almost did to Sarah. Other staff quickly takes the Multiplier away, for what I worry will be an even rougher booking than usual. This makes me feel even guiltier about the unnecessary pain I put him through before bringing him here. I'm better than that, or at least, I'm supposed to be.

Halpern eventually composes himself and reassures his co-workers that he's fine and can be let go. The other Agency employees release him and return to their various stations inside the control room. I need to get back to the arena and make sure Sarah is all right, but before I have a chance to dash off, Halpern approaches me.

"Omni," he says to my back as I'm heading toward the teleportation grid, "wait up a minute."

I stop in my tracks and turn to face him.

He reaches out and puts a hand on my shoulder. "I just wanted to thank you for what you did tonight."

"Just doing my job," I blurt out before I have time to think of anything else to say.

"No, you're not," he says.

"Excuse me?" I ask after a brief but uncomfortable silence.

"You're not doing your job. No one gave you the job of watching out for other people and taking care of them," he says.

I'm starting to get nervous.

"You decided to do that on your own. No one is making or even asking you to do any of these things, but you do them anyway."

"I don't know what else I would do."

"It was my job tonight to make sure that my ... " Halpern

begins before stopping himself, realizing that he was about to reveal that a family member was in the audience tonight, and committing a huge, *huge* breach of The Agency's draconian rules regarding the separation between work and private life.

Revealing such a personal aspect about himself, even to a somewhat "trusted" meta like me, could result in all kinds of trouble for him. According to Derrick, Agency members whose identities are exposed are moved as far as possible from their posts. They and their families are uprooted, given new lives, and told to start all over again. This is especially hard on the families, considering they're supposedly always kept in the dark about what it is their loved one actually does for a living. There are cameras, microphones, and sensors everywhere inside this building. A slip like that could easily lead to the Millers disappearing forever from Bay View City.

"Sir?" I ask Halpern, who is stunned at the fact that he almost dropped such a crucial piece of information.

"Sorry. I'm just a little frazzled. That was a big fish you caught today for us, and those people in the arena tonight owe you a huge debt of gratitude. So do I ... on behalf of The Agency," he says as he puts out his hand for me to shake.

"Of course. Just doing what I can," I say gripping his hand to shake it.

"Well, thank you for that."

After leaving Silver Island, my immediate concern is Sarah. Midnight has already reassured me via my earpiece that she got out of the arena safe and sound, despite the mass confusion and panic that set in amongst the audience. I forgot that to them, it looked like The Multiplier simply disappeared. I was moving too fast for the human eye to have possibly seen anything more than a blur right before I got up to speed, but even that's unlikely. They just saw The Multiplier disappear, followed by his copies disappearing less than a second later. In reality, they likely saw these two events happen simultaneously, considering the speed at which the connection between him and his clones was broken.

Not wanting to risk teleporting to the arena and possibly end up colliding with what I'm sure are tons of helicopters circling the area, I opt to fly there instead. I'm close enough to get there quickly, and it gives me a better opportunity to find an isolated area to power down.

I fly over the bay, only a few feet over the water, creating a small wake behind me. It occurs to me that the only way Midnight could know for sure that Sarah is safe would be that he's there. The cameras allowed the world to see what was going on inside the arena, but once The Multiplier disappeared, there must have been absolute mayhem as everyone ran as quickly as they could for the nearest exit.

Midnight is likely hiding out on a nearby rooftop, binoculars in hand, watching Sarah. Though, I guess it's possible that he's actually on the ground. He's worn disguises before to blend in with crowds. Hell, he doesn't even have to wear a disguise, considering I don't even know what he looks like. Wherever he is, I owe him for keeping an eye on Sarah. If he's hiding in plain sight, I owe it to him not to try and sniff him out. This isn't the time, and that's not a very nice "thank you" for someone who just helped me save my girlfriend's life.

There's a small park opposite the arena that looks desolate from a few hundred feet above. I spot a wooded area that looks perfect and slowly bring myself down, trying not to attract any unnecessary attention. After landing and determining that there aren't any prying eyes nearby, I deactivate my metabands and my Omni suit retreats back into them before they fade away. Now that I'm Connor again, I'm running as fast as my regular human body will let me.

It's only been about twenty minutes since I stopped the attack, but a lot has happened. That's always going to be the case when you're able to move as fast as I can, or at least as fast as Omni can. I need to find Sarah and make sure she's okay with my own eyes.

There are ambulances and reporters everywhere. With them are more than a few metas. Some are here to genuinely help; others are opportunistic and simply see a way to get on TV. Situations like this can quickly become dangerous since they have the potential to be a lightning rod for metas with bad intentions looking to take advantage of a chaotic situation. In the sky, I recognize a handful of metas that I've seen in online videos before. They're some of the "good guys," and I feel better knowing that they're here keeping an eye on everything from afar in case anything bad should happen.

In the distance, I see Sarah. She's wrapped in a blanket and speaking with a meta wearing a bright blue and red suit. In fact, it's the uniform that catches my eye first. It's only after seeing him that I notice the person he's talking to is Sarah. I'm running toward them before I give it any further thought.

Sarah doesn't see me until I'm practically a foot in front of her face.

I grab her tight and hug her. "Thank goodness you're all right. I was so worried."

There's no response from Sarah, she must still be in shock at what happened.

"Is this guy bothering you?" The blue and red meta asks Sarah.

I turn quickly and glare into his eyes. He's wearing the same style cowl I wear as Omni, but his does not cover the top of his head, allowing his thick, dirty blond hair to flow out over the top.

"She's fine. I'm her boyfriend," I say.

"Connor," Sarah finally says after taking a moment to take in the fact that it's actually me, "I thought you were..."

It hadn't even occurred to me that she would be worried about me. I'm so used to being Omni and not having to worry about myself, that I forget the people who care about me and don't know my secret still worry. It's fine day to day, but in situations where death is present, it can be a little more than disconcerting for others.

"I'm fine. I'm fine," I say as I pull back to look her in the eyes and reassure her. "Everything's fine. We're all set here, now. Thanks," I say to the meta next to her, making little attempt to hide my contempt.

There's something about him I don't like. Aside from the fact that there're thousands of shaken up people here, for some reason, this pretty boy meta decided to personally help out my upset and vulnerable girlfriend, who just happened to be on TV no less than half and hour ago.

"All right then, I'll leave you to it. Have a good night, Sarah. I hope to run into you under better circumstances someday," he says as he turns to the sky and flies away.

Sarah waits until he's out of earshot, or at least reasonable earshot for a normal human being.

"Where were you?" she asks.

"I was getting food when everything happened. Before I knew it, there was a guy in front of me holding a knife to my throat. I couldn't get back to you. I'm so, so sorry Sarah," I say.

"I mean, where were you just now? How did you wind up so far away from everyone else?" she asks.

Crap. I didn't have time to think all of this through.

"I was looking for you," I say.

"In the park?"

"I couldn't find you anywhere. I panicked."

"Are you sure you didn't run for cover?"

"What? Yes. I'm sure I didn't run for cover. I was looking for you."

"It just doesn't make sense, that's all. Why were you so

mean to that meta just now? He was just trying to help."

"Yeah, sure he was," I say, barely able to contain my frustration with this entire situation. "I'm sorry. I'm glad he was here. I wanted to be here; I just couldn't find you."

"I think you should take me home. I'm tired and rattled. I think I just want to go to bed."

The drive to Sarah's house is quiet. I try to start a conversation, but it's difficult. She doesn't want to talk about what happened, which I can completely understand, but talking about anything else seems completely trite and mundane on a night where she came within seconds of almost certain death. I'm so relieved that she's all right, but I'm startled and shaken myself. To Sarah, I went through only a fraction of the trauma she did tonight, but of course, that's not true. I stared death in the face as well and took one of the biggest risks I have ever taken. I risked the lives of thousands to save hers. I can justify it a million different ways. I can assure myself that I did it to stop any number of murders that could have happened if The Multiplier had gotten his way, or if the public had decided to negotiate with a terrorist on a macro scale, but deep down, I know the truth; I took that risk because I wouldn't have been able to live with myself if something ever happened to Sarah and I had done nothing to stop it.

When we pull up to her house, her dad is running out the front door toward the car before I can even pull to a stop. He would have had to leave Silver Island immediately after I saw him to have gotten home so quickly, but I'm not completely surprised, considering it seemed like few people wanted him around after how emotional he was acting, regardless of whether or not it was justified. For the record, it was.

"Sarah!" he yells out as she opens the door and meets him in a huge hug.

They're holding each other tight. The way only a family

who has lost someone and feared losing the only other person they have left does. I'm feeling slightly awkward being here, but it would be about a hundred times more awkward for me to just get in my car and drive off, so I just wait without saying a word.

Finally, they pull apart and Halpern, err, Mr. Miller asks Sarah to go inside for a minute while he talks to me. This can't be good. I thought my adrenal gland had called it a night after having to take out The Multiplier, but I can still feel my nerves overreacting at the idea of my girlfriend's father wanting to speak with me ... alone.

He walks over to me and looks back to Sarah. He waits until she's entered the house and the screen door shuts behind her before he says anything.

"Explain to me why I should ever let me daughter spend time with you again," he says.

Turns out my nerves weren't overreacting after all.

"Uhhh ..." I say instinctively to fill the dead air.

"'Uhhh' isn't an answer, Connor. You took my little girl to a very, very dangerous place tonight, and as a result, she almost got killed," he says in a hushed, but deeply serious tone.

"I didn't know any of that was going to happen," I blurt out. I want to tell him that it wasn't even my idea, they were her tickets, but I don't think that will help the situation.

"Of course you didn't know any of that would happen," he says in a condescending tone. "Trust me, if I thought you knew anything even remotely close to what happened tonight was going to happen, if I thought you thought that there was even a *chance* of something like that happening, we'd be having a very different conversation right now. Your ignorance is the only thing keeping me from putting my foot up your ass."

Yikes. Who is this guy? It's hard to look at someone through the same eyes and not have them see you as the same person. Less than an hour ago, this same man was shaking my hand and thanking me for saving his daughter. Now, he's threatening to beat the hell out of me for putting his daughter in danger. If I had any doubts that he suspected Omni and I are one and the same, they've surely been squelched now.

"You're lucky she's fine," he says to me.

"I'm sorry. I don't know what else I can say."

He takes one last hard look at me, turns without saying a word, and walks back up to his house. The front door is slammed hard as if to put an exclamation point on what he just said to me.

Mr. Miller hates Connor and Halpern can't thank Omni enough. It was confusing keeping my two identities straight.

It's a long ride home by myself with plenty of time to think about everything that happened tonight. I hate it. The right thing was ultimately done, but at the cost of possibly ruining my relationship with Sarah and her dad. If I didn't have powers, tonight might have played out much differently, but at least it wouldn't have seemed like I just ran away at the first sign of trouble. I'm suspicious that the reason emotions are running so high at their household tonight has something to do with whatever happened between Sarah's mom and the meta she's with.

For a minute, I consider calling Midnight. He's the only other person I can reach out to who has even a vague idea of what it's like to live two different lives. Except, I'm becoming less and less sure that he actually does lead two different lives. The more I get to know about him, the less there seems to be another side to him at all. Maybe there was at one point, but now only Midnight seems to exist. On top of that, the idea of calling Midnight to talk about my girl problems and not having that conversation end with him hanging up the phone on me seems far-fetched.

The only other person who I can even remotely talk to about all of this is, of course, Derrick. It's late, even for Derrick, but considering everything that's happened tonight, I can't imagine that he's already called it a day and headed home from the office, even if it is Friday night. There's a sense of relief when I pull up to our building and see the lights on all the way up on the top floor before pulling into the underground parking garage. Guess he decided to go home before the sun came up after all.

The elevator goes right to the entryway of our apartment, as long as you have the key. I told you it was fancy. On the ride up, I feel a wave of exhaustion come over me. It's been a very long day, even for a superhero. I'm starting to question if I even want to get into all of this with Derrick tonight, or if I just want to cut my losses and head to bed. Maybe Sarah will feel differently about everything after having a night to sleep on it.

The elevator doors open to the apartment, and I walk out. Most of the lights are off. Only one by the couch, in the sunken living room, is still on, and even that is turned down low. The remains of some half-eaten Chinese food are on the coffee table. It's not unusual for Derrick to leave a mess, but what is unusual is that the TV isn't on. If Derrick is home and awake, the TV is *always* on.

Walking farther into the living room, I find more evidence that starts my heart beating just a little bit faster. On the counter is Derrick's phone. He is never *ever* without his phone. If he were asleep, which he wouldn't be this early anyway, the phone would be on the nightstand next to him. In fact, I'm not even sure if that's true. I suspect he might actually fall asleep with it in his hand. That's how glued to it he is. There's absolutely no way in hell he would have left the apartment without taking it with him. But it's the last thing I see that really geta my pulse racing: shattered glass all over the hardwood floor closest to the couch.

There's been some type of struggle here. I'm about to shout out Derrick's name when I realize doing so will alert whoever might be here to my presence. Does someone know who I am? Is it another meta, a friend of The Multiplier's that's here to get revenge? Did Sarah's dad put two and two together and figure out who I am, sending the same team he partnered me up with to come and "retrieve" me?

Creeping quietly through the apartment I don't hear any voices. It's too quiet. If someone's here, they might realize I'm here also and be planning to surprise me. Just then, I hear a quiet, almost unperceivable noise from the bathroom. It's the sound of the wood floor creaking ever so slightly, but enough that I'm positive it's a person and not just the apartment settling. Do apartments even settle?

Turning the corner, my suspicions are confirmed. There's a light on inside the bathroom that I can see leaking out through the bottom of the door. Briefly, a shadow crosses through the light. There's someone in there. My heart is still pounding, but I momentarily feel some relief that it has to be Derrick in there. He probably cut himself on the glass and is in there cleaning himself up. But why would he close the door? He never closes the door, much to my discomfort, even when I'm home. He'd never close the door if he were here alone. Something just doesn't make sense.

"You must be Connor," a voice says from behind me in the hallway.

I turn on my heel to face it, but just as I do, the knob on the bathroom door turns, distracting me for just an instant. I'm overwhelmed and instinct takes over as I turn back to the voice behind me that poses the most immediate threat. I consider thrusting my arms out summoning my metabands, but Midnight has done a good job of knocking that instinct/bad habit out of my brain. If it's not a threat, I'll have blown my cover for nothing. Before I can even fully turn around, a hand tightly grips my wrist, stopping any hope I have of summoning them anyway.

In front of me is a woman in her late twenties. She's somewhat professionally dressed, Asian, and has black hair that falls to her chin with bangs that just touch her eyebrows. Who the hell is this?

"Hey! Connor!" Derrick says, still grabbing my hand as he closes the bathroom door behind him. I turn back and look at him, extremely confused about what is going on.

"I've heard so much about you. I'm Veronica," she says as she extends her hand to shake mine. "I hope you don't mind. I was just taking a look at the photos you have up in the hallway. You guys were adorable when you were little!"

"And we're not adorable now?" Derrick asks with a smile.

There's a sweet smell lingering in the air from Derrick's breath that I recognize.

"Are you drunk?" I ask Derrick.

"Nooooooo," Derrick says, the way a drunk person would.

Veronica giggles behind me. I exhale, still confused, but relieved that one fight is all tonight had in store for me.

Wait. There's a girl here? And she's with Derrick?

"Did that work?" Veronica asks Derrick.

"No," Derrick replies sheepishly, rubbing at a purple stain on his polo shirt.

Since when does Derrick wear polo shirts?

"I told you, you have to use seltzer water. It does the trick every time," Veronica says.

"Okay, I'll try it. Let me see if I have any," Derrick says as he walks past me with a slight stumble and heads down the hall toward the kitchen.

"Sorry if we scared you. Your brother's had a little bit too much wine," Veronica says to me in a loud whisper.

"I heard that," Derrick shouts from down the hallway in the kitchen.

"I'm sorry. Who are you?" I finally ask, realizing there's probably a less rude way to ask that question, but it's already too late as the words have left my mouth.

Veronica laughs, though. It seems like she's had a bit to drink tonight too.

"I'm Derrick's friend. We met at the panel he was speaking on today down at the university. I'm a professor there in metahuman studies, and I've always been a big fan of his work. I managed to rope him into getting a drink with me afterward so I could continue to pick his brain," Veronica tells me.

"Hey, you were right, it worked!" Derrick says as he re-enters the living area, proudly displaying his now spot-free shirt.

In the decade I've lived with Derrick, he's had dates here and there, but this is the first time that I've actually met one of them. It was kinda difficult to meet any of them when he refused to ever bring them by the house. I guess things are changing now that I'm older and now that he has a million-dollar apartment to come back to, probably more the latter than the former.

"So, Veronica was just telling me that you were telling her all about me?" I say to Derrick, my back turned to Veronica so I can clearly show Derrick that I'm stretching my eyes very wide in an effort to wordlessly convey, "you didn't tell her too much did you, you drunk idiot?"

"Oh yeah, I was telling her all about your adventures," Derrick replies.

"My adventures?" I ask, my voice now also conveying the emotion I had tried to show with my eyes, which was apparently lost on Derrick before.

"With Sarah, your giiiiiiirlfriend," Derrick says in a teasing tone

Veronica is laughing again.

"Stop, Derrick. Don't tease him, Connor, and she's got herself quite a catch with you, according to the bragging your brother's done about you tonight," Veronica says with a smile before directing her eyes back at Derrick.

They've both had too much wine, but it's apparent now, at least, that Derrick hasn't spilled the beans about my *career*. I would hope that it'd take more than a bottle of wine and a pretty girl to do that, but considering I've never seen Derrick tested by either, let alone both simultaneously, I couldn't be completely sure.

"Yeah, well, we'll see if she's still my girlfriend tomorrow," I say as I start to pick up the bits of shattered wine glass that are still all over the floor.

"What does that mean?" Derrick asks.

I look up at him, then at his phone on the counter and the TV's blank screen, and put it together.

"You didn't see what happened tonight?" I ask.

The look I get back tells me he has absolutely no idea what I'm talking about. Wow, he must really like this Veronica woman to have completely unplugged like this.

Before saying another word, I grab the remote control off the coffee table and flip on the television. The screen comes on immediately and is already tuned to one of the meta news channels, which it always is if Derrick's left alone long enough. The reporter on the screen is live at the arena and going over the night's events.

Most of the emergency crew is gone now with mostly just gawkers hanging around, looking to get in the background of the live shot and be on TV for a few seconds. A scrolling ticker at the bottom of the screen summarizes the event: "Tens of thousands held hostage earlier tonight at Meta Circus. One dead and seventeen injured. Unknown metahuman responsible for ending ransom situation created by meta criminal known as "The Multiplier.""

"Holy crap," Derrick says, his hand immediately going for his phone on the kitchen countertop. "You were there tonight?!" he asks, the look in his eye indicating that he's asking about both my normal, everyday self and the me that has superpowers.

"Yeah, I was. I'm okay though, obviously. Sarah's okay too, but pretty shaken up."

As if on cue, the television switches to a shot of Sarah being brought down the arena steps seconds before The Multiplier disappears in a blur of red. Derrick's hand goes to his mouth in disbelief.

Veronica looks at Derrick, then back at me before asking, "Wait. Is that your girlfriend?"

"Well, she was at the time," I say.

"Oh my God. I have ninety three missed calls," Derrick says. "I'm really sorry about this, Veronica, but I have to go to the office."

"Of course, don't worry about it. Perhaps another time then?" she asks.

"Absolutely. I'll walk you downstairs and grab you a cab," Derrick replies.

"That's sweet of you, but you've got more pressing issues right now. I'm a big girl. I can find my way home," she says with a smile as she grabs her purse off a stool near the kitchen counter and pulls out a piece of scrap paper, which she scribbles on and hands to Derrick. "I assume you'd be able to figure out how to find me, but just in case. I don't want to leave it to chance," she says to Derrick as she hands him the paper that presumably has her phone number or email address on it. "It was very nice meeting you, Connor. I'm glad to see you're all right after what happened at the circus tonight."

"Thank you," I say.

"Goodnight boys," Veronica says with a wave as she closes the door behind her.

Derrick smiles and waves back until the second the door clicks shut. That's when he spins on his heel toward me and blurts out, "What the hell happened?"

"I'm fine. It's fine. I mean it's not fine. People were hurt and killed, but a lot more could have been if I hadn't done something," I reply. "You should head to the office."

"What? You're not going to fill me in on the details?" he practically yells.

"I don't think that'd be a very good idea," I calmly reply.

"Says who? Midnight?"

"Says me. I'm just looking out for you, Derrick. I can't tell you the details of what happened tonight and have you somehow "find out" a bunch of stuff that no one else seems to be able to. Someone could start putting it together and realize that you know me."

"Wow," Derrick says, leaving it to hang in the air in uncomfortable silence. "I thought you knew I was smarter than that."

"It has nothing to do with that. I'm just trying to look out for—" I manage to get out before I'm interrupted by Derrick.

"It's fine. Whatever. I'll figure it out on my own," Derrick says as he grabs his coat and heads out the door.

For the second time tonight, someone I care about slams a door on me.

TWENTY

The next morning, I wake up to a very quiet apartment. It's early, but I'm not surprised since I couldn't sleep last night. I lay in bed for a while, trying desperately to catch a couple more hours of sleep, but eventually, I have to give it up. It's useless to think that I can sleep in on a Saturday when there's so much on my mind.

The apartment is still a mess from Derrick's little impromptu date the night before, so I keep myself busy cleaning for a while. Even that only takes about a half hour, though, and I'm once again left with empty time to fill. It's too early in the morning to call or text Jim. Hell, that'd be true on a Saturday even if it were noon. I look at my phone for a long while with my thumb hovering over Sarah's number. Ultimately, I decide that not only does she probably not want to talk yet, but she probably also doesn't want to be woken up at seven AM, so that option is out.

Derrick must still be at the office. If he's there this late/early, it means either he's really busy, or he's asleep underneath his desk. Either way, I don't want to bother him right now and incur the wrath of either a busy or a sleeping Derrick. I learned that lesson a long time ago.

There's one person left whose contact number I have in my phone who might be awake, only because as far as I can tell, he doesn't sleep, and that's Midnight. Of course I don't actually have his phone number any more. After the new metabands fell from the sky a few months ago, his paranoia went to the next level, so now I have to contact him through a specially designed app. Excuse me, a specially designed app that *he* designed, naturally. Anything less would run the risk of having some flaw or compromise that he couldn't account for. It's a slight inconvenience, but much, much easier than the intermediary solution, which involved multiple phone numbers, anonymous posts to random message boards, etc. just to verify that I was who I claimed to be.

HEY. ARE YOU UP? I type out and then hit the send button.

A reply comes back a few seconds later: YES.

CAN I COME BY? I ask.

WHY? Comes the reply I could have predicted.

BORED.

There's a pause in the rhythm of the texts that implies he's thinking, or that I'm just not going to get another reply. Midnight isn't one for entertaining, especially when I'm being as upfront as I am that I'm really just looking for something to keep my mind occupied, at least for a little while.

After a full minute, I get my reply: OK.

I'm surprised and a little nervous that Midnight is taking that as an excuse for me to come by and just hang out. Maybe he's growing a heart after all?

Nope. He's not growing a heart. This realization comes about twenty minutes after arriving at his water tower. He didn't tell me before I arrived, but my coming over came with a condition: Saturday mornings are training time. Friday nights are apparently pretty busy for Midnight. He doesn't elaborate, but I imagine this is more crime-related than him going out on the town. So, Saturday mornings are spent training. Considering Saturday nights are also supposedly pretty busy crime-wise, I don't understand why he'd spend his morning training rather than resting. I don't even want to know what he spends the rest of the week doing if this is how he relaxes.

I'm game at first, but by the tenth time I've been thrown head over heels onto the mats, I'm ready to call it a morning. I probably won't be able to sleep now that I'm bruised black and blue all over, but being alone with my thoughts is more of an alluring proposition than spending the rest of the day getting my ass kicked.

"All right, I think I'm done for today," I say.

"Are you serious? We haven't even warmed up yet," Midnight protests. "Don't come over here to practice if you're just going to quit at the first tinge of pain."

"That's easy for you to say. You're not the one getting thrown all over the place."

"Fine. Put your bands on then."

"What's the point of that?"

"Dampen them. Turn them down so you don't punch a hole through my head, but high enough that you're not going to cry every time a strong breeze blows through."

"Fine," I say as I thrust my arms out to my side to summon my metabands. They appear instantly, and I bring them together to activate. My suit spills out from the bands and covers my body almost instantly.

"Is the suit really necessary?" Midnight asks.

"Is yours?" I retort.

All that comes back is a grunt and a stare, but he's not wrong. I might not know who Midnight really is, but he knows damn well who I am, so there's not much point in rocking the tights right now. I close my eyes briefly to concentrate, and the suit retreats back into my metabands.

"Better?" I ask Midnight.

"Ahem," he coughs as he points to the bands on my wrists, indicating that I have yet to turn down the power on them. I bring the index and middle finger on my left hand to my right wrist and swipe down. A series of ten green lights dim one at a time until only one remains.

"Now, is that better?" I ask again.

My response comes immediately in the form of a right jab square on my nose.

"What the hell was that for?" I ask, holding my nose, which hurts like hell, but isn't broken.

"Have to make sure they work somehow," Midnight says.

Before the sentence is even finished the pain is completely gone.

"Yeah, they work."

"Good," Midnight says an instant before he goes to throw the same exact punch to the same exact place: my face.

Instinctually, my left arm swings up and meets Midnight's forearm mid-air, deflecting it away.

"Very good," he says.

I smile at the accomplishment of actually blocking Midnight, right before a left hook hits me in the jaw.

This goes on for hours and well into the late afternoon. Midnight's attacks are relentless, and he never seems to get tired. He also never seems to lose his patience, which is good, because all of this is new to me. I ask him at one point why it even matters that I know how to fight or not. It doesn't really matter if my technique is perfect when at the end of the day, I could slap someone and still send them careening through a brick wall.

Midnight has an immediate answer for this: there will come a day when I'll meet someone who is not only as powerful as I am, but probably even more so. If and when that day comes, the only hope I'll have is that I've trained harder, that I've put the time into learning how to fight, and that I'm smarter than my opponent.

Midnight is also concerned that completely relying on my metabands is dangerous. As I've found out a few times already, it's not always exactly convenient to make two alien objects that can transform me into a superhuman appear out of thin air. Sometimes situations require a more delicate touch. I shouldn't have to constantly worry about exposing my secret because I have absolutely no way to defend myself or anyone else otherwise.

And besides, this is fun. It's keeping my mind off of Sarah, and there's a real sense of accomplishment in learning from

Midnight. Despite his normally icy disposition, he actually hands out some praise throughout our practice. He seems genuinely surprised that I'm learning so quickly. After he catches me with a move once, I'm able to defend against it and often counter again and again. His compliments come to an abrupt stop when he hypothesizes that the speed of my learning is coming from the metabands and not natural ability.

It fits into Midnight's hypothesis that the bands enhance the innate, natural abilities of their owners. Even with them running on a setting low enough to prevent Midnight from giving me a concussion, it's still enough power to enhance my natural muscle memory and defense instincts. At least, while I'm wearing the bands, that is.

By the time Midnight finally wants to take a break, I'm regularly countering his blows and throwing him to the mat. Not every time, but enough. It's certainly more than I've ever seen anyone else accomplish against him. While he still credits the metabands, there's what seems like a slight sense of pride in the results of his training. Even if it's not "me" learning, he still seems pretty pleased with himself that he's an efficient teacher.

"Not bad," he says as he grabs a towel and two bottles of water from the small refrigerator that I have never before noticed along the stainless steel wall on the east side of the room.

He throws one of the bottles to me. I catch it from across the room before placing it on the ground to power down my metabands.

"What do you mean, 'not bad'? I had you more than a few times," I say as I slip my metabands off my wrists and walk to the nearby table to set them down for a moment while I towel off.

Keeping my metabands running on low power might have prevented me from breaking an arm when Midnight put me in a submission hold that would make a normal person cry, but they didn't do much to prevent me from sweating like a pig.

"You're just pissed that someone beat you."

"You didn't beat anyone," I hear Midnight say behind me.

Even though I have my back to him, I can tell he's no longer on the other side of the room and is instead only a few feet away from me. The next thing I know, I'm looking at the ceiling. He got me, I think to myself. In the split second I'm in the air, I assume that he's swept my legs or thrown me over his shoulder. Now I'm just waiting to feel my back hit the mat.

Except the ceiling is still moving, the room itself is upside down now, and in another instant, it's right side up once again. I'm on my feet. Midnight is not. He's crouched down, finishing a sweep kick right where my ankles were milliseconds ago. He was trying to sneak up on me, take me out, teach me a lesson about respect or whatever, but he missed. Or rather, I dodged it.

Midnight stands up and looks at me. We both have the same look of confusion on our faces. At least I think we do since I can't see much of his. I'm the first one to look over at the table where my metabands are resting. Midnight quickly follows my line of sight and sees them too.

"That's not possible," Midnight says, softer than I've ever heard him speak before.

"I ... I don't know. I just reacted," I stutter back.

Midnight picks up the metabands and examines them. I have no idea what he's looking for. When they're off me, which they rarely are due to Midnight's orders, they're completely plain and uninteresting looking.

"Do you feel any different?" Midnight asks me.

I think for a moment, taking a mental inventory of how I'm feeling. "No," I say after a few seconds, once I'm sure.

"I had a hunch that the metabands would allow for

increased muscle memory and motor skill learning, but this.... You've somehow retained what you've learned today even without the metabands active or even present," he says, slumping down into a chair, genuinely shocked.

"So, I have my powers without the bands now?" I ask.

"Pick that up," he commands as he gestures toward a concrete slab covering a maintenance access point on the other side of the room.

I rush over to it and take hold, excited that my powers are seemingly no longer limited to having to wear my metabands. That excitement doesn't last long, though, as I nearly throw my back out trying to heave the immovable slab.

"It won't budge," I say before I sense something wrong.

Turning around, I catch a very large textbook on quantum mechanics that Midnight's hurled at me and was inches away from smashing into the back of my head.

"Hmm," Midnight says as he rises from his chair and walks over to me.

"What if I didn't catch that?" I ask, frustrated.

"It would have hit you in the head. Maybe even knocked you out," Midnight answers.

I don't know why I even ask questions like this any more.

"So, I don't have my strength, but somehow I have superhuman reflexes?" I ask, not sure if Midnight has any more idea of what's going on than I do right now.

"No. Not superhuman. Heightened, but not superhuman. Today's training altered the pathways in your brain. The metabands have allowed you to learn quicker than you would have ever been able to under any other circumstance. This is something I accounted for. What I didn't expect is that these learned behaviors have seemingly been permanently retained," Midnight says.

"So what you're saying is that you're not the only bad ass around here any more, huh?"

Before I know what's happened, my head smashes into the mat so hard that it bounces. I'm flat on my back with my left arm twisted and completely immovable, being held down by Midnight, who also has his right knee firmly dug into my back.

"I didn't teach you everything, kid."

"Fair enough. Uncle."

TWENTY-ONE

It's late now, and I've spent the vast majority of my Saturday getting my ass handed to me by Midnight in his water tower. I say the vast part and not the entirety because the last few hours of sparring are more or less even, often ending in stalemates where one of us eventually calls for a timeout so we can grab some water and rest.

My metabands have come on and off during the day as Midnight has taught me. Although I'd never tell him, mostly because I'm sure the sentiment wouldn't be appreciated, it means a lot that he trusts me enough to spar even when I have my powers activated. It hasn't been easy to learn how to control them, so the confidence Midnight has in my abilities, and more importantly, restraint, isn't something I've overlooked. Either that, or he just thinks he can still take me out, metabands or not. I'll give him the benefit of the doubt and assume it's the first one.

"Not bad," Midnight says, picking himself up from the mat for the tenth time in a row. It's the closest thing I've gotten to a compliment in hours. "You're retaining what you're learning well. Computer," he says out loud to the room itself, "time since metaband deactivation."

"Four hours, thirty two minutes, sixteen seconds," a computerized voice replies from unseen speakers somewhere in the ceiling.

"Four and a half hours since you've taken your metabands off, and you're almost able to keep up with me," Midnight says as he grabs a towel and wipes the sweat off the little bit of his face that's exposed through his mask.

"*Almost* keep up? The only thing I'm not keeping up with you on is falling on my ass," I reply.

Midnight's white eyes narrow as he glares at me, indicating he doesn't find my smack talk very amusing.

"This isn't a true test though. We don't know if what you've learned today is permanent, or if it'll eventually fade away once your metabands are off."

"What does it matter? I've got the metabands, sooooo I'm not really getting the point of training so hard without them."

"Because there will be a time when you're without them. There will be a time when you can't activate them, and you'll still need to step up."

"Right, but I'm only going to be trying to diffuse a situation long enough for me to run into a phone booth or whatever and activate these bands. I get the training, but this seems excessive. Once I activate my metabands, it's game over for anyone who's still looking to pick a fight, especially if they're just some normal person."

"And what happens if you lose your bands tomorrow?"

"Already planning the end of my career?"

"Exactly. In your mind, your metabands are what make you an ally to those who need one most. If your metabands are all that make you a hero, then you'll never actually be one," Midnight says as he throws the towel into a bin at the edge of the training area.

"What is that supposed to mean?" I ask.

"It means that this, all of this," Midnight says, motioning toward the training mats and around the tower, "doesn't mean anything if you're only in this because you've got those stupid gadgets on your wrists."

"So now they're just stupid gadgets?" I ask, raising my voice. "I don't remember them being so stupid the time I used them to take out the Brute who would have turned you into wall pizza had I not had them."

"What good are they if that's all you are?" Midnight asks rhetorically.

There's a small silence where I don't know what to say next, but I can feel my blood beginning to boil.

"Why? Why? Because it's not exactly normal to keep your face hidden from the world throughout your entire life. You've kept it hidden from me all this time, even when you've let me in on so many of the other secrets about you. Why would you keep what your face looks like from me if I wouldn't even know you from a random person on the street?"

"So I can stay that random person on the street. It's dangerous to both of us for you to know who I am. Now I'm not anonymous to you. You no longer have plausible deniability if you're ever compromised. You can't pass me in the street without a flicker of recognition in your eyes. That makes you knowing who I am, even just what my face looks like, a liability."

"Then why show me?"

"Because, right now, it's more dangerous for you not to trust me than it is for you to know what I really look like underneath. Do you trust me now?" he asks.

"I never stopped trusting you."

"Good," Midnight says as he grabs a pile of gray fabric from a motorized drawer that slides out from a seamless stainless steel wall. He examines the fabric for a moment before throwing it to me. "Then let's go have some fun."

TWENTY-TWO

"Soooo, what do we do now?" I ask.

"We wait. Stop asking," Midnight replies.

Night's fallen, and we're both perched on top of a five-story building. Midnight took the faster, more dangerous way up: jumping to it from another not-so-nearby rooftop. I opted for the fire escape. Despite my insistence that I wouldn't use them, Midnight has *insisted* that I leave my metabands back at his water tower. *Insisted* might be too delicate of a word for how he actually put it to me.

I should be more nervous about being out here, waiting for whatever it is we're waiting for, without my metabands, but I'm trying to put that out of my head for the moment. I've had them on and off most of the day to help with my training, and while I feel great, they probably need a little bit of a rest to recharge. This is the only true way to tell if the training from this afternoon, with the metabands on, will actually stick with me permanently or even for an extended period of time.

Since my normal suit actually comes from the metabands, wearing it tonight wasn't an option. Luckily for me, Midnight had a change of clothes: a suit made of some type of optical camouflage that allows me to blend into the nearby surroundings seamlessly. A simple gray, domino-style mask with white lenses is all that obscures my identity, but Midnight says it's enough. It's not like he has extra cowls lying around in a variety of sizes, and as Midnight put it, my "head is too big anyway." Thanks a lot for that. He also had concerns about my ability to stay aware of my surroundings if I wore anything bulkier over my face.

"Where did you get this camo suit? It's ridiculous," I ask.

Midnight doesn't respond, he just continues looking out over the city through a small pair of binoculars that he procured from somewhere on his uniform. Where, I'll probably never figure out.

"How come you don't wear it?" I ask, trying to find a question that maybe he'll be a little more open to answering.

"Don't need it," he replies.

"Yeah, but it couldn't hurt," I reply.

"The suit you're wearing weighs almost one kilogram more than the suit I have on due to the electronics and sensors embedded throughout. That kilogram would slow me down."

"Come on. It couldn't possibly slow you down that much."

"Fractions of a second matter when you're not invulnerable."

"Oh, right. I guess I wasn't factoring that in," I say. "So, when do I find out what exactly it is we're doing here?"

"We're here to help."

Great. Perfectly vague answer. Midnight puts down his binoculars for a moment and turns to me.

"Do you know this neighborhood?" he asks.

"I know it's a bad one. Other than that, not really," I say.

"It's an area that the police don't come to anymore," Midnight tells me.

"Why not? It's bad, but it's not that bad."

"They don't come here anymore because it's crawling with metas."

"That doesn't make any sense. If it were crawling with metas, I would know about it."

"It's not crawling with the types of metas you encounter. These metas usually can't fly, or walk through walls, or any of the other neat little tricks that get you notoriety. These metas are just bruisers. Strength and some invulnerability, no flashy powers. They have no interest in being heroes or villains; all they care about is what they can get for themselves. They're low-level thugs who don't bother with the flashy suits and code names. They're too powerful for the police to deal with and too mundane to attract other metas for a fight. As long as they keep to this neighborhood, they can do whatever they please."

"And what is that?"

"Extortion. Robberies. Muggings. Drugs. No daring bank heists or diabolical schemes here. Just scum picking on the easiest prey in society, and no one thinks they're important enough to do anything about it."

"And we're just going to clean up an entire neighborhood in a night then?"

Midnight turns his head to me. "That's exactly the attitude that let's these animals get away with what they've been doing. Those that are in a position to help think that this neighborhood is too far gone for anyone to make a difference, so they leave it alone. To rot."

"Fair enough. Where do we start then?"

"That's a better question, and your answer is heading down Washington Place right now."

Below us, on an otherwise empty street, is a lumbering brick wall of a man walking down the sidewalk almost three blocks away. His suit is old and ill fitting for his overweight body. If I had to guess, I would say he's in his early forties, but his face looks like it's at least ten years older thanks to hard living.

"Who is that?" I ask.

"Frankie Botticelli. He used to be a low-level thug in the Scolari crime family."

"Used to be?"

"He struck out on his own a month back when he happened to find a set of metabands hidden under the floorboards of a local shop that was owned by someone who owed his boss money. The shop owner intended to sell the bands to pay back his gambling debts, but he couldn't find a buyer willing to pay what he was asking."

"How much was he asking?" I ask.

"Ten thousand dollars," Midnight replies as he picks up his binoculars to take another look at the end of the street.

"Ten thousands dollars? You're kidding, right? There's no way someone wouldn't be able to get rid of a pair of metabands for ten grand. Don't get me wrong, ten thousand dollars is a lot of money, but there are oil tycoons paying millions for these things on the black market."

"Does this look like the type of neighborhood where people have contacts with oil tycoons? The gambler was desperate and untrustworthy. Hard to prove your goods are the real deal without the customer testing them out to make sure."

"Yeah, but then you just promise them their money back if they don't work."

"And if you're the owner of a new set of metabands, what stops you from just taking the money back by force any way?"

"I didn't think of that. Why wouldn't he just use the metabands himself then? He'd be able to fight off any enforcers coming to collect at the very least."

"Maybe, or maybe the metabands he found didn't have any type of physical powers attached to them. What if all they did was give him enhanced vision or hearing? Hard to use those to protect yourself from a crowbar to the side of your head."

"Is that what happened?"

"Yes."

"Ugh."

"Frankie's only gotten worse since then. Turns out, the metabands are somewhat powerful and their new owner has increased strength and invulnerability. He's since used those powers to branch out on his own."

"Let's go back to the water tower and get my metabands, then. This guy would be a piece of cake for me. I can make sure he doesn't hurt anyone else ever again."

"We're going to do that, but we're going to do it without your bands."

"How?" I ask as I watch Frankie walk up to the front door of a large apartment building, take out his keys, open the door, and go inside.

Midnight doesn't respond.

I sigh and start to turn to him again. "You know, the whole not answering my simple questions thing is getting kinda ol —" Never mind. He's not there.

I jump to my feet and swivel my head around the rooftop, looking for him. Out of my peripheral vision, I see movement below. It's Midnight sliding down the side of the building across from us and landing on the ground below without a sound.

"I'm going to go follow Frankie, Connor. Do you want to come? Sure, I'd love to Midnight. Thank you so much for asking. That's very polite of you," I say to myself mockingly as I find my way back to the fire escape and begin heading down the steps as quietly as I can manage.

The front door of the apartment building is slightly open when I reach it on the ground. I'm guessing this is Midnight's way of telling me to follow him. The hallway inside is dark and narrow. The only sound I hear is Frankie's footsteps as he plods his way down the hall, presumably to the front door of whatever hellhole apartment belongs to him. Midnight is in here too, but I'm not surprised that I don't hear his footsteps. He's pretty good at hiding things like that, or at least a hell of a lot better than Frankie. In Frankie's defense, though, he doesn't know that he has a reason to be hiding the sound of his footsteps. Something tells me that there isn't a hell of a lot that Frankie's afraid of, even before "finding" his set of metabands.

Frankie's footsteps stop on the fourth floor of the cramped, walkup apartment building, and one flight above where I am right now on the stairwell landing. Above me, I hear the jangling of his keys as he pulls them out of his pocket followed by the clicking sound of the key sliding into the keyhole before he turns the knob and enters his apartment. I wait a few seconds after the door closes behind him before I slowly grab the stairwell railing and turn the corner to climb up the flight of stairs to Frankie's floor. I'm not sure where Midnight is, but if I were a betting man, I'd say he's already inside the apartment waiting for Frankie to power down his metabands.

The hallway outside of Frankie's apartment is empty. It's old wooden floors creak under my feet despite my efforts to remain as silent as possible. I pass under a small archway as I tiptoe down the hall, my eyes darting back and forth along the corridor that's lit with only one forty-watt light bulb, hanging exposed, all the way at the other end.

"Shhhhh," I hear almost inaudibly from behind me. Spinning on my heel, I turn to find nothing but darkness. What was that? A second later, I have my answer in the form of a soft "ahem," coming from above. I should have known is all I can think as I tilt my head up to see a barely visible Midnight in the corner of the archway, pressing his feet and back against opposite walls to keep himself wedged three feet above my head. He puts one finger up to his mouth to indicate to me to keep my mouth shut.

In the blink of an eye, he's back on the ground, standing in front of me. Somehow, I couldn't even walk down the hall without making so much noise that I thought Frankie would come flying out of his apartment to find me any second, but Midnight can drop from nine feet in the air and land without making a sound. He motions with his hand for me to follow him back down the stairwell. I take one step, and immediately the floor beneath me creaks even louder than before. Midnight stops in his tracks and turns back to give me an angry look.

"Sorry," I half mouth, half whisper to him.

He turns back toward the stairs, and I follow, being extra, extra careful to avoid any plank that looks especially creaky. Once we're down the flight of stairs, Midnight turns again to address me.

"Are you ready?" Midnight asks.

"Ready? Ready for what? I thought we were leaving."

"We're not going anywhere yet; we just need to wait somewhere you can't make so much noise."

"Sorry I'm not a ninja, Midnight."

"It's okay."

"That was a joke," I say.

Nothing back. It's like talking to a wall sometimes.

"I've been monitoring Frankie for the past few weeks," Midnight begins, completely ignoring my joke. "He's not too smart, but he has a routine. Every night, he comes home and does the same thing, without fail. He walks inside, pours himself about a pint's worth of vodka, takes a big swig, uses the bathroom, then powers down his metabands before sitting back in his recliner to watch TV where he usually passes out for the night."

"Fascinating."

"You're not paying attention. Most nights, he blasts the volume on the TV so loud the neighbors complain the next day. It's a surefire sign that he's fallen asleep or passed out. His routine is our opportunity to seize him when he's most vulnerable."

"So we just wait until we hear the TV, and we know he's got his metabands off and ambush him?"

"That's better," Midnight says.

As if on cue, the canned laughter of an old sitcom comes blaring down the hallway. Frankie's sitting in his recliner, metabands off, and has no idea what's about to happen. Midnight turns to me slightly.

"Ready?" he asks.

I get the feeling that whether I'm ready or not, he's going in in about two seconds. I nod and wait for his cue.

Before the cue comes, though, there's the muffled sound of voices wafting down the hallway from Frankie's front door. It's hard to tell at first, but after a few seconds, it's obvious that the voices aren't coming from the television. Midnight's eyes narrow as he tries to decipher what they're saying to each other, and who exactly they are. Or at least, I assume that's what he's doing since that's what I'm trying to figure out.

The volume of the voices rises suddenly. Whoever is in there is being yelled at by Frankie, which strongly implies that this person isn't exactly his friend.

"We're going in," Midnight says to me without waiting for me to agree or protest.

Before we can even move, though, the sound of the television and the yelling is cut by the distinctive sound of shattering glass.

"Now!" Midnight yells as he breaks into a sprint.

I run behind him as fast as my legs will carry me. In front of me, Midnight doesn't break his stride as he leaps into the air, battering his shoulder into Frankie's front door. The door splinters apart as though it were made out of balsa wood. At first, I can barely tell what's happening, but inside, through the dimly lit apartment, I can see a figure. It's slender and obviously not Frankie. Past the figure is a shattered window that leads to an alleyway outside. I'm no detective, but it doesn't take much to deduce that whoever this person is, they're responsible for that broken window. Or rather, Frankie's responsible for breaking the window, but this is the person who pushed him through it.

"Grab him!" Midnight yells back at me as he again leaps into the air and through the shattered window, missing the jagged edges of the broken glass now protruding from the wooden frame.

The figure inside Frankie's apartment is stunned by the fact that a masked vigilante just came bursting through the front door, and it takes him a second to process the words that just came out of Midnight's mouth and realize that he's not alone.

There's only an instant before I make contact with the figure where I get a good look at him. I'm running on adrenaline at this point, and although my optic camo makes me hard to spot from a distance, it doesn't make me invisible. Especially when I'm moving. Even more especially when I'm moving as fast as I am. My training and instincts take over, and I leap into the air, thrusting both of my feet in front of me toward the figure. Right before I make contact, the figure turns to me, and I see his face, or rather, lack of face.

He's a Blank. I've heard rumors about them from Derrick but wasn't completely sure I believed them until right now, when I'm actually staring at one. According to him, they started popping up only a few weeks ago. A gang of anti-meta vigilantes who all wear the same lead-lined, mirrored masks to protect their anonymity.

I can't see the expression on this Blank's face thanks to the mask he's wearing, but I imagine it's one of surprise as my feet slam into his chest and knock him backward into the television, shattering it instantly. He slumps down onto the floor as I pick myself up. He's alive, but hurting. I approach and rip off the reflective mask. The face of the man underneath it is mostly unremarkable. Late twenties, shaved head. He has neck tattoos that I can't immediately decipher. He could be a gang member or a hipster coffee barista. So hard to tell nowadays.

"Get down here!" Midnight's voice echoes from the street below.

We weren't expecting much trouble tonight, so we didn't go through the hassle of figuring out what my codename should be. Calling me Omni would give away my alter ego, and yelling "Connor" would be about a million times worse. In any case, when I hear Midnight yell, I can only assume he's talking to me. Before I give my brain too much time to think, I take off running toward the broken windowpane, unsure of what's waiting down below.

"Here we go," I say out loud to no one, but I swear I hear a faint grunt of recognition from the nearly unconscious Blank lying on the ground before I leap into the air and sail clean through the window, missing the jagged pieces of glass sticking out and threatening to shred whatever part of my body they might catch.

No metabands, which means no rapid healing. It'd be easy to think I can't take any chances tonight, but right now, taking chances is the only choice I've got.

The funny thing about jumping out of a fourth floor window without thinking about what you're doing is that the fall takes a lot longer than you anticipated. It feels like I'm hanging in mid-air forever before inertia takes over and I start falling to the alley below. Looking toward the ground, I see what it was that Midnight wanted help with: there are dozens and dozens of Blanks canvassing the alley and surrounding Midnight.

The one directly in front of Midnight is bigger than the others, and he's holding up a bloodied and badly injured Frankie by the back of his torn shirt.

"Ladder!" Midnight yells to me, causing all of the Blanks to look up and see me cannonballing out of a fourth floor window without much of a plan.

There's only an instant to process what Midnight's shouted to me, but it's enough. I see the rusted fire escape ladder directly ahead of me and reach out both arms to grab onto it like I've never grabbed onto anything before.

At first, it feels as though my arms are going to rip right out of their sockets, but before they have a chance to, my momentum swings me forward, causing the ladder to break free from its lock and begin sliding down to street level. This would be great for me, if I were able to stop my body from still flying forward. I hang on as tightly as I can when my legs swing out in front of me. They reach the same level as my head and my fingers give out, flipping me head over heels into the air.

The next thing I know, before I have time to even think, both feet are planted firmly on the ground. I don't even wobble. Whoa. I guess that training from today decided to stick around in my head for a while after all. It takes a few long seconds of disbelief on my end before I realize that everyone, including all of the Blanks, are staring at me. Apparently, they can't believe what I just did either. Scanning the crowd, I eventually find Midnight directly to my left. He gives me a look that says "not bad" as he nods in approval before very subtly tapping an unseen button on his left forearm.

The instant he taps the button, there's a small popping noise, and everything goes white. I'm completely and utterly blinded. Judging from the screams I hear all around me, it sounds like the Blanks are too. The yelling is quickly drowned out by the sounds of fists hitting meat and bones breaking. I rub my eyes as hard as I can to try to regain some of my vision and help Midnight out before he takes this entire mob out by himself.

Luckily for him, a punch directly to my gut from an unseen assailant helps speed up the recovery process. My vision isn't completely back yet; there're a lot of spots floating in front of my vision from the flash, but it's back enough for me to start hurting people rather than them getting in cheap shots at me.

The training that Midnight has given me kicks in, and I instinctually start taking down Blank after Blank.

A command is shouted from one of the leaders: "Don't hold back. They're meta sympathizers! Blank Four, kill

Botticelli before they have a chance to give him back his powers."

That doesn't sound good. Botticelli is a bad person, but we're not here to let someone get killed on our watch.

A punch comes within centimeters of my nose, but I pull my head back just in time for it to go sailing past. Without thinking, I grab the would-be nose breaker's arm and pull it downward, striking him in the sternum with my knee hard enough to put him down, but I'm still careful not to cause permanent damage. These guys are lucky they're coming after me because I don't think Midnight is being as gentle.

That's when I feel an all-consuming, searing pain across the length of my back. I turn to see a Blank holding a plank of wood he's either brought with him for this special occasion, or he's found lying around somewhere. It doesn't really matter where it came from because my back hurts like hell. I'd almost forgotten what this type of pain feels like thanks to my metabands. It's all I can think about, and the instant it starts to subside, the pain is replaced by rage. I can't see the face of the person behind the reflective, blank, metal mask he's wearing, but I have to assume he has a look of terror after seeing how angry he's made me.

In one fluid motion, I grab the plank out of his hand and drop it to the ground, bringing my left leg behind both of his to sweep his feet out from under him. His legs are taken out from under him so quickly that he's almost parallel to the ground. I'm back on my feet before he hits the ground, grabbing the Blank by the throat and slamming him hard onto his back and into the pavement.

All I can see is red, and all I can think about is how much my back hurts. If he'd hit me in the head, I would have been knocked out for sure, possibly even killed. Whether he missed or intentionally made an effort *not* to kill me, barely enters my mind. All I can think about is this pain and how badly I want this coward to feel it too.

His back takes the brunt of the fall. Good. Hope it hurts even half as much as mine does. His mask flies off and goes skittering across the alleyway.

Jim. It's Jim underneath the mask. The pain in my back is replaced by dizziness from what I'm seeing. How? How could this be? I must be seeing things or imagining them. Jim is a Blank? Why?

"Please, please don't hurt me. I give up. I surrender!" Jim pleads with me, nearly in tears.

"Get Botticelli out of here!" Midnight yells as he throws another Blank off his back and into a nearby wall, before reaching behind his back and pulling out two metabands that he throws toward me.

Midnight was holding out on me. He brought my metabands after all. I'm not exactly surprised that he managed to swipe them out of the safe he had me place them in before we left. I never trusted that the safe wasn't a place he could access without me never even knowing or seeing him do so.

The metabands fly up into the air after Midnight tosses them, but in midair, they seem to defy the laws of gravity and redirect course. They align themselves perfectly with my hands and are drawn toward them; it's as if my hands are magnetized. My arms actually jerk backward when the metabands slide onto my wrists because they hit me with such force. After finding their proper places, they constrict around my wrists and are ready.

I bring my wrists together to activate them, and in the next instant, my powers and my suit are back. So much for keeping a low profile. The remaining vision problems I had are gone, and I can accurately see everything that is going on around me. Midnight continues to take out multiple Blanks at a time, but more keep on coming. Around the corner of the alleyway, dozens more are sprinting from a nearby street. Reinforcements.

"Omni! Get him out of here!" Midnight yells at me again as multiple Blanks jump on his back.

For a second, I think about helping him instead of listening to his command. I don't have long to think about it, though, because an instant later, Midnight explodes out of a pile of Blanks, sending them flying into the air in every direction. He can take care of himself. Time to get Botticelli out of here before someone takes him out permanently.

I glance down at Jim one last time. He's terrified. He thinks I'm going to finish him off. Make him pay for hurting me. There isn't a way to tell him that I would never, ever want to hurt him. That he's one of the people I care most about in this world, and that I'm so confused right now about what he's doing here. I know he was becoming increasingly upset about the metas in our city, but this? To become radicalized to the point where he's become part of a mob, essentially a gang, that has taken it upon themselves to be judge, jury, and executioner? Only pure hatred can cause this type of reaction.

There isn't time to think about all of that now, though. I need to get Botticelli out of here before someone decides to take advantage of the chaos and snap his neck. I wade through a group of Blanks blocking my path, not even bothering to fight them. Their fists, kicks, knives, and baseball bats strike my body but do nothing. Blank after Blank reels backward, holding their now broken hand or foot and howling in pain.

Once I'm past enough of them that have either incapacitated themselves or run away, I find Frankie slumped over next to a Dumpster. In all the confusion, no one has even remembered why they had come here in the first place: to get Frankie Botticelli. Instead, they focused on trying to take out, or maybe even kill, Midnight and me, two people who want the same thing for this neighborhood as they do. For it to be safe, and for the people who live here to be happy and not have to constantly worry about being the victims of crimes, meta or otherwise.

"Get up, Frankie. We're going for a ride," I say as I grab him by the collar and lift him to his feet.

He's barely conscious and can't stand under his own significant weight. Still holding him with one hand, I use the other to tap the right side of my cowl and activate my comm device.

"Silver Island, this is Omni. Requesting clearance for drop-off. Level one, metabands deactivated and disarmed."

"Confirmed. Cleared for arrival, coordinates B-84."

TWENTY-THREE

The booking process at Silver Island goes much more smoothly when you bring in a meta who already has his bands deactivated. Most give up their bands after seeing what the alternative is firsthand, but it's rare to bring one in who doesn't have his metabands on at all. At least, it is for me.

The agent that processes Frankie is one that I've seen a few times. Rodriguez, I think is his name. Unfortunately for him, he seems to get stuck with the Saturday night shifts a lot. Two guards come through the solid steel gate sealing off the main detention center from the Arrival Zone and take Frankie away before he's even regained consciousness. I'm just about to turn around and head back out when the guard calls to get my attention.

"Hey, Omni?" Rodriguez asks.

"Yeah?"

Rodriguez looks over his shoulder to make sure we're alone and approaches me nervously. "Listen, buddy. Would you mind doing a round?"

"Huh? Why?"

"I'm a little short staffed here tonight. Two of the metas that were supposed to be on guard duty never showed up."

This is surprisingly not an uncommon occurrence. Most metas don't get paid very much for their work at Silver Island. Therefore, skipping a shift isn't unusual. It's not like metas are somehow automatically more reliable than regular people. It's also not like The Agency can "fire" them if they don't show up for work. Add to that the fact that even the real excuses for being late or missing a shift sound completely unbelievable anywhere else. "I would have been here on time, but I had to fly a bomb into outer space before it detonated," or "There was an attempted military coup in

181

South America that I had to stop."

A lot of the metas that work guard duty here feel very strongly that it's just for show anyway. The entire facility has been designed so that a break out, or break in for that matter, is nearly impossible. The metas housed here are either contained and buried far underground, completely out of sight from everyone, even the guards, or they've had their metabands removed. In those cases, they're not much more than a common prisoner of the federal government who just so happens to formerly be a meta.

"Why don't you just bring in whoever's on call?" I ask Rodriguez. Since no shows are so common, there's a long list of "alternates" who can be, and frequently are, called to fill in if need be.

"Haven't you noticed that things seem a little quiet around here tonight?" he asks me.

I've been so fixated on having just learned that Jim is a Blank and that he was part of a mob fueled by murder tonight, that I hadn't even noticed that the Arrival Zone is completely empty except for me and Rodriguez.

"What's going on?" I ask as I continue to scan the room. For a moment, I try to look through the walls before remembering that they're lead-lined and completely impenetrable.

"There's some big meeting going on. Higher ups from Washington are in town. I'm not exactly sure what it is, but I know I got the shaft getting stuck out here watching the doggy door. No offense."

"None taken."

"Most of them have been crammed in one of the communication rooms for the last three hours. I need authorization from my superior if I need to call an alternate. Hell, I can't even physically call them myself without her being here to verify the request with a hand scan."

"That's a really dumb system."

"I know, but they're afraid of a rogue guard calling in a bunch of metas at once to clear them off the streets or lure them into a trap. At least, that's what I've always been told. I'd go ask for authorization, but Scott already got himself fired tonight just for knocking on the door earlier. The prisoners should all be fine; I'd just feel better if a meta could do a round. Some of these guys, they pick up on these types of things. They count rounds and keep track of faces and names. Maybe I'm just being paranoid. It's not like any of them have their powers anymore, but it'd just put my mind at ease if I knew they weren't aware that we're short staffed tonight. You know?"

There's some hesitation on my part. It's not like a facility like Silver Island to be so lax with their security protocols. Something about tonight makes me feel uneasy. Maybe it's just what happened earlier with Jim, but I can't shake it. What if what I'm feeling is the same exact same thing Rodriguez is afraid of: that without the threat of metas guarding the facility, this might prove the perfect opportunity for an escape or worse.

Scanning Rodriguez's body puts my fears somewhat at ease, though. Pulse rate and blood pressure are slightly elevated, but not to the degree they would be if a person were lying, especially if they're lying to a being that has the ability to crush them like a fly if he wanted. He's telling the truth and genuinely is just nervous about losing his job tonight if he embarrasses the wrong person in front of the wrong big league Washington guy. I haven't done rounds here in a few weeks, mostly because they've been plenty happy with me just bringing in guys, but there's not much to them. Walk through the general population block where all of the prisoners have had their metabands confiscated and are behind Plexiglas-encased, steel bars. Just make sure none of them are using a spoon to dig a hole to China.

* * *

It's lights out at Silver Island, meaning every cell I've walked by has been dark. Occasionally, one or two of the inmates are up, using the stainless steel toilet inside their single occupancy cell, or just staring at the walls or ceiling. I'm not sure what they're thinking about, but if I had to guess, I'd imagine it would be something about the fact that they're basically going to be imprisoned here indefinitely.

While The Agency might have their metabands under lock and key, there's no way to ever definitively destroy them. And as long as the metabands exist, it's always possible, even if extremely unlikely, that an inmate could find a way to get his back if he were ever allowed back out into the real world again.

My round is almost done when I hear his voice. At first, I can't place it, but I know it's familiar. Familiar enough to stop me in my tracks at the very least, and not just because he seems to know me.

Desmond Keane.

"How are you doing, young man?" he asks me.

I pause momentarily; terrified that he somehow knows who I am because he called me a young man. He doesn't know who I am, who I really am, I reassure myself. He only called me a young man because he assumes that I'm younger than him.

"Oh come on, don't tell me you've forgotten me already. You obviously haven't been on that many raids, considering how poorly that one ended."

"It didn't have to end like that. You could have just done what you were told to do."

"Do you really believe that? Do you really believe that if I'd just done what I was told to do by a bunch of men shouting at me that anything would have been different than how it is now?"

"I'm sorry about your wife," I say.

I'm not entirely sure why that's what comes blurting out of

my mouth, but it feels impossibly rude not to say it. This man broke the law, committed crimes, and stole. It's easy to think that he only stole from other rich people, people who more or less wouldn't miss the money. It's hard to shed a tear for someone who went from being a billionaire to simply a millionaire because of this man, but that's not the entire story. For every rich, old money socialite that got screwed over by this man, there were a thousand regular people who saw their life savings and retirement funds disappear. And for what? He already had more money than he could spend in twenty lifetimes, but it just wasn't enough, I guess.

"Do you want to know something?" Desmond asks me. He doesn't wait for my response before just telling me anyway. "You're the first person who has said that."

"Who has said what?" I ask.

"Who has said that they're sorry for what happened to my wife. Everyone else either pretends like it didn't happen, or that it was my fault."

"If you hadn't done what you did, we would have never been there."

"You're absolutely right, but does that mean that everything that's happened from then on out is just one hundred percent on me? If that's the case, why even have police officers and The Agency at all? Why not just allow for martial law if we're not going to hold those who police us accountable for their actions?" Keane asks.

"That's not my decision."

"Oh, but it is, young man. It's everyone's decision. The attitude that it's not your decision, that it's the decision of men and women older than you, more experienced, more highly educated, is what is wrong with this world. No one believes that anything is actually up to them. The idea of individual choice and responsibility is a thing of the past. Nothing is ever anyone else's problem any more. That's why they threw me in this cage. Why they forbid me from receiving a trial. Why go through all of that when I can just be locked away and made to be no one else's problem any more?"

I approach the Plexiglas wall of the cell Desmond is in so I can look into his eyes, even if he can't see into mine. He's made some points that have caused me to stop and think, but in the back of my mind, I remember that his man is an expert at manipulating people. Even before he acquired his metabands, which *allegedly* gave him some type of limited mind control and the ability to control the decisions of others, he was still a very persuasive man. It's not like he rose up from nothing to all of a sudden be running Wall Street after getting his metabands. He was already the CEO of a top one hundred company long before that. The metabands just greased the wheels for him to completely take over.

"And what exactly do you want me to do about it?" I ask.

"Who said I expect you to do anything about it? Can't a man just talk and express his thoughts, or is that right being taken away from me as well? The truth is that the 'powers that be' didn't want me to have those metabands, you see. They don't like the idea of an outsider having their intellect enhanced by metabands. They're much more comfortable with those who simply use them to bash the daylights out of each other. That, at least, can be easily understood by the sheep," Desmond says.

I decide I've heard enough and turn to walk away.

"Do you even know how those bands on your wrists work?" Desmond asks, stopping me in my tracks.

He doesn't know how they work. He couldn't. But he also had metabands that were unlike any that had ever been seen before. Is it possible that his metabands gave him some insight into how the bands actually work? Where they came from? He's manipulating me, I know he is, but if he has even vague answers, I want to know them.

"You're saying you do?" I ask.

"No, no, I was just a simple owner, like you. But just because we don't understand how something works, doesn't mean that we are limited in how we use it. Do you understand the inner workings of your touchscreen phone?" he asks me.

Worried that he's asking personal questions of me to try to glean more information about who I really am, I don't respond.

"Of course you don't. Your phone is infinitely more complicated than any machine created by man up to perhaps only twenty or so years ago. It was designed by a team of hundreds, maybe even thousands, of individuals, all building upon the shared knowledge of our culture that has taken thousands of years to take shape. If I asked you to make me a smartphone from scratch, or even explain to me in detail how it works, how the screen senses your finger, or how a webpage is relayed via radio waves to its internal antennas, you wouldn't be able to."

"What's your point?"

"Just because you can't explain to me how it works, doesn't mean you can't figure out how to use it. What makes that so remarkable is that even if you traveled ten thousand years back in time and showed it to a caveman, they would eventually figure out how to operate it. It would confuse and bewilder them, but in time, they would learn how the device responds to their touch and how to control parts of it, even if they never fully master it. At the end of the day, they would still believe that the phone was magic. They would still be afraid of it, and that fear is what would keep them from ever fully understanding it's power and full potential."

"Hey, what part of lights out don't you understand?" a prison guard yells from down the corridor.

I'm more startled by the guard than Desmond is, having completely forgotten that of course there are regular guards here at all times. Meta rounds are more for show of force than anything else.

"Well, it would appear I've overstayed your welcome," Desmond says to me.

"Yeah, something like that," I reply as I walk down the dimly lit corridor and out of the Containment area of Silver Island.

Twenty-Four

By the time I get home, it's late, even for me, even lately. I land on the private rooftop terrace of the apartment Derrick and I share. Okay, the apartment he owns and lets me live in. I let myself in through the rooftop entrance after using my enhanced vision to quickly scan the skyline and make sure I'm not being watched. On my way down the set of spiral stairs leading into our living space, I click my metabands together and deactivate them, allowing my suit to retract into the bands before phase shifting them off my wrists and out of sight.

"Connor!" Derrick yelps as I hit the light switch.

"Ah!" I yelp back. It's not immediately obvious which one of us has startled the other one more, but I'm glad I used the bathroom before I came home.

"What are you doing here?" he asks.

"Uhh, I live here? I know I don't pay rent or anything, but I didn't know I had to start announcing myself to you whenever I planned on coming home," I say.

"Shhh, turn off that light!" Derrick orders in a hushed tone.

"What?"

"The light! The light!" Derrick whispers again before he becomes impatient and rushes toward me to turn off the light switch himself.

"Jeez, all right. Calm down," I say to Derrick. He looks around the apartment nervously. "What's with you? I checked before I came down. No one followed me. I'm sure of it."

"I'm not worried about someone following you. I'm worried about them following me," Derrick says as he motions his head toward his office.

I give him an inquisitive look, basically asking him

nonverbally, "Are you serious right now?" He doesn't answer and instead just stares at me. The look in his eyes is the same one he gave me when he told me he knew I was Omni. It's a deadly serious look that I never expected to see again.

Derrick ushers me into his office and closes the door behind us. His laptop is partially shut on top of his desk, but the glow of the screen reflecting off the keyboard lights the otherwise pitch-black room. The blinds are closed tight.

"Phone," Derrick says to me, holding his hand out, waiting.

"Seriously? Fine, I'll turn it off," I say as I reluctantly pull my phone out of my pocket and move my finger toward the off switch.

Before I have a chance to even tap "OK" to confirm that I want to turn the phone off, Derrick snags it out of my hand. Without hesitation, he drops the phone in a glass of water sitting on the desk. The phone's screen slowly dims before completely shutting off.

"What the hell, Derrick! Are you out of your mind?" I yell. "That phone cost me—"

"Shut up," Derrick says to silence me. "I'll buy you a new one. It's not important."

"But ..." I begin before Derrick interrupts me again.

"Sit," he commands.

I do as he says since he's starting to scare me a little. I've never seen him so serious. Derrick takes his computer desk chair and sits next to me while pulling over his laptop and opening it. The laptop wakes up and Derrick turns to face me again.

"I received an anonymous tip today. Actually, more than an anonymous tip."

"A non-anonymous tip, then?" I ask sarcastically, still pretty pissed off that Derrick drowned my freaking phone for no reason.

"Connor, I'm not joking around. The information I

received today is dangerous. I'm not sure who sent it, or why they sent it to me, but it can have major implications if it gets out," Derrick says.

"Okay," I say, becoming a little more serious after seeing how rattled Derrick is. "What is it then?"

"Watch," Derrick says as he double clicks a file on the screen that then opens inside a video player.

On the screen is a somewhat grainy green and black night vision image split into nine squares. Each square has it's own video. Some are seemingly from the point of view of a person, while others are from high in the sky, looking down. All of the videos are synchronized and showing the same event: a tactical team armed to the teeth, running stealthily through a barren desert landscape, past small huts and shacks.

"What is this, Derrick? Is that the same tactical team that —"

"Just watch," he says, motioning for my attention to return to the screen in front of me and turning up the volume on the computer.

With the volume turned up, voices can now be heard, however the voices do not belong to the men on screen. Instead, they seem to belong to men watching the same feed we are, but the slight static over some of the voices seems to indicate that these men are not in the same room and that at least one of them is remote.

What I hear next is horrifying.

"Commander, we have incoming hostiles detected overhead by drone."

"What is their ETA?"

"Two minutes, sir."

"And what is our team's extraction ETA?"

"Nine minutes, sir."

"..."

"Sir?"

"Is there any chance that Alpha Team can defend their position against incoming hostiles?"

"Not likely, sir. Incoming hostiles outnumber Alpha Team by the hundreds and are carrying heavy artillery."

"Execute failsafe protocol."

"Sir, are you certain?"

"Execute it dammit!"

The screen goes black.

"Wow," I say.

"Do you understand what happened?" Derrick asks me in a solemn tone.

"Not really."

Derrick sighs and closes the video player, moving his mouse pointer quickly to a minimized web browser window. He clicks to expand the window, and the headline of news website screams, *TERRORISTS ACCIDENTALLY DETONATE NUCLEAR BOMB IN USKZIL.*

"Now do you understand?" Derrick asks me.

"Umm, nope. Not really still," I tell him truthfully.

"Are you serious? How can you not be aware of the biggest story in the world right now?" Derrick asks, no longer trying as hard to keep his voice down.

"In case you forgot, Derrick, I can kind of get a little preoccupied during the day, what with the whole superhero thing and all."

"A nuclear bomb exploded in the desert today in a small village in Uskzil. Immediately, the news reported it as having been the work of a terrorist organization looking to target the United States. They said this group has obtained the materials necessary to build the bomb, but that they accidentally blew it up themselves when trying to arm it. There were approximately one hundred deaths, but no one is being allowed anywhere near the town due to the threat of radiation poisoning. Satellite imagery shows that the explosion was extremely contained. Too contained and specific to have been the work of an accident, so I started digging. Someone must have noticed my digging, or just assumed I would be digging, and sent me that video. It's proof that I'm right."

"Right about what?"

"That it was too convenient. That it wasn't an accident. The Agency sent Alpha Team in there to retrieve an unknown number of metabands that have been found in the desert. A local warlord who had arranged to have them sold to a terrorist organization was holding the metabands. That's who was on their way to the site in the video you just saw, but obviously they never got there. Someone was monitoring that operation. They saw what was about to happen: that Alpha Team was too late and the metabands were about to fall into the wrong hands. They made the decision to nuke the entire place, including the Special Forces team, in order to make sure those metabands didn't fall into the wrong hands."

"That's crazy, though. Why wouldn't they have just done that in the first place? Why send in Americans just to have them killed?" I ask Derrick.

"Because the metabands must have been deemed too important to destroy. Hell, even those nukes probably didn't destroy them. Someone wants those metabands, either because there's something different about them, or because there're a large number of them, or something. I'm not quite sure what the reason is yet, but it's serious. You think the government really wants to drop nukes? Do you have any idea what the consequences will be if it's uncovered that we dropped the first nuclear bomb on another county in over half a century, sacrificing the lives of our own soldiers in the process?" Derrick asks me.

"So are you going to put the video out there?" I ask.

After a brief pause, he tells, "I'm not sure yet. I'm used to leaking things that are dangerous, things that can get me in trouble, but this? This is a whole other level. This is the type of thing wars get started over. I don't know if I can have that on my conscience."

"But people have a right to know. They have a right to know what our country did, don't they?"

"I'm not sure, Connor. I always believed that, but now that the power to do something about it is in my hands, I'm just not sure. This isn't just an ideological stance. This is the real world. I don't know all of the details here. I'm just putting together what I can figure out from this video and from what's been publicly reported. For all I know, this video is a fake. I have absolutely no idea. I can't just put out something like this, knowing the consequences could start a war, when I'm not even sure if it's real!" Derrick yells, beginning to become borderline hysterical.

"All right, all right. Calm down. There's no reason you have to do anything about it tonight," I say.

"How can I sleep knowing that this has happened, though? What if I'm way off about all of this, and it wasn't even our government that had a hand in this? What if it was some other group, another government's military, or hell, what if it was another terrorist organization? What if it was someone *looking* to start a war?" Derrick asks.

"What do you mean?" I ask.

"I'm saying, what if the idea that this terrorist organization having access to nuclear weapons actually *starts* a war? We're going to have to respond to this, right? We're going to send our military into Uskzil to round up whatever remnants of this group are left, aren't we? What if all of that happens under false pretenses? How can we ever possibly know for sure? No doubt whatever is actually happening, the wheels are already in motion to cover it up."

"When did this happen?" I ask Derrick.

"About four hours ago, according to the reports that can be trusted."

"Then they couldn't have gotten very far in their cover-up,

could they?"

"No. Like I said, no one can even get close to that area right now. It's radioactive. Even the United States government can't get the kind of equipment that would be needed to safely enter that area in so little time."

"That's true, but I don't need equipment."

"What are you saying?"

"I'm saying I could go there. I can see it for myself and let you know what I find. From there, you can decide what to do."

"Is it safe?"

"Is anything I do safe?"

"You've got a point, I guess. You can't teleport there though."

"Sure I can. I saw what the area looks like in the video; that's enough for me to get there."

"That's not what I mean. I mean you can't just suddenly appear in that area. It's too hot. Too dangerous. We don't know what the effects of the radiation would have on you. You need to be smart about this. If you approach the area from the south, you'll avoid the fallout and be able to move slowly enough that you can get out of there quickly if something doesn't feel right."

"That's a good idea," I say.

"I'm older than you. I'm full of good ideas," Derrick says with a smirk. "I won't be able to maintain contact with you once you're close. The radioactivity will knock out all radio and satellite communications for sure. You'll be one hundred percent on your own."

"Were you planning on coming to get me five thousand miles away in a nuclear wasteland in case something did go wrong?"

"No, I just don't like the idea of you flying in there blind and me not having eyes or ears on you."

"I'll be fine. Don't worry."

"I don't care if you're a metahuman, you're still my little brother. It's my job to worry. It's been my job to worry about you for the past ten years," Derrick says.

"Look, if anything is weird or doesn't feel right, I'll get out of there."

"Promise me."

"I promise."

TWENTY-FIVE

If I kept promises like the one I just gave Derrick, I'd be a pretty terrible superhero. I'm not stupid, and I have no intention of unnecessarily risking my neck, but flying around the world to investigate the site of a nuclear detonation isn't very high up there on the "smart, safe things to do" list. So, if I were worried about being safe, it wouldn't have been a good idea to come out here in the first place, especially this soon after a nuclear detonation, and especially when I have no idea what to expect.

The first six thousand miles or so go by in a blur. At this point, I'm pretty familiar with the Pacific Ocean and don't need to worry about taking it slow when I fly over, as long as I keep my altitude between five hundred and thousand feet. High enough so that I don't create a tidal wave as I fly at Mach whatever, but still low enough that I don't accidentally slice a plane in half.

It's happened before during the First Wave. An unknown meta flew straight into a passenger plane flying at thirty five thousand feet. He put a hole clean through the cabin so quickly that the plane just exploded due to the sudden change in cabin pressure. Everyone on board died, and it wasn't until months later that the pieces were put together, and it was discovered that a meta was the cause. This was at the very beginning of the First Wave. The incident happened when metas were just a rumor, an urban legend. No one believed they actually existed, and by the time it became public knowledge, the crash was a distant memory for most. By the time a meta had been pinned as the cause, there were already a number of villainous metas, like Jones, all over the world, causing the kind of havoc that made an airplane crash look insignificant by comparison.

The last few hundred miles I take slowly, careful not to

overshoot my target, but I'm also careful not to fly myself into a situation where I'm not fully prepared for what to expect. In the distance, I can see the faint remnants of a mushroom cloud. If this isn't the right place, I'll eat my metabands. As I get closer, I feel pins and needles all over my body. The sensation isn't painful, but it isn't exactly pleasant either, especially when I'm not used to feeling a whole hell of a lot with these bands activated. It must be the radiation from the nuclear fallout. I'd better not stick around here too long, just in case.

The air is thick with smoke and dust. The closer and closer I fly to where the bomb went off, the less I can see. Time to switch over to X-ray and infrared vision. X-ray offers almost nothing, a desolate wasteland in an area where there was never too much to begin with. An infrared scan reveals a little bit more. What I see, though, I don't like.

There's a white-hot area approximately where the bomb went off. In the few months I've had the ability to see things along the infrared spectrum, I've ever seen anything quite like it. The color is unlike anything I've ever seen before. A white brighter than any white I could ever imagine. Looking into it feels like looking into the sun. I've never seen the aftermath of a nuclear explosion before, and I hope I never will again.

Something feels wrong. Even a bomb couldn't produce this kind of energy. It's not like the government has never tried using nuclear technology to destroy, or at the very least break apart, metabands before, but it's never had any effect. The metabands always emerged from the tests without so much as a scratch on them.

Something very bad happened when they dropped that bomb, though. There must have been a reaction with the metabands. I can't get close enough to see what that reaction is. I'm still at least five miles away, but I can tell that it's something that shouldn't have been done.

TWENTY-SIX

I hate Mondays. Not in the Garfield kinda way, but in the "I spent all weekend being a superhero and now I just want to sleep instead of learn calculus" kinda way. Yesterday's trip to the nuclear detonation site affected me in ways I'm not sure about yet, both mentally and physically. It was hard seeing that type of destruction and knowing so many innocent people were essentially murdered for the sake of protecting metabands.

I have to keep telling myself that the havoc those metabands could have caused in the wrong hands would have been a hundredfold worse. That team knew they were risking their lives every time they embarked on a mission like that, but it still doesn't make it any easier to stop thinking about. For every positive the metabands have brought, there's been dozens of negatives. For every cat saved out of a tree, there's some mass murder in a shopping mall or town square because someone is trying to rob a bank and can't control his or her new powers.

Derrick drops me off early before heading downtown for work. He's a little more than paranoid about the information he was given over the weekend and understandably doesn't want to be home when a metahuman who's related to him, and thereby somewhat bound to protect him, isn't home too. I feel like I'm still half asleep as I find my way to my locker, desperate to get rid of my heavy backpack.

"Hey," I hear a voice say from behind me. I turn. It's Sarah.

"Hey," I say back, sounding a little more excited to see her than she is to see me.

"Can we talk for a minute?" she asks.

"Sure, as long as this isn't one of those 'I don't think this is working' type talks," I say with a laugh. The laugh hits the floor dead. Sarah winces slightly and frowns. This is one of those talks, isn't it? Both my stomach and heart drop.

"Let's go somewhere a little more private," Sarah says, and I follow her around the corner and away from the busy lockers.

"Connor, I really like you. I hope you know that," she begins.

"I really like you too, Sarah. I'm sorry that I haven't always been—" It's all I get out before she interrupts me.

"It's not that, Connor. It's just that I'm not sure if this is a great time, for either of us. You're busy, and I totally understand that. I'm busy too. It's not either of our faults. It's just not the right time, I think."

"I'm sorry. I know I'm not around as much as I should be. I can work on that."

"But you weren't around when I really needed you. You weren't around when that psychopath almost killed me at the circus."

"I know, I know. Believe me, I wish I'd never gone to get that burger. I regret that constantly," I say, only half meaning it. I wish I had been there for Sarah, next to her, comforting her. But the reality is that if I had been there, I wouldn't have been able to activate my metabands without exposing my identity. And if I hadn't activated my metabands, she might very well be dead right now.

"It's not just that. I'm sorry. I shouldn't have even brought that up. It's actually more complicated than that," she says.

"What is it then?" I ask in return.

"It's my dad," she says.

I exhale in slight frustration. She doesn't even know who her dad is, or what he really does.

"Your dad doesn't like me," I say, more of a statement than a question since I feel like I already know the truth.

"No, it's not that at all. Actually, he does kinda like you."

"Great, maybe I can date him then," I say in a bad

attempt at lightening a pretty dark situation.

"This isn't funny, Connor. Do you think this is easy for me? I really care about you. I really wanted this to work. It's just that it can't. Not right now."

"Then when?" I ask.

"I'm not sure. I'm not sure if it ever can."

"Where is all of this coming from?" I ask.

"You didn't let me finish before. I started telling you it had to do with my dad. He wants to pull me out of school."

"What?"

"He says it's getting too dangerous here. That we're right in the middle of the city and the meta attacks are getting worse and worse. He's worried about me."

"So what, you're just not going to go to school anymore?" I ask.

"No. I've already been accepted into Burgundy University next year."

"What? How? We're only juniors. You're already accepted into an Ivy league school?" I ask, somewhat incredulously.

"You don't believe that I could get into such a good school?"

"No, I expected you to get into a great school. You're the smartest person I know," I say. This actually is a lie. Midnight's the smartest person I know, but if we're going to take everything into account, Sarah's by far the smartest *well adjusted* person I know. In other words, she's the smartest person I know who doesn't spend the majority of her time on rooftops. "So you're just going to leave then? Go off to college at sixteen?"

"Well, no. The fall semester has already begun, so I'd have to wait until at least the spring, if not the following fall. I'm not entirely sure yet. My dad and I are still trying to work out the exact details."

"And you're just not going to go to school in the meantime?" I ask.

"Well, no. Not exactly. My dad arranged for me to get an internship at his job."

My jaw nearly hits the ground. The room seems like it's spinning. Time seems to slow down, but not in the good way where it actually *is* slowing down, when I have the metabands on and I'm moving at supersonic speed. What is actually happening is my brain can't comprehend what I'm being told and is desperately trying to work out all the permutations of what Sarah has just told me. All the while, Sarah is standing in front of me, likely wondering why I'm so shocked by this. There's only one question I can think to ask.

"At the accounting firm?"

"Yeah," she says, but her eyes quickly dart off to the left.

Midnight hasn't trained me as much as he's wanted to, but between his training and having lived for sixteen years on Earth, I can tell she's lying. I wasn't sure if her father had informed her of the entire truth about where he actually works, but her expression says it all. She knows damn well what he does now. Her insecurity with lying to me indicates she just recently found out for herself what it is that her dad spends his long hours doing.

Suddenly, everything makes sense. Of course she can't have a boyfriend while she's *interning* at a top-secret government facility, working on God knows what. My natural instinct is to blurt out that I already know everything about her dad. Well, not everything, but more than she thinks I know. Obviously this would be probably the absolute worst thing I could do in this situation, so the idea doesn't stay at the forefront of my mind for very long.

"I'm sorry, Connor," Sarah says, and I can tell it's sincere. Her eyes are almost welling up with tears.

What do I do? I can't tell her who I really am. Even if I could, how would that even change the situation? I can't sit here and argue her back into wanting to be with me.

"I am too, Sarah," I say, finding myself choking up a bit

too.

This sucks. This really sucks. What is the damn point to having these powers if I can't even have a girlfriend? I knew that my life wasn't going to be the same with these things, but I was hoping to at least have this. Just my luck that the first time in my life I have a real girlfriend, I lose her, and it's all because of these bands.

"We can still be friends though, right?" she asks.

"Yeah, of course," I reply, knowing full well that if she's not going to school here any more and working at Silver Island, it's very possible I'll never even see her again. Or at least, I won't ever see her again as Connor, only as Omni.

"Okay, well I should probably go," Sarah says. "I have to go down to the office to fill out a bunch of paperwork."

"Yeah. Of course," I say.

"See you around?" she says more than asks.

"See you around," I reply, defeated.

I watch as she walks away, desperately trying to think of something else to say. Something that can save this relationship. Sure, it hasn't been very long, but I've cared about Sarah since the first time I saw her. Back when I was just the weird new kid in school that no one else seemed to bother with except her. It just doesn't feel right for things to end this way.

Down the hallway, I see Jim for the first time since I saw him in that alleyway with the Blanks. I really need a friend right now, and something tells me that Midnight's shoulder isn't the most comfortable to cry on. I also feel extreme guilt over what's happening with Jim. He shouldn't be involved with the Blanks. They might mean well on paper, but their methods are no different than some of the worst metas out there. I understand Jim's rage, his hatred. I felt a lot of the same things growing up as a kid whose parents were killed as the result of metas fighting without any regard for the human beings around them. If anyone can understand how

Jim's feeling right now, it's certainly me. And if anyone can get through to him, I hope that would also be me.

He's down the hall from me, transferring texts and notebooks from his locker to his backpack. He looks tired, almost like a zombie. I'm not surprised, considering that I now know how he spends his nights. That's something else I understand better than most, even if it's a part of my life that I can't exactly let Jim in on. At least not yet. Maybe, hopefully, one day, though.

As I approach a few doors down from Jim's locker, I see him begin to zip up his backpack and close the locker door. He hasn't seen me yet, likely because he's barely awake, when he turns and head down the hallway in the opposite direction from where I am approaching.

"Hey, Jim!" I shout down the hallway, hoping to get his attention.

He stops and turns, obviously hearing me, when suddenly a loud cracking sound steals the attention of everyone in the hallway all at once. It's coming from outside, almost like lightning in the sky, even though it's a cloudless, beautiful morning. Just as everyone decides it was nothing and turns to continue on with their mornings, it happens.

The explosion is deafening and blinding. My ears are ringing, but through the ringing I can hear screams and chaos. Everything is rubble. My first thought is that a bomb has gone off somewhere. The early autumn sun shines down from where the roof used to be and through the cement dust hanging in the air. Where there aren't screams, there's coughing as students try to make their way back to their feet through the gray cloud.

I yell Jim's name, but I can barely hear my own voice over the ringing in my ears. It sounds distant and far away, like it belongs to someone else. The world is just beginning to come back into focus when I see part of the rubble in front of me moving. The pieces of concrete are at least a foot thick and heavy. Whatever is moving under there, under that type of weight, is not human. Before I have a chance to give it any further thought, my questions about what could have caused this, and what's happening in general, are answered.

Through the haze a figure appears. A hulking, gigantic figure. Some type of Brute, shirtless with a chest so hairy it looks like he's wearing a sweater. Two black, curved horns protrude out of his forehead and wrap around the back of his oversized skull. He's picking himself up and brushing off large pieces of concrete as if they're nothing.

Above me the sky darkens. The sunlight shining in through the newly ripped hole in the ceiling is blocked out by a silhouette. Another meta, this one wearing a green and orange suit, descends slowly from the sky. His face is entirely obscured by a mask, without even an opening for his mouth. Only two white dots are where his eyes should be. It's hard to tell where he's focusing his attention without real eyes, but it's a safe bet that it's on the meta who just came crashing through the roof.

"Stop!" a voice yells through the chaos. It's come from Marcus, a guy I recognize from homeroom, but I've barely spoken to since coming to Bay View High School last year.

Marcus is running toward the horned Brute, attempting to get in front of him in the hopes of at least getting him out of the school. The Brute doesn't even look in Marcus's direction before throwing one of his huge fists out to the side as he continues down the hallway without breaking his stride. Marcus is embedded into the nearby lockers, killed instantly.

The green and orange suited meta reaches the ground and lands gently. I've never seen him before, but I hope he can put an end to this quickly. That hope is dashed when he picks up the nearest student by his head, a guy named Russ that was in my chemistry class last year, and hurls him directly at the horned Brute. Russ bounces off the meta's chest and falls to the ground with a sickening thump. If he's not dead, he's gravely injured.

My bearings are back, and I need to do something. There's screaming everywhere as students rush past me and head into the nearest classrooms. Some are pounding on the doors, the students and teachers inside apprehensive about unlocking their doors and risking the horror that's happening in the hallways getting inside.

The two metas rush toward each other down the hallway. I barely have time to turn my head before they collide and send even more wreckage hurtling in all directions, no doubt causing even more injuries. I look around for Sarah in desperation. Wherever she is, I need to get her out of here. That's my first priority. These two can wait to have their heads bashed in until Sarah is safe.

But Sarah's nowhere to be found. Seeing anything is extremely difficult with the dust and falling debris in the air, though. I scream out her name, but the sound doesn't seem to make it very far with all the noise bouncing off the walls around me. Where is she?

There's another cracking sound as the two metas collide again. Whatever their powers are, they seem to be equally matched. This is bad. Very bad. Two metas who match each other in strength usually means a prolonged battle. In a metropolitan area, this can mean massive destruction and death. If the damage and casualties I've seen already are anything to go by, this is going to be bad.

The thought of transforming keeps overwhelming all the other thoughts in my brain. There's a line where I need to put the lives of those around me in front of keeping my true identity a secret. I've never known exactly where that line is since it always meant endangering the people around me who I care about most, but right now, two of those people, Sarah and Jim, are somewhere in this building, and I'm quickly finding out exactly where that line is.

I'm about to yell Sarah's name again when through the

haze of cement dust in the air, I hear coughing. Coughing so loud and hard that it sounds as though whoever is behind it is about to cough their lungs right out of their chest. Impulsively, I rush toward the sound, unable to ignore someone who sounds like they are in the throes of death. Making my way through the haze, I find myself behind a figure doubled over in a coughing fit. It's the green and orange meta. He's surrounded by the bodies of my fellow classmates. Some of them are dead, and the rest barely cling to life. Before I can think, my training kicks in and I'm at the meta's throat.

My subconscious has put the pieces together faster than my brain: if this meta is coughing due to the cement dust in the air, that means they are not impervious to a lack of oxygen. He might possess super strength and a level of invulnerability, but he still needs to breathe. I've already figured out what I need to do, metabands activated or not, and that's to stop this meta from breathing until he submits and relinquishes his metabands, ending this bloodshed.

In an instant, my forearm is wrapped around the meta's windpipe from behind. My other arm is perpendicular, acting as leverage to pull my forearm harder into his throat. He takes a desperate, wheezing gasp, but no air enters his lungs.

"Stop this, stop this right now!" I scream as loud as I can manage directly into his right ear from only an inch or two away. Blowing out his eardrums should be the least of my, or his, concerns right now.

"Power down! Now! Power down, or I swear to God, I will —" Before I can finish my threat, the meta reaches over his head with both arms, grabs me by the collar of my shirt, and hurls me in front of him as hard as he can manage in his weakened state. Unfortunately, that's still hard enough to send me flying at least twenty feet and directly into a concrete brick wall.

That's it. I have to put a stop to this, even if it means exposing my identity. There's no time to find a more secluded area to transform. I've already wasted enough time and let enough people get hurt or worse. As I lie on the linoleum tile floor, I concentrate on my metabands and they appear on my wrists, ready to activate. Except my arms won't move. I can see my right arm, laid out to the side of me, but no matter how hard I try it won't move. I can't even feel it. A wave of horror washes over me as I realize I can't feel my left arm either. My entire body is numb.

I'm paralyzed.

When that monster threw me into the brick wall, he broke my back. There's no pain, just the complete lack of any sensation whatsoever, which is even more terrifying. And right now, the worst part is that I have a front row seat to these metas battling it out without any regard of whom they hurt, and there's nothing I can do to stop them. Even breathing is a struggle, and I'm lucky to have at least summoned my metabands quickly enough that they can begin repairing my broken body. They're not active, but at least they'll start to heal me, even if it's brutally slow. Another few seconds and I would have started losing consciousness for sure.

Still, it's enough to ensure that I can't activate my metabands. If only I could bring my wrists together. I'd be healed instantly and have absolutely no problem taking these two out. It was stupid of me to worry about risking my identity instead of just activating my bands right away. Midnight trained me to fight without the bands active in the hopes that I'd never have to fall back on it, but instead, I foolishly and arrogantly thought I no longer needed them.

There's a slight sensation in my toes, almost like the pins and needles feeling you get when you fall asleep on your arm. I can't move my foot, but it's there. It's something. It's hope.

The two metas continue beating on each other, throwing each other through walls and into what I at least hope are now abandoned classrooms. Small electrical fires have broken out and smoke is now filling the halls, making it even harder to tell what's happening, or to see if there's any hope that Sarah's safe.

"That's enough!" a voice bellows from above.

I can't make out the face of the meta descending from the sky as the morning sun backlights her. The two metas stop their fight for a moment and turn their attention to the new challenger. Just then, her face comes into focus.

It's Iris.

And she's pissed.

She rushes toward the Brute, the closer of the two metas, and slides into his feet, taking them out from under him and landing him directly on his ass. In the same movement, she comes back up to her feet and roundhouse kicks the other meta, sending him spinning into the nearest wall.

"You want a fight? You've got it, but let's take it outside like gentlemen," Iris says to the two metas, lying on opposite sides of what used to be the cafeteria.

Each slowly rises to his feet, shakes the dizziness out of his head, and reassesses the situation. Unfortunately for them, their assessment doesn't conclude in them deciding to listen to Iris, and they instead decide it's best to keep the fight right where it is.

The Brute charges at Iris, taking no consideration for the path in front of him, littered with injured and dead students. He tramples many of their bodies, others are merely kicked aside as he gains speed and momentum. Iris is screaming for him to stop, but it's no use. He just keeps coming, lowering his head as he prepares to ram her. Iris's white eyes glow brightly as she thrusts out her hands and releases pure, white energy toward the Brute.

He stops and falls to his knees. His head is now missing

entirely, vaporized off his shoulders in an instant. Iris screams out in frustration as she pulls her hands back in. She couldn't control what she just did, but she didn't see an alternative. She's mad at herself for it. I know because I've been there before. Her shoulders sink as she bows her head, ashamed of what she's just done. Just then, the other meta flies into the air, looking to bring both his fists down on Iris's back.

I struggle to pull air into my lungs and scream out her name to warn her, but instead of "Iris," a different name comes out. "Sarah."

For a split second, I think it's just because I'm worried about Sarah, more worried than I've ever been, and her name is on my mind. But then I realize what I think must be the truth.

That Iris is Sarah.

Somewhere deep down, I knew it all along. How else could Iris have gotten here so fast? Where else could Sarah have gone moments ago? She's not leaving school because her dad is worried; she's leaving school because her dad knows the truth. He probably knew the truth all along, and it's only now, when the world is full of metas and he can no longer help keep her safe, that he's demanding she be closer to him.

There's a loud crack and a pop, followed by a scream of my own. My vertebrae are realigning themselves thanks to the metabands on my wrists, but the bands aren't doing anything for the pain. My eyes are watering uncontrollably, and I feel like I can't breathe, that's how badly everything hurts as sensation begins to return. The sound attracts Iris's attention as she turns to me and quickly glances at the metabands on my wrists. She might not realize that I'm Omni, but she now knows that I'm a meta too. The distraction has opened her up to an attack from the other meta who is still alive and apparently hasn't learned his lesson from what just happened to his former enemy.

Iris hears him coming, though, and swiftly moves to the side, wrapping her right arms around the meta's neck as he passes, and then pulls him backward so that he's pinned backward over her knee.

"Yield!" she screams in his face, but it does nothing.

He continues to try to fight, clawing at her arms and head, and trying desperately to break free. His hands keep grasping around him until he finds something to grab onto: Lucy Friedman, another classmate of mine from homeroom, who's already pinned under a cafeteria table and barely alive when the meta pulls her up by the throat.

"Let her go. This is your only warning!" Iris yells into his face.

His eyes look right through her and his expression doesn't change as the barely conscious Lucy begins making a faint gurgling sound. He's squeezing her throat, choking her to death.

"Let her go!" Iris screams one last time.

Lucy's face is turning a deep shade of purple. I try to yell to stop them, but I can only grunt. My motor skills are beginning to return as I try to use my legs to push me along the waxed floor, hoping to stop her in time.

"Damn you for making me do this," Iris says before she exhales, and twists her shoulder, snapping the meta's neck over her knee.

An instant later, she's gone.

TWENTY-SEVEN

There were five dead and over three dozen injured when all was said and done. Seven dead, if you include the two metas who Iris killed.

By the time the police arrive, my metabands have fully healed me, and I go back to hiding them. Explaining that I'm a meta is something I never want to have to do. Explaining that I'm a meta, and I let something like this happen while I could have done something ... I can't even think about it right now.

Between the police, medics, news crews, and opportunistic metas looking to "help" now that the danger is over, it's nearly impossible to find anyone. That's why I'm so happy when I finally find Jim and see that he's okay. Or at least, not physically hurt.

"How could they do that, Connor?" he asks me.

"I don't know, Jim. It's horrible," I say.

"I was there. I was right there when a piece of the wall landed on a guy. Killed him instantly. Blood everywhere. And the most horrible sound I've ever heard."

"I'm sorry, Jim."

"Do they even know why they did all of this?" Jim asks me, but I don't have the answer. "I don't know how much longer I can take this, Connor."

"Have you seen Sarah?" I ask Jim.

"Yeah. Her dad came to pick her up. She was pretty shaken up. I don't know where they went."

"I do."

I'm above Silver Island now; Omni suit fully in place. In the past few hours, I've reassured Derrick that everything's fine and he doesn't need to worry about me. I've also called Sarah's phone about a million times, give or take a few hundred thousand. She hasn't answered, which has me worried. Maybe I was wrong. Maybe she isn't Iris after all. They're still digging through the rubble that was my former high school, and the idea that she's somewhere underneath all of that has me terrified to the point that I can't even think about it right now. Jim said she's okay, though. I have to keep reminding myself of that.

I radio in to Silver Island, requesting teleportation coordinates. It takes three requests before I get a call back.

"What is your purpose for entry?" I'm asked. I've never been asked this before.

"I need to speak with Halpern," I reply. There's a long silence.

"Teleportation coordinates are available only to metas transporting potential prisoners. All other inquiries must be made through ..." the voice on the other end says.

"To hell with your other inquiries. I need to talk to him!" I scream into my receiver.

"I'm sorry. Access has been denied," the voice on the other end says without emotion.

"Goddammit, half the people in there right now are there because I brought them in! You're seriously going to tell me that I can't come in there without a prisoner?" I scream again.

There's no response on the other end.

For a moment, I consider the idea of finding a new prisoner. The night is young, and there certainly must be some meta out there in the city causing problems. If I can find them and bring them in, I'd have reason to enter Silver Island. Certainly, they wouldn't refuse a known "good" meta bringing in a bad one. But even still, it's a long shot. I don't even know if Halpern is there; let alone Sarah. I cruised over their house briefly on my way to Silver Island, but I didn't see either of them inside. I felt like a bit of a creeper even doing that. No, if I'm going to confront Sarah about my suspicion that she's actually Iris, I want to do it in person, and I want to ask her directly. I'm not sure why, but the idea of hearing the admission from her directly is more important to me than catching her in the act.

But right now, Silver Island is no use. The facility is purposefully impenetrable. There are ways in, of course, for a meta there's almost always a way in, but no way that wouldn't trigger a full military response and possibly cause the deaths of many of the metas there who have yet to receive a fair trial.

Silver Island learned from the first wave of metas that when it comes to super-powered beings, the idea of "fair" is subjective. There were a lot of metas sprung from prisons during the First Wave a decade ago, when security was lax. Well, not lax, but not built to the specifications that imprisoning metas requires. Between the First and Second Waves, many of the organizations subcontracted by the government in the case of a Second Wave spent the majority of their time and resources coming up with ways to imprison metas, if ever the need should arise again.

Beyond the idea of just imprisoning metas, many brilliant men and women thought of ways to shut down the prisons entirely in an emergency, even if all of the elaborate perimeters had been breached.

There's a crackle over my earpiece, and a new voice comes on. It's Halpern.

"Omni, I'm clearing you for arrival. Coordinates G-13. Come see me when you're in."

I haven't given much thought as to what I'm going to say to Halpern when I confront him. "I know your daughter is a meta?" What if he doesn't know himself? How is it my place to blow someone's identity? No one has done that to me, at least not yet. So suddenly, I'm having a crisis of faith over what I should do. I watched Iris kill. Is this really a conversation I want to have with someone about his daughter? I rushed in here full of anger and concern, but now that I'm here, finding the right words is much harder than I assumed it would be.

After teleporting into Silver Island, I quickly find Halpern; he's already waiting for me outside the Processing area of the facility.

"So you've heard?" he asks me.

For a second, I'm about to blurt out that I know the truth about Sarah, but I question why he's asked if I've heard. I didn't *hear* it from anyone; I saw it for myself. In this situation, it's always best to play dumb. Except when it's best to play smart. I decide to go somewhere in-between.

"I've heard a little. Why don't you start from the top," I say, very proud of myself for figuring out such a clever way of getting the information I need without Halpern thinking I'm not in the loop.

"You haven't heard, have you?" Halpern asks. Guess that didn't work as well as I thought. "Why are you here then?" he asks.

By this time, we're walking down the hallway together toward his office, and I can tell by the buzz of people coming in and out of different offices, all looking like they're in a hurry, that obviously something is going on. I decide to pull that thread.

"Well, it's obvious something's happening," I say. This seems to satisfy Halpern's curiosity about why I'm here, at least for the time being.

"Desmond Keane is being granted a release pending his trial," Halpern tells me.

"What? Why? How?"

"You forgot where and when. He's rich and powerful, even without metabands. Keane hired the best lawyers in the world, and they've compelled the court to question whether his metabands are even real."

"But they are; I saw them appear!"

"Which would be great if we could use your testimony in court, but it's not going to be admissible as evidence if you're not sworn in under your real identity. They don't like the idea of someone sitting up on the stand in tights and a mask."

"They're not ti—"

"I know, I know. The bottom line is that Keane is getting released. People don't get released from Silver Island, in case you hadn't noticed."

"I had."

It was hard not to notice that there is a whole wing of Silver Island that isn't accessible, or isn't accessible to me, at least. According to Derrick, the east wing is where all the prisoners from the first wave of metas are kept. Both those that forfeited their metabands and the ones who didn't are buried deep under the facility. When metas first started appearing, people were amazed, but frightened. When the first ones started committing criminal acts, laws were passed quickly to ensure life sentences for any metas determined to have used their abilities for harm. No possibility of parole, no trial, nothing. If The Agency said you did something bad, and they caught you, well that was it.

"As you've probably guessed, while we've figured out a pretty good way to get prisoners *into* Silver Island, we've never had to deal with getting them out, safely at least," Halpern says. "We were hoping you could help with that."

"How?"

"We want you and another meta we trust to teleport Keane to his home. He's to remain there under house arrest until such time that a trial can be arranged. There are a lot of threats to his life coming in from all over the place. People aren't happy he's being released, so we can't exactly walk him out the front door."

"And then what? Once he's out of here he'll magically be

safe at his house?"

"Probably not. That's why he's already hired a number of metas to guard him. We'll be providing additional security as well."

"And what if I refuse?"

"I can't make you do anything you don't want to do, Omni," Halpern says as he turns the corner and swipes his access card at a security gate, entering one of the many areas of Silver Island that I'm excluded from.

"Excuse me," a voice calls as I am walking back through the Processing area to Arrivals so I can teleport out of here. "You're Omni, aren't you?"

I turn and find Sarah sitting behind a computer terminal in the glass-enclosed workstation nearest the teleportation port. For a second, I'm at a complete loss for words. I want to confront her about everything. To find out if my suspicions are true that she's Iris, and if she is, why she did that.

But I don't. There are cameras and microphones everywhere. This is a beyond high security facility. Every physical being that can be recorded in here, is. To confront her now would reveal my own identity; there's no doubt about it.

"Yeah, I'm Omni," I say, realizing that this is the first time I'm having a conversation with someone who knows Connor, but doesn't know we're the same person.

"Sorry, I know you're probably sick of hearing this, and it might not be appropriate since I work here. Well, technically I'm just an intern, but anyway, my point was going to be that I'm a really big fan of yours," Sarah tells me as she blushes slightly.

"Oh," I say, stalling for time to think of something to say since this is pretty high up there on the list of things I hadn't expected to come out of her mouth. "Thanks," I finally arrive at.

Not exactly the most creative response to someone who just said something nice to you.

"Also, I'm supposed to schedule you to come back here tomorrow? It doesn't say why. Apparently that's above my security clearance, but it says here," she says, gesturing to her computer screen, which is facing the opposite direction from where I'm standing, "to confirm a seven a.m. arrival with you. Is that okay?"

"Yeah, that's fine," I say in return.

"Great. Just call in beforehand and we'll give you teleportation coordinates. Jeez, what am I thinking, telling you that? You already know all this stuff."

"Don't worry about it."

"Okay, see you then, Omni!" Sarah says with a slight cheer in her voice.

"See you then."

The only place I can think to go to next is Midnight's water tower. I teleport in. Midnight doesn't like me coming in through the other entrances during the daytime. He says I'm not stealthy enough to make sure no one's following or watching. He's not here, but I'm not exactly surprised. So I wait. It isn't long before he arrives through the trapdoor in the ceiling disguised to look like a valve from the outside.

"What are you doing here?" he asks.

"What, don't like surprises?"

"No. And it's hard to surprise someone who's got his water tower covered in surveillance equipment."

"It was a joke. I know you have this places decked out with cameras and lasers and ... more lasers or whatever. I figured I'd save myself the trouble of calling since you're more likely to show up if I just invite myself over."

"This is about what happened at your school today, I assume?" Midnight asks.

"Sarah is Iris," I say.

There's a long silence before Midnight says anything back.

"No, she isn't."

"What? How do you know that?"

"She just isn't."

Midnight brushes past me and heads over to his computer terminal. He removes his cowl and sits down. He pulls up maps and security cameras from around the city and watches various metas fly through the city sky like fireflies on a summer night. He's trying his best to ignore me, thinking it will get me to drop it and just go away. A frequent tactic of his that never works on me.

"Then who is Iris?"

"It doesn't matter. She isn't Sarah, though."

"So you do know who she is?"

"That's not important."

"How is that not important?" I begin to argue. "My school got destroyed today, people died, and Iris magically shows up and starts murdering bad guys. That's pretty important in my book."

"And why did it get to that point? Why didn't you do something to stop it?"

"What? Are you serious? Now this is my fault?" I ask.

"What Iris does is her business. What *you* do is mine."

"But what you know about Iris is none of my business? You know what? Forget this. I came here trying to find some answers or at the very least some sympathy, but I should have known by now how stupid it is to think I'd find either of those here."

Before Midnight has a chance to respond, if he was even going to, I teleport out of there to the skies over Bay View City. It's almost night time now, and I can see glimpses of some of the metas who were just on Midnight's screen, darting around above the city, silhouetted by the setting sun. No doubt some of them are up to no good, but it's not my place to do anything about that. I can't be the savior of this entire city twenty-four hours a day. If anything has taught me that, it's today.

Twenty-Eight

It's early the next morning when I arrive at Silver Island for Desmond Keane's transport. Really early. Like, I didn't know this hour even existed early. I don't know if "luckily" is the appropriate word to use, but luckily I don't have school this morning due to everything that's happened. Otherwise, I'm up so early that I wouldn't even make it through homeroom without falling asleep. There's already been too many calls home to Derrick because of me missing class, being late, or falling asleep. You name it. If he didn't already know I'm a meta, he would have figured it out within the first week of school starting

Classes are canceled for the foreseeable future to allow everyone time to grieve, but also because the building isn't structurally sound anymore. They're not sure if they're going to try to fix it, or just tear the whole thing down and start over. In the meantime, it sounds like we're all going to get split up and sent to neighboring schools. Probably for the rest of the year at least if I had to guess. That's how bad the damage is.

I don't get the luxury of time to grieve. I feel like I haven't for my entire life. After Mom and Dad were killed in The Battle, I had to grow up quickly. Not as quickly as Derrick, though. Overnight, he went from being a college student to the legal guardian of a six year-old. There wasn't time for either of us to grieve. With no other family, we were immediately on our own. Derrick had to quickly prove that he was capable of taking care of me to child services so that I wasn't taken away and placed in a foster home. Again, I hate to use the word "luckily" here, but luckily, there were so many deaths that day and so much confusion in general, they barely had time to find homes for all the new orphans let alone follow up with the ones who had homes and family to go to, like me.

After dragging my ass out of bed this morning, I felt a million times better once I turned on my metabands. It's like having a quadruple espresso but without the jitters. Nothing quite wakes you up like activating strange alien technology that gives you super powers. That being said, I feel like I need another few hours of sleep before dealing with the meta I find out I'm teamed up with.

"Hey there, buddy. Name's Elastico," the meta wearing florescent orange and green says as he extends his hand for me to shake.

I'm no expert on style, but even I can tell that this costume is butt ugly. If the metabands hadn't woken me up this morning, one look at this god-awful uniform would have. We're outside the Silver Island facility, just in front of a pair of large metal gates in what looks like a loading dock, likely for ships bringing supplies onto the island. It's a sunny day in the bay, and the seagulls are already up and squawking overhead.

"Hi. Omni," I say, shaking his hand.

"So, what's your deal?" he asks.

"What do you mean? I'm here to transport Keane. Isn't that why you're here?"

"Duh. I know that. I mean, what's your *deal*. What are your powers, bro?"

Yup, it's way too early in the morning to be dealing with this. This guy doesn't know who I am? Seriously? I'm not trying to be vain or something, but I *was* kinda a big deal for a while there. Ugh. Everyone forgets so quickly, especially when you're no longer one of the only metas in the world.

"I've got a little of everything," I say, trying to politely end the conversation so we can just wait here until they're ready to release Keane so we can teleport him out of here and I can go back to my nice comfy bed.

"Pfft," Elastico replies.

I really don't want to deal with this right now.

"What is that supposed to mean?" I ask, against my better judgment.

"Nothing. Just you guys with multiple powers think you're better than everyone else."

"I didn't say that."

"No, but I'm sure you think it."

"Hey, listen. You don't know me, and I don't know you. We're both just here to do a job. Why are you trying to pick a fight with me?" I ask. I'm in no mood.

"I'm not trying to pick a fight with you. I'm just making an observation."

"Whatever. Let's just drop it then."

"Well aren't you going to ask me what my powers are?"

"I don't really care to be honest."

Wow, maybe I do need a coffee after all.

"See! There it is. That's exactly what I'm talking about. '*I don't really care to be honest,*'" Elastico says in a mocking tone.

Why did I even say anything?

"Okay, fine. What are your powers?" I ask.

"You're not asking like you really mean it. You don't care," he says. Really? This is how this morning is going to go? What a baby.

"Sure I do. What are your powers?" I ask again.

Elastico turns to me and smiles. I really just want this morning to be over. Without warning, he suddenly throws both hands into the air. I say he throws them into the air, because that's literally what he does. His arms extend what must be hundreds of feet in a matter of seconds as his hands reach higher and higher into the air.

"You're a Changer," I say.

Elastico just smiles back at me. While Changers aren't exactly the most impressive metas, they're some of the rarest you'll see. Their powers vary slightly from meta to meta, but basically, they're able to manipulate their own body in pretty crazy ways. Some, like Elastico here, are able to extend their body like it was made out of rubber. This can lead to all kinds of fun, if not exactly practical, abilities like using your limbs to tie up a bad guy or making yourself really flat to slide under doors or glide through the air.

Other Changers have even more complex abilities. Some are able to transform their bodies into actual mechanical shapes. They can become complex machines. Others can change their bodies into animals, sometimes even animals that don't exist in the real world, like say, a flying giraffe. That's a real example; he's all over the Internet.

There are still other Changers who can control their size and mass, meaning they can shrink down to the molecular level or grow themselves to be the size of a building. The guys who can shrink are in ultra high demand in the medical field since they can go inside the human body and actually physically fight diseases and cancer. When the super rich get sick, they don't take medicine. They hire a meta that can shrink to the size of a molecule and go inside of them to physically fight alongside white blood cells to beat whatever ails them.

The metas who can grow usually work in more blue-collar jobs, often in lumber or other natural resource gathering jobs. Companies would love to use them in building construction, but no city will issue the permits required since a Changer tripped over his own shoelaces and wound up taking out the skyscraper he was building during the First Wave. They've since been strictly forbidden from using their powers inside populated areas.

I glance down at where my watch would be, before realizing that, of course, I'm not wearing a watch, just a slightly ridiculous-looking full body suit. It wouldn't look ridiculous if I were flying or fighting or doing anything cool, but it doesn't suit just standing around outside a loading dock.

"Do you know when they're supposed to be bringing him out?" I ask Elastico.

"Why, you got a hot date?" he asks back.

I'm slowly starting to realize that I'm not going to get anything except smart ass answers back from this guy, so maybe I'd be best served to just keep my stupid mouth shut until this is all over. As if on cue, I hear a lock click behind me from one of the steel doors to the facility. It swings open and Desmond Keane emerges, still wearing his orange prison jumpsuit and shackles and surrounded by heavily armored security. Most of the guards immediately retreat back into the facility the second Keane is outside its walls, slamming the steel door behind them with a solid thud.

One of the two armored guards who remain comes over toward us.

"Henderson, right?" I ask him, thinking I recognize him from my guard duties.

"Ha, yeah that's right, Omni. Good memory," he says back.

I can't place a name to a face for the life of me without these metabands on, but along with being able to make me fly and punch through walls, they seem to help me remember names too. A great bonus in social situations, but unfortunately, I don't spend very much time just hanging out with my metabands on, so it's rare they actually help. Behind Henderson, the other guard is using a key to unlock and remove the shackles keeping Desmond's ankles and wrists connected to a chain around his waist. These are fairly simple constraints like you would see on any regular prisoner since after all, Desmond is exactly that now that he's been stripped of his metabands and powers.

The only reason for the heightened security is the fear that something could go wrong during the transfer that could compromise the integrity of the entire facility. They don't really know what to expect and seem to have prepared for every situation, just in case. Desmond Keane might be innocent in the eyes of the law, or at least presumed innocent for the time being, but those working for The Agency and Silver Island think he's anything but, even if they can't prove it.

"We'll have him out of those cuffs in just a minute. Then he's all yours, and we can get back to wrangling the other monsters inside," Henderson says.

"Don't worry officer, myself and my companion here have your back. You're safe with us," Elastico says.

Companion? Is he freaking kidding me? I can't wait for this morning to just be over already.

"Are you quite done, guard?" Desmond asks the man unshackling him.

He seems to be having a little bit of trouble with the last lock. Can't blame the guy; it's not that often that they even use these things. Once you're thrown into your cell here, you're pretty much in solitary confinement in order to maintain the security of the entire place. The sanity, comfort, rights, and everything else of the men and women imprisoned here is secondary to security. Always.

"There you go, and it's still 'officer' to you, Keane," the prison official says as he releases the last cuff from Desmond Keane's ankle and pulls away the entire apparatus. "He's all yours now, boys. Have fun."

"All right, let's just get this over with. Grab onto me," I say to Desmond and Elastico.

"What?" Elastico asks. "Sorry, buddy. I don't go *that way*."

I give Elastico a look of disgust. He's lucky I don't just throw him into the ocean right now.

"You've really got a comment for everything, don't you?" I ask rhetorically. "I'm sorry to disappoint you, but I'm not interested in you either. You're going to need to grab onto me so I can teleport you both out of here and to Keane's estate."

"I'm not teleporting," Keane says nonchalantly, as though

I'm the pool boy at his country club asking him to use the same public entrance as everyone else.

"What do you mean, you're not teleporting?" I ask.

"Yeah, I'm not teleporting either," Elastico says. This gains a nod from Keane, which in return causes Elastico to smile. Someone's already angling for a position on Keane's meta bodyguard staff.

"It's emasculating," Keane says.

"What is it with you two and the macho stuff? Are you both really that insecure?" I ask.

"I'm not relying on someone else to use magical powers to get me where I need to go. I can do it on my own," Keane says.

"On your own with us protecting your ass, is what you mean to say," I reply.

"It's a rights issue. I have the right not to have a meta use their powers on me. That is a basic, inalienable human right, or do you think those types of rules don't apply to you, Omni? Do you think you have the right to just do as you please to anyone else?"

"That's not what I said. Listen, you wanted me here to babysit you on your way home, and if you want me to protect you, then we do things my way," I say, surprising myself a little bit. I guess Midnight really is rubbing off on me. Not sure if that's a good thing or a bad thing.

The previously closed door to the Silver Island facility opens back up and the two guards reemerge.

"Listen boys, as much as we enjoy watching you bicker on the security monitors, you all gotta get out of here," Henderson says.

"I know. Come on, Keane. We're teleporting out of here right now," I reply as I begin walking over to grab him.

"That's bett—" Before the officer can finish his sentence, a blast of blue energy slams into his chest and leaves a foot-wide hole. He falls to his knees before toppling over, face first to the ground, dead before he even hits it.

I spin my head around to see where it came from, but my eyes can't believe what they're seeing.

It's Beta, from the Alpha Team. He's alive, and he's a hundred feet in the air with two shiny metallic cuffs around his wrists.

Metabands.

"What the ..." Henderson begins as he brings his gun up to aim at Beta.

Before I can get in front of him, Beta lets another blast of blue energy loose from his fists, killing Henderson instantly.

"Don't even think about trying to teleport. I'll blow Keane's head clean off his body before you have a chance to move a muscle," Beta says to me.

Keane is too far away from me to get to him in time, even moving at supersonic speed. I have no idea how quick Beta is right now. It's not a risk worth taking. Yet.

"What do you want?" I yell toward Beta.

"I want Keane. Alive. That's all," he yells back.

"Why? He's nobody. He's nothing," I respond.

"I couldn't agree with you more. Which is why I'm going to need you to stand aside."

"I can't do that."

"I'm afraid you don't have a choice in the matter. You see, this man, this *thing*, he killed my wife. He killed her in cold blood as some sick, perverse sort of revenge."

"I did nothing of the sort!" Keane yells out.

"Liar!" Beta screams back before shooting a blast of energy in Keane's direction. I react without thinking and dive at Keane, pushing him out of the way of the blast.

"That was foolish. What has this piece of human garbage ever done to deserve such compassion?" Beta asks.

"All right ladies. I think I've heard about enough chit-chat. You want a fight buddy, bring it," Elastico says.

His body begins expanding, rapidly. It grows in all

directions, becoming longer and longer until he's stretched to the point of being as tall as the height at which Beta is flying. He's maybe a hundred or so feet in the air. Although Elastico is gigantic now, he's literally stretched thin. It's as though his body gained no mass, but instead was just pulled in every direction like a rubber band.

"This isn't a game, son. Stand aside, now," Beta demands of Elastico.

"No way, José," he replies.

"Fine, have it your way then," Beta says as he begins to glow a deep, bright blueish color all over his body.

Even though he's high in the air, the ground all around us is beginning to tremble. There is a look of hesitation on Elastico's face, as though he's just had second thoughts about what he's done and the challenge he's thrown down. It was a very, very bad idea, and he's finally realized that a few seconds too late.

With a primal scream, Beta's legs and arms are thrown out to his sides as the blue energy gathers at his outstretched hands before bringing them back together and shooting the energy at his target: Elastico's metabands. In the blinding blink of an eye, Elastico's metabands simply vaporize. They disintegrate right before my eyes, and Elastico reverts back to his human form, a teenage boy no older than me.

I now have two problems. The first, and most grave concern, is that I just witnessed a pair of metabands seemingly be destroyed. Maybe they weren't. Maybe they were just teleported away somewhere or temporarily hidden, but even that has dire consequences.

Metabands that have been powered up cannot be removed by anyone, except their users. On top of that, there has never, ever been a case of metabands being destroyed. The closest case there has ever been was when The Governor threw Jones into the sun, and even then, it's only assumed that his metabands were destroyed. There's no proof. For all we know, there's still a pair of metabands somewhere inside that huge cloud of gas without a scratch on them.

The second, and more pressing concern, is that without his metabands, Elastico, or rather the guy who used to be Elastico, is now simply a regular dude a hundred feet in the air with nothing holding him there except for time, and that's only about a second or two. Instinctually, I bound into the air, carefully timing my trajectory so that I'm able to catch him and still give myself enough room to slow my descent. Catching him near the ground isn't going to be a much better option than just letting him hit the concrete, so I have to time everything just right.

And I do. I time it perfectly, catching the person who used to be Elastico and who will likely never be him again, at least saving him from death by gravity. There isn't a second to celebrate before I realize what else I have done. I've left Desmond Keane vulnerable. I turn to look at Beta. He looks displeased that I've saved Elastico, but an instant later, I can see all over his face that he's had same thought I've just had. He turns his attention back to Keane.

I'm still at least twenty feet in the air. Far too high to simply drop Elastico and expect him to live after bouncing off the concrete below. Beta is already charging up again, his body bathed in a growing florescent blue glow. There isn't a need to summon this type of power, the type of power that can destroy a metaband, just to take out a single, simple human being. But this isn't a rational person. This is a person bent on vengeance. He has nearly limitless power. Why choose to limit it now when he's about to destroy his enemy?

I allow myself to drop to the ground, knowing that I'll be able to absorb the fall with my knees while holding Elastico safely across the chest. Once I hit the ground, Elastico is placed on the concrete, unconscious but breathing, and I turn my attention back to Beta. Getting in between him and Keane is a surefire way to ensure my metabands suffer the same fate as Elastico's. I can't let Keane die on my watch, but I'm not going to do either of us any good if I don't have my metabands five seconds from now. Whatever is different about Beta that is allowing him to do this, I'm not sure yet, but I realize that his power is far from fully depleted from the energy blast that destroyed Elastico's metabands. If I block his next energy blast, it doesn't mean Beta won't have anything left in the tank to vaporize both of us two seconds later.

My only hope is getting Keane out of the way of the blast. Time slows down and I begin running. There's a bright flash and the blue pulse begins gathering at Beta's hands and pooling there before arcing outward toward Keane. Even I'm not fast enough to outrun electricity, but I have to try.

There are only a few feet separating me from Keane when in the blink of an eye, Iris appears in between the both of us. She's teleported in and is about to grab Keane, presumably to teleport back out with him, when the blue pulse reaches her.

Time returns to its normal speed just as the explosion occurs in a brilliant combination of blues and whites. I'm easily thrown a hundred feet. My hearing and vision both become foggy, like they're rebooting and slowly coming back online. I try hard to regain my senses and assess the situation. There's debris and dust everywhere. I can't find Beta in the sky, but after scanning the horizon, I spot Iris on the other side of the loading docks. She's facedown, her body crumpled on the ground. The first thing I notice is her outstretched arms, and what they're missing: her metabands. She wasn't fast enough. Beta destroyed them.

Keane's whereabouts are unknown to me, but my first priority is getting Iris out of here. She would do the same for me. I concentrate on teleportation, knowing that will be the quickest way to get to her since I can see exactly where she is. My body begins to disappear, but then blinks back into the same spot. I try again, and again I remain in the same exact place. Looking down at my feet I can see them begin to shift out of focus, but then snap right back into place with a digital artifact-like appearance, as though they're glitching or something.

Soon, I notice a much bigger concern. My metabands. They're almost down to zero power, and this isn't a good time for that. My suit is intact, though, and when I take off running, time once again slows down around me. I reach Iris almost instantly. At least that's still working, which means my metabands aren't completely depleted.

When I find Iris, she's still face down and still not moving. I kneel down and turn her over, afraid of what I might find. What I do find shocks me. While she's definitely hurt and parts of her clothing are torn and bloody, her suit is still intact. I'm momentarily confused as I try to wrap my head around what I'm looking at. The question of whether her suit isn't a part of her metabands enters my mind, but it's quickly dismissed when I see her suit begin stitching itself back together. Her wounds begin to heal right in front of my eyes. She opens her eyes and looks at me. They're still glowing pure white.

Her metabands are gone, but her powers remain. My head begins to hurt just trying to figure out what's happening. I must be hallucinating.

Keane. I turn back to find him confused and relieved that Iris isn't dead. Behind me, I see Beta approaching a wounded Keane who's sitting up against the steel wall of the Silver Island facility, holding his gut as though he's been gravely injured as well. I don't know how the hell I'm supposed to stop Beta, but I have to try.

Pulling myself back up to my feet, I start to run, except I'm not moving any faster than I would be if I didn't have my metabands on. I look down at them, fearing the worst, and find that I'm not too far off. The indicator light is blinking at me solemnly. They're used up. My limited power is being redirected, solely focused on keeping me alive and repairing my injuries. Still, I have to try. I have to do something, so I keep running.

Up ahead of me, I can hear Beta talking to Keane as he approaches.

"You're all out of friends, Desmond. This is the end of the line. It's time to pay for your sins, and it's time for you to pay in the only way you can't afford, with your life. Before I execute you, I'm going to give you the dignity that you never gave my family so you'll know when you go to hell that I'm a better person than you. Any last words for the world you're about to leave?"

"Yes," Desmond struggles to say as he hobbles to his feet, seemingly accepting of the fate he's about to receive.

My thighs and calves are burning as I run, struggling to get there before the deathblow is dealt. My powers are gone, but there's still a chance that maybe I can talk Beta out of this. That maybe, in the next few seconds it'll take me to reach them, I'll somehow magically come up with a plan.

"Do you know the saying, 'The greatest trick the devil ever pulled was making the world believe he didn't exist?'" Desmond asks Beta. "Do you know what the greatest trick I ever pulled is? Making the world believe I only had one pair of metabands."

A look of confusion crosses Beta's face. He hasn't had time to process what Keane has said, but he realizes very quickly that it wasn't good. He lifts his hands to kill Keane, but's too late. Keane already has his arms spread and metabands have already materialized. In another flash, the metabands are together and an all-white suit materializes over Keane's body.

Before Beta's energy can flow from his hands and outward, Keane's already sidestepped the blast and moved behind Beta. There's not a moment's hesitation as Keane wraps his hands around Beta's forehead and chin and twists. The snap echoes across the loading dock and over the bay. There's no sound other than the reverberations of the crack that signifies Beta's neck has been broken.

The surprise at what I've just witnessed causes me to stumble and trip, falling to my hands and knees. Before I can rise up, I hear a voice, Desmond's voice, over me saying, "Don't get up."

I can barely see him standing directly in front of the early morning sun above me.

"I appreciate what you tried to do, young man. Don't think that will be forgotten, but today's battle is over. Go home. Lick your wounds. You'll fight another day," he says before turning and walking away from me.

"What do you want?" I ask, not even sure if there's anything Desmond Keane wants other than just his own interests to be served.

Surprisingly, Keane stops dead in his tracks. Nice to know that a guy like him still has time for a little guy like me, especially since I just saved his life.

"What do I want?" he asks me. "That's a strange question."

"How is it strange? You just killed a man."

"Yes, a man who was intent on killing me. A man who almost killed you, I might add."

"Don't worry about me. I can take care of myself."

"Yes, that seems apparent. Tell me, how is that broken right femur?"

Well it looks like I'm not the only one with X-ray vision on this loading dock.

"It'll be fine, thanks for your concern, though. Answer my question," I say.

"What I want is all anyone wants. Liberty. Freedom. Happiness."

"You have all of those things."

"Do I? You tell me. You just escorted me from a jail where

I was held without trial for over a month. A jail where I was not permitted to see the sun, breathe fresh air, or have visitors. A jail where I was held despite there being no evidence whatsoever that I've done *anything* wrong. A jail where I was held simply for the crime of possessing metabands, metabands I legally obtained while the man who murdered my wife was allowed to walk free."

"That was an accident, and you know it was."

"An accident?" Keane screams at me, coming closer. "An accident is when you spill a cup of coffee on your shirt right before an important job interview. Putting a forty-caliber bullet through an innocent person's spine is not an accident. I would have cooperated. I would have talked to them. I would have given them any information they wanted, if it had been requested in a right and legal manner. If they had issued me a subpoena, if they had gone through the court system.

"But no, because I possess these bands, I was considered dangerous without any further discussion. And why? Because I chose not to don a silly costume and use my abilities 'for good,' as determined by The Agency? How I use my abilities is my business, not The Agency's. Not anyone's. But that's not how they see it. They see it as you're either with them or you're against them. And if you're against them, they're going to find a way to put you in a hole in there," Keane says, gesturing toward the main Silver Island facility behind us.

"I tried to play by the rules. I tried to keep to myself. I didn't choose to be one of those so-called heroes that cause more harm than good most of the time. Has anyone even stopped to think that maybe if these idiots weren't flying around the city 'saving' people that maybe there wouldn't be as many lunatics out there endangering people just for the attention?"

"It's not that simple," I argue back.

"Of course it's not that simple! That's my whole point. This whole damn world wants to make everything black and white. It wants to separate us out by deciding we're either good or bad. There's no gray. There's no room for anything in between in this new world. So be it, then. I'll put on a costume. I'll play by the rules. Now we'll see how good and righteous all of you really are when push comes to shove," Desmond says before moving incredibly fast over to Iris.

She's sitting up now, but obviously still badly injured.

"It's all right, sweetheart. I've got you," Keane says as he puts his hands under her, gently lifting her body up to his chest. Her eyes are only half open, but she instinctively puts her arms around Keane's neck to help support herself. His gaze turns skyward a second before he takes off with her still in his arms. They shoot straight up into the air. In another second, they're completely gone from sight.

I drag myself across the concrete loading dock toward Beta, intent on seeing if there's anything I can do for him, if there's even the slightest chance he's still alive. Before I can reach him, pain and the lack of metaband capacities overwhelms me. The last thing I see is the view in front of me turning the same color as the pavement below: gray. Slowly, my eyes close, and I lose unconsciousness.

Twenty-Nine

When I wake up, I'm in a familiar place. Well, maybe not necessarily a familiar place, but a familiar scenario: regaining consciousness inside of Midnight's headquarters. I'm on a cot, and my slowly recharging metabands are still working to help me recover and repair my broken body. Turning to my right, I see Midnight standing with his arms crossed, watching.

It's not like him to wait. Any other time I've been here, I've always seemed like maybe the third or fourth most important thing on his plate at that moment. He's always been at his computer or tinkering with some gadget, but not right now. Right now, he's just standing there, not doing anything except staring.

"Admiring the view?" I ask sarcastically as I lift my head and feel a tremendous pounding as blood tries desperately to reach my brain now that I'm in a somewhat vertical position. Midnight doesn't laugh, or move for that matter.

Glad to see that at least his sense of humor, or lack thereof, hasn't changed.

"Start at the beginning," he says as he clicks a button without looking over at the computer behind him. Presumably, the button is meant to start recording what he expects me to say.

"No," I say, groaning as I swing my legs over the cot and sit upright. My head feels like it's made of lead, and I can feel every individual heartbeat inside of it; they all hurt.

"I'm not telling you anything," I begin, taking a moment to let out a brief grunt of pain, "until you tell me what the hell you know."

Midnight's stance and posture do not change. He just stands there, staring at me. Waiting. He's a patient man, and I know I have no chance with him in a staring contest. So, I continue, whether he'll acknowledge me or not.

"You know something. No, not *something*. You know a few things, and you're keeping them from me. You knew Iris wasn't Sarah. You were sure of it. How could you have been so sure?"

"She was your girlfriend. I tracked her movements and communications. It became obvious very quickly that she wasn't Iris."

"Bull!" I yell. "Well, I believe that you followed her because that's your style, but I don't buy that that's the only way you know Sarah isn't Iris. I think you know Sarah isn't Iris because you know who Iris actually is."

"Even if I did, what makes you think you would deserve to know her identity? What makes her different than you? Why should you be afforded privacy and a normal, everyday identity to live your life, but she shouldn't?"

"You think I lead a normal, everyday life when I'm Connor? I'm referring to myself in the third person again for God's sake. Is that normal? What on Earth could possibly make you think that anything about my life is ordinary anymore? I'm basically on the verge of being suspended for skipping or being late to school, my girlfriend dumped me because she thinks I'm a coward, and my best friend would disown me if he knew I was a meta. Explain to me on what planet that would be considered a normal, everyday life?"

Midnight doesn't respond. Not at first. He just stands there with his back to me, and I can tell he's agonizing over his decision. I want to know. I have a right to know. He's on the ropes, and I'm close to finding out the truth. There's no way I'm letting go of this now.

"Sit down," Midnight softly asks without turning around.

"I don't want to ..."

"Sit down!" he shouts.

I sit.

"You want to know the truth? You want to know who your

little friend really is? Once you know, there's no going back. There's no forgetting about it or seeing her as you see her now any longer."

"But you already know who she is, and you don't see her as some horrible person, whatever it is. If you can see her that way, then I can too."

"Iris is Jones's daughter," Midnight says.

It feels like time grinds to a halt as my brain works those four words over and over in my head, trying to make sense of them. Anyway I put them together, though, it just does not compute.

"How ..." I begin.

"That's why she doesn't have metabands. She doesn't require them. She inherited her abilities through her father. Passed down through his metaband-altered DNA. The metabands she wears are a decoy. Simple aluminum alloy bracelets, nothing more."

"I don't understand."

"I don't expect you to. It's a lot to take in."

"And The Battle?" I ask.

"She had nothing to do with The Battle. I promise you that, Connor."

"How do you know all of this?"

"It's not the right time to tell you that, yet."

At this point, I've heard so many excuses I don't even bother to push further. Iris is the daughter of Jones, the man who killed my parents, the man who killed tens of thousands of innocent people.

"Is she like him?" I ask, fearing what the answer will be.

"I'm not sure yet. She has the potential not to be. She has good in her. You've seen that yourself. She also has whatever it was that haunted him in her too."

"And what about her powers?"

"I don't know everything about them. Not yet. That's the truth. I've been studying her since she popped up, cataloging all of her sightings and demonstrated abilities. She doesn't know that I know her secret. I'm not sure if she even knows her secret."

"I thought you knew her, though? Why did she help us take out The Controller if you don't know her?"

"I thought I knew her. I'd reached out to her, just as I had you. Before I found out who she was, I could see the potential in her. I knew there was something different about her. I knew whether she used her powers for good or for evil that she was going to be a force to be reckoned with. She resisted my guidance, insisted that she didn't need my help, because I'm not a meta. She said there was nothing she could learn from me. I haven't spoken with her since the showdown with The Controller. That's the truth."

"Every time you tell me something is 'the truth,' it makes me think everything else you've told me is a lie."

"I've told you what I know."

"And what about my metabands?" I ask.

"They're in bad shape."

"Thanks a lot for that, Sherlock."

"I don't know anything beyond what you know about their current state. I've analyzed them as extensively as possible, but I can't find anything out of the ordinary."

"The ordinary being that you can't detect any type of energy within them anyway?"

"Not necessarily. There are some readings I'm able to get off of metabands."

"Well, you're just full of revelations today, aren't you? I should almost get killed more often."

"The information I have about metabands, and specifically how they work, could be extremely dangerous in the wrong hands."

"I know, I know."

"You don't know. I'm not just talking about metabands used as weapons kind of dangerous. I'm talking about accidentally boring a hole through the Earth kind of dangerous."

"Oh," I say. That shuts me up.

"Whatever depleted your metabands was not just extremely powerful, it was specifically tuned to the way they work. Yes, it was strong, very strong, but no stronger than the energy you were able to generate when you put a hole through The Controller."

"So it can destroy metabands? I thought nothing on Earth could destroy metabands?"

"Nothing that we knew of. These metas aren't like any we've ever seen before."

"Metas? As in plural?"

"Yes. I've picked up similar energy signatures throughout the globe. Three to be exact."

"It's Alpha Team. It has to be. That was Beta there today, but according to Derrick, they're all dead. They were killed during a mission trying to retrieve a cache of metabands in Uskzil. How could they be alive and have this kind of power? It doesn't make sense."

"No, it doesn't, but there's one possibility I've come up with that might explain both of these circumstances."

"I'm all ears."

"It's possible that the members of Alpha Team recovered and activated the metabands themselves prior to the missile strike. If that were the case, it would explain how they were able to survive the blast. There's a precedent for metas surviving nuclear blasts."

"You're talking about Destroyer."

"You know your history."

"Are you forgetting who my brother is?"

Destroyer was a meta during the first wave. His story isn't that well known outside of Russia since the Russian government, to this day, has never officially acknowledged it. According to the story, Destroyer was a somewhat dimwitted local farmer who happened upon a pair of metabands and was quickly discovered by the Russian government. At first, they tried to integrate him into the Foreign Intelligence Service, intending to use him as insurance against the United States in case the Cold War ever sparked up again.

Fortunately for us, but unfortunately for them, Destroyer turned out to be even stupider than they thought. He's rumored to have accidentally killed over a hundred soldiers during training exercise accidents. Apparently, most of those accidents didn't even happen during training exercises. They happened during downtime. He was a sleepwalker and would activate his metabands in his sleep, destroying entire barracks. Even after he removed his metabands under their orders and put them in a secure location at night, there were still incidents during the day when his bands were active. He trampled other soldiers during marches, squeezed tanks full of commanders like tinfoil when he was asked to move them onto aircraft carriers, etc.

Eventually, it got to the point where no soldier would go near him, and no branch of the military wanted him under their command. The Russian government refused to waste such a useful tool, despite having trouble getting him to follow simple orders. A plan was devised to squeeze the last bit of usefulness out of Destroyer before they were done with him.

He was ordered to the middle of the Siberian forest for a special training exercise. A solo exercise, he was told. What he was not told was that the training exercise was just an excuse to lure him out to the middle of nowhere so the government could "safely" drop a nuclear bomb on him. They didn't do this to get rid of him, there are cheaper and easier ways to do that, including just ordering him to surrender his metabands. No, they did it because they wanted to see what would happen. The world's superpowers were racing to convince metas to fight for their side if World

War III ever happened, but also to figure out how to destroy a meta if the need ever arose.

The blast leveled a ten-mile radius and was seen hundreds, if not thousands, of miles away. What it didn't do was kill Destroyer. However, it did make him very, very angry. It took him a week to find his way back to civilization. Again, he wasn't very smart, but once he did return, he took out his full rage and vengeance on everything in his path. Entire villages were leveled, and cars were found miles away from where their owners had left them.

It wasn't until they found a trusted bunkmate from his early training days that they were able to stop him and convince him that the attack had not come from his own government, but instead from the United States of America. Destroyer immediately tried to swim to America to continue his rampage, but was convinced by his former bunkmate that he should take advantage of one of the nearby Russian rockets to help him get there faster instead.

The Russians blasted him into space and never looked back.

"The timing of the bombing in Uskzil could explain what you saw today. It's possible that the metabands were exposed to the energy of the nuclear blast shortly after being activated. If that was the case, who knows what type of effect it could have had. The time immediately following their initial activation seems to be very important, and is also potentially the time when the metabands are first programmed to the individual's DNA," Midnight says.

"They're tied to DNA?"

"Or something like it that we haven't discovered yet as a species. It explains the limitations of other individuals being unable to use a set of metabands once they've been paired to a specific person. It also explains how Iris is able to still possess her abilities without having a pair of metabands. The abilities are hardwired into her DNA through her parentage.

Jones's abilities could have been passed down genetically, inherited the same way you got your green eyes."

"But that's impossible. Iris has to be at least my age. That would mean she was born before Jones was first sighted. Hell, it'd make her older than the first sightings of any metas."

"I'm aware. It would mean metas have been around longer than we've suspected, living in secret."

"Yeah, I've heard this one from Derrick before."

"The timeline for their first appearances is hazy at best. There are lots of reports of sightings before the first one was ever caught on camera. Not to mention previously unexplained events that many suspect were the work of metas in hiding."

"You mean Bigfoot and all that stuff?"

"Exactly. Jones may have been around for a long time before he made himself known."

Suddenly, there's an alarm sounding in the room. The words "Incoming Media Alert" are displayed on all the monitors surrounding the inside of the water tower. A moment later, the televisions switch over to all of the major broadcast news channels.

"What is this?" I ask.

"If more than two networks run an identical newsfeed, the computer is set to switch to them automatically. It usually indicates a breaking story that might be of interest," Midnight replies.

The screens flicker past different channels before all arriving at the same feed. It's Charlie from Alpha Team, except he looks different. Enhanced. His military helmet and mask remain intact, but they've been streamlined. Somehow changed and enhanced by his metabands. His once baggy camouflage fatigues are now as tight as my uniform and darker in color. The fact that he's on TV strikes me as bad. Very bad. I doubt he's taken over all of the media feeds just to introduce himself.

"Residents of Bay View City. You don't know me, but I have looked after and protected you for a long time. I have protected this city from metahuman threats that you were never even aware of," Charlie says.

"What is it with these guys? Is videotaping themselves the only way they can get attention?" I ask sarcastically, trying to get a laugh out of a guy I've never heard laugh, because I'm actually terrified of what I'm about to hear.

"Look," Midnight says. The television camera is slowly zooming out, showing that Charlie is in what looks to be the city center, and speaking to a group of reporters who are gathered in front of him. "He's not hiding," Midnight continues. "He's out there in broad daylight. This isn't like the others who hide in their homes, ranting in front of a webcam. Whatever he's saying, he doesn't care who comes to challenge him over it."

"Recently, myself and my compatriots were tasked with returning a number of metabands to the United States from the hands of foreign terrorists. We were unable to complete this task because The Agency decided to terminate the mission before it could be completed. The way in which they terminated the mission was by dropping a nuclear bomb on my team in the hopes of eradicating both the metabands and the terrorists wishing to retrieve them. We have gone into every single mission knowing that it might be our last, knowing that we might not come home.

"None of us ever expected our own government to be responsible for our deaths, but we also never expected our own government to free a monster like Desmond Keane either. He murdered our families in cold blood, and for that he has received no punishment, no justice," Charlie says. He takes a deep breath, trying to compose himself after the troubling words that just came out of his mouth. The media that are present use this brief pause as an opportunity to jump in with their questions.

"How do you know he killed your families?" asks a reporter who happens to be loudest, getting Charlie's attention.

"How do I know?" he responds. "How could I not know? Our wives, husbands, and children were all killed within weeks of Desmond Keane's capture."

"But the circumstances of their deaths don't indicate foul play or that Keane was responsible," the reporter continues.

Charlie is quiet for a moment. The type of quiet that happens right before an explosion. He's trying his best to control his temper before continuing.

"Desmond Keane is one of the richest men in the world. He could afford anything, including being able to arrange for a series of murders that were all made to look like accidents," Charlie says.

"Is what he's saying possible? Beta said the same thing to Keane at Silver Island today," I tell Midnight.

"It's possible," Midnight responds. I'm dumbfounded. "I've been investigating their deaths on my own. The circumstances are all varied. Car accidents, suicide, drug overdoses, cancer. Not the typical M.O. of an assassin, but Keane isn't a typical client either."

"I'm calling for Desmond Keane to turn himself in to us within the next twenty-four hours, or we will be going after him. Additionally, we are demanding that all metas within Bay View City forfeit their metabands to us within the same time period or risk suffering severe consequences," Charlie says.

There are gasps throughout the crowd, and all the reporters begin talking at once, shouting questions at Charlie. Camera flashes illuminate his unblinking face as he waits for silence.

"Metas have no place in our society. There are no such things as heroes and villains within their ranks. All of them are dangerous. Look at the damage they have caused to our world. City after city where buildings have been knocked down, homes set on fire, innocent lives lost, all because of metas and the menace they bring. None of us has asked for this.

"The world was a safer, better place before metas. We know this. We've seen what the world was like during the First Wave. We've seen The Battle and the lives of thousands and thousands of innocents lost for no reason. But we've also seen what the world was like without them. That was the world we all shared until two months ago when they returned. I ask you, is a world of metas really one that we want to go back to? A world of cowering in fear every time the air raid sirens go off? A world of uncertainty over whether or not a meta who is having a bad day might kill you without discrimination or remorse?

"We have the ability to destroy these devices. You may have heard the news that we recently did so at Silver Island. For the first time since these horrible things have appeared, we have the ability to destroy them for good. To put the human race back on a level playing field," Charlie says.

"And what if a meta refuses?" a reporter near the front asks during the brief pause in Charlie's speech.

"Then their metabands will be destroyed by force. Our priority is eliminating these bands, and we cannot guarantee the safety of anyone who stands in our way. We will not treat so-called heroes differently from criminals if they do not abide by our demand."

There is another flurry of questions lobbed at Charlie from the assembled mass, but he simply ignores them and instead gives one last statement.

"Noon tomorrow. Leave your metabands here in Central Square. If you do not and you choose to stay in Bay View City, we will find you, and we will destroy your metabands. It's up to you whether or not we do so while they're attached to you. This is your final warning," Charlie finishes.

Immediately after finishing his statement, he turns his head to the sky, and in a blur of black and gray, he's gone, launched high into the sky. The TV cameras follow him before all of them cut back to their respective newsrooms for further coverage from the studio. The televisions in Midnight's water tower all mute themselves automatically.

"This is bad," I say, stating the obvious.

"Mmm," Midnight replies back, deep in thought and barely acknowledging me. "You need to decide what you're going to do."

"What do you mean I need to decide? I'm not giving into this lunatic," I reply.

"Connor, you need to think about this long and hard. These men can destroy your metabands with little more than a simple thought. This isn't a game. If you choose not to give up your metabands, I'm not going to be able to protect you."

"I know that, but I'm not giving up my metabands. I'm not bowing down to them. They're no different than any other meta. Once they've destroyed all the other metabands in the city, what's to stop them from doing anything they want because they're the only metas around?"

"Good. I was hoping you'd say that," Midnight says with a faint grin.

THIRTY

"You're home," Derrick says as I walk through the front door of our apartment.

"Yeah, I still live here too," I say.

"Really? I hadn't noticed," Derrick says as he comes over and gives me a hug followed by a punch on the arm.

"Ow, what was that for?" I ask.

"For not calling your big brother or answering your phone after he hears there's a group of psychopaths looking to kill him," he says.

"They're only looking to kill me if I don't give up my metabands."

"So, you're going to give up your metabands?"

"Hell no."

"Yeah, that's what I thought. Listen, there's some new information," Derrick says in a conspiratorial way as he waves me into his home office again. Once inside, he closes the door behind us. I don't think I've ever seen this door closed since we moved in, even when Derrick is on the phone, and I have to listen to his loud phone voice when I'm just trying to watch TV.

"What's going on?" I ask.

"So, I assume your buddy Midnight has come to the same conclusion I have about this Alpha Team and the nuclear bomb having an effect on their meta abilities?"

"Yeah. I mean, he's not one hundred percent sure about it or anything, but it certainly seems to make the most sense."

"Well there's another twist to it. I've been doing some research and talking with my contacts, and they're not sure it was The Agency that ordered the nuclear strike."

"What? How would that even be possible? If they didn't do it, then who did?"

"That's the question, isn't it?"

"Why would they let everyone believe that they dropped a nuclear bomb on these guys if they didn't?" I ask.

"I'm not sure. They haven't come out and officially said it was them. It's only speculation. Speculation that's been further fueled by Alpha Team stating that to be the case, but it's still just speculation. However, there are a lot of other reasons to stay quiet about it. Especially if The Agency doesn't want anyone else aware of others who might be tracking loose metabands and can also get their hands on nuclear weapons. That's probably about the only thing that could scare people more than the current situation right about now."

I'm about to ask more questions when suddenly I hear a very soft, barely inaudible click. I look into Derrick's eyes, and without saying a word, I can tell that he's heard it too. A second later, I can hear the creaking of the floorboards by the entryway of our apartment.

Someone is inside. I flick my wrists and summon my damaged, but still functioning, metabands. Derrick looks at them, then at me, and shakes his head "no." I begin to open my mouth to object, but he puts his finger to his lips to instruct me to be quiet instead. I don't like this. For once, Derrick's crazy paranoia seems to have been right. Someone is watching us, and we aren't safe.

Derrick's head swivels around the room, looking for something. He settles on a desk lamp that he quietly unplugs from the wall and grips like a baseball bat. I mouth the words, "What the hell?" to him, indicating that if he's going to have a weapon, then I sure as hell should have one too. He looks around the room again and grabs a coffee mug, which he then hands to me. I mouth the word, "Really?" to him and am again shushed.

Looks like I'm going to have to defend myself against whoever's out there with a coffee mug instead of my metabands. Great.

The creaking sound of the wood floors gets closer, and it's apparent that whoever is out there is close to the office door. Derrick looks at me and starts mouthing the words, "Three. Two ... One!"

He kicks open the office door and jumps into the hallway with the lamp held high over his head, ready to bring it down and crack open the skull of ... Veronica?

Veronica screams and puts her hands in front of her face, bracing for the blow from the lamp. Luckily, it never comes as Derrick realizes who she is and pulls back just in time.

"What the hell are you doing?" Veronica screams at Derrick. He's now dropped the lamp and has his hands up in the air.

"Sorry, sorry, sorry!" he says to her at a rapid pace.

I gently place the coffee mug I was about to use to brain Veronica back on Derrick's desk before she notices. No reason for both of us need to get screamed at, right?

"We heard someone come in and were worried that it might have been ..." Derrick trails off, realizing he can't say much more unless he wants to give away some of his secrets.

Obviously, Veronica knows that Derrick's a journalist, but it becomes apparent pretty quickly that Derrick hasn't clued her in to the theories and intel he's made me aware of for reasons pertaining to both our safety and the stability of their relationship. I don't know much about girls, but I do know that generally speaking, they're not crazy about staying up all night listening to their boyfriend rant and ramble about shadow governments and lizard people.

"You thought it was what?" Veronica asks.

"Just an intruder. You know," Derrick answers.

"An intruder? That's a little paranoid, even for you," she says.

"Wait. Veronica has a key?" I ask, not really thinking before the words tumble out of my mouth. Veronica blushes and looks down at her feet. Derrick looks over at me.

"Uhhh, yeah. I meant to mention that to you. You're cool with that, right?" he asks.

"Yeah, sure. I mean, you're paying the rent, so I'm not sure how much of a say I have. And I just realized that I'm talking to you like Veronica isn't standing two feet away from both of us."

"It's okay. I can give you guys some space if you need to talk. I was just stopping by to grab something I forgot the other night," Veronica says, looking for an exit.

"No, no. It's fine. I was actually just on my way out," I say.

"Umm, Connor? Are you going to, uh, think about that thing that we just talked about?" he says, giving me a very unsubtle wink.

"Yeah," I sigh. "I'll definitely think about it."

"Umm, and maybe mention it to our mutual friend?" he asks.

I give him a confused look since I'm not really sure who he's talking about. He makes his eyes bug out slightly at me, asking me to think a little harder, when I realize that he's talking about Midnight.

"Oh! Oh, yeah. Sure. I'll ask 'our friend' about it," I say.

"You guys are so weird," Veronica finally feels compelled to say, as she laughs it off and heads into Derrick's office, presumably looking for whatever it is she left here. Maybe the coffee mug? Hopefully not the lamp because I'm pretty sure that's broken now.

"Okay, that's my cue. See you guys later," I say to Derrick, who's still giving me a look.

Once Veronica is inside the office and out of sight, he mouths the word "Midnight" to me. I roll my eyes, exhausted now, and mouth back, "I know!"

"Okay. Bye," Derrick mouths back.

"Bye," I mouth, before realizing I don't need to mouth that. "Bye," I say again, but out loud this time.

"Oh, right. Bye," Derrick says, realizing the same.

THIRTY-ONE

Midnight sends an encrypted message to my phone, asking me to meet him tonight. This is convenient since I've been more or less kicked out of my apartment for the evening and going out to cruise the city as Omni just became a lot more dangerous. The unusual thing about his request is that it came with a set of coordinates, indicating that he didn't want to meet at his water tower. Since I've learned of the water tower, there's rarely been a time he hasn't asked to meet there. After all, you don't go through the trouble of setting up a secret lair inside a water tower if you're not going to use it.

It takes downloading a special GPS app to find out where exactly he wants me to meet him. It'd be easy to just send me an address or a cross street, but Midnight is rarely easy. He's also rarely imprecise. There's a reason why he sent me *exact* GPS coordinates, so I'd better follow them.

I decide to do so as myself rather than Omni. Midnight hadn't indicated that there would be any danger in meeting him, and being out and about as a meta is dangerous right now. The media is all over any meta they can find since most have decided to lay low after Alpha Team's declaration. Many have already left their metabands in a pile at the square where Charlie gave his speech.

The coordinates bring me to a dark alley. This does not surprise me; it is Midnight after all. It takes a few minutes to locate the exact coordinates he's sent, though. Finally, after walking around with my head buried in my phone's screen for a few minutes, I find the exact spot he sent me. It's on top of a sewer cap. So I decide to just stand here and wait.

I'm standing here waiting for close to five minutes, ready to give up, when suddenly the sewer cap moves slightly. There's a buzzing noise and the sound of hydraulic pistons.

Before I know what's happening, the sewer cap I'm standing on is dropping beneath my feet, just slow enough that I'm not in complete free fall. Within what must only be a second or two, it comes to a controlled and cushioned stop. There's nothing but darkness all around me, except for the small bit of light streaming in front the hole above me that I just came through. In another second, the manhole cover closes, and I'm in pitch-black darkness.

A few floodlights come on and I'm temporarily blinded. Midnight never had a thing for making someone feel welcome. A number of lasers scan my face and body before a disembodied computer voice says, "Identity verified, Connor Connolly." The floodlights shut off with a loud click and a moment later, after my eyes readjust to the darkness, I see a pathway illuminated by a series of footlights. They lead to a closed doorway, but I decide they're my best bet for getting to wherever it is Midnight wants me to go. Turns out my guess was right since the door slides open automatically as soon as I approach it.

Through the doorway, a short hall opens up to a gigantic abandoned subway station. The architecture of the place clearly indicates that it's very old, and the cobwebs and dust all over the place tell me that it hasn't been used in a very long time. I don't remember there ever being a subway station around this neighborhood either. So it's pretty clear that wherever I am, I'm one of the few people to have been here in the past few decades.

"Took you long enough to find it," Midnight says through the dark on the other side of the station.

I might be one of the few to have been here in a long time, but who knows how long Midnight's been holed up here. I've lost count of the various bases he's set up throughout the city, and I'm no longer surprised at the abandoned places he's found to set up shop.

"Yeah, the buzzer outside wasn't working. I think you

should have someone take a look at that," I say back.

Midnight doesn't laugh. Typical.

"Come here. I need to show you something," he says.

I walk across the station and through pools of light streaming in through old stained glass windows that at one time lead to the outside world. Now they just house makeshift work and floodlights Midnight has set up to make sure this place isn't in complete and total darkness.

"What is it?" I ask. "If you haven't noticed, today's been a little busy for me."

"I know it has, and that's why we have to put it to an end."

"Okay. I'm game. What do you have planned?"

"My intelligence indicates that Alpha Team will strike at Silver Island. Soon. Their goal is to eliminate all known metahumans from Bay View City. Simply demanding that metas either forfeit their bands or leave the city will only accomplish part of that goal."

"Okay ..."

"To fully realize their goal, they'll need to eliminate all the metas being held in the Silver Island facility."

"Why would they bother doing that? All of those metas are either already disarmed or imprisoned hundreds of feet under steel and concrete with their bands essentially disabled."

"They're also exactly the type of metas that Alpha Team hates and would be looking to make an example of. They're the worst of the worst, the ones who have killed and caused the most damage. Simply demanding that metas leave the city while allowing these criminals to remain in the city under lock and key doesn't seem to be their style."

"So what can we do about it?"

"We can make our stand at Silver Island."

"Me and you? What are you, crazy? I mean, I know you're crazy, look at where we are, but this is like next level crazy."

"I'm not crazy. I have a plan. I'm going to take them out."

"Like with a bomb or something?"

"No. By myself."

I'm silent for a moment, trying to understand exactly what he means. He's always somewhat cryptic, but unless he has a weapon or gadget he hasn't clued me in to before, I have absolutely no idea how he can possibly think he'd take on three of the strongest metas the world has ever seen by himself. It's right about now that I wonder if he actually is crazy. Before I'm able to raise an objection or ask another question, he seems to sense my apprehension.

"I said I needed to show you something," Midnight says.

He taps a few keys into a nearby computer terminal. Once that's done, a glass plate slides out from the console. He takes the black glove off his right hand and presses it into the plate. The plate lights up briefly, reading his palm print. Once it's done, another piece of machinery emerges from the console that was previously hidden behind a seamless metal slab. Midnight removes his cowl and the long cylindrical piece slides out and runs a blue laser over his eyes.

"Final voice approval," a computerized voice says over a speaker somewhere in the room.

"Midnight. Voice approval granted," he says.

As soon as the last syllable leaves his mouth, a series of pistons and hydraulics hiss all around me. The ground trembles slowly as the wall farthest from both of us recedes into the floor below. Even for Midnight, this is some pretty serious stuff going on.

From the area behind where the wall previously stood, the outline of a huge bipedal, human-esque figure emerges. As the figure is pushed out farther and farther into the abandoned subway station by machinery hidden within the walls, it becomes more and more obvious what exactly I'm looking at. It's some kind of robot, maybe about eight feet in height. The outside is painted matte black, making it hard to pick out its details even now that it's more or less in direct light.

"Holy ... you made a robot?" I ask, my jaw hanging halfway to the ground in amazement at this ... thing standing in front of me.

"It's not a robot," Midnight says.

Right on cue, the various sections of the robot begin to move and shift. Within no more than a few seconds, it has reconfigured itself. The front of the machine is now completely open. Every surface has peeled back to reveal the inside, to reveal space for a person.

It's not a robot at all; it's a suit.

"Okay, now I have about twenty more questions," I say to Midnight.

Again, as if on cue, although not nearly as cool this time, a series of alarms begin sounding throughout the subway station. White lights change to red.

"What is it? What's going on?" I ask.

"Dammit. I thought we'd have more time," Midnight says. "It's Silver Island. It's under attack."

"What are we going to do about it?" I ask.

"You're going to get inside. You need to evacuate everyone you can to safety. You're no good to me or anyone else if one of those Alphas destroys your metabands the second they get the chance."

"You can't take those things on by yourself. I don't care how impressive this armor is. They're metas, hell, they're *more* than metas. What on Earth could possibly make this thing able to beat them?" I ask.

Midnight confidently strides across the room to another section of the wall. This one appears to be simple, exposed brick. Of course, nothing is simple when Midnight's behind it, I think as he begins typing a passkey into the brick itself. The keys emit a blue light behind the brick facade with each tap. When he's done, one of the bricks slides out toward him, revealing a small drawer. Midnight reaches inside and pulls out a single, pristine metaband.

"What's that for?" I ask.

"It's for powering this thing," he says as he walks back to the armored suit and inserts the metaband into a previously unseen slot on what would be the front of the suit when it's closed back up.

The metaband clicks into place, and two small metal arms clamp over the top of it, keeping it in place. It's inserted vertically, making an O-shaped cutout in the armor not too dissimilar from the circle on my chest.

"You've figured out how to draw power from a metaband? Are you serious? No one has *ever* figured out how to do that! This is insane. Why didn't you tell me this earlier? Whose metaband is that?" I ask.

"It's mine," Midnight says.

Before I can respond, he props himself up into the armored suit. A series of braces and restraints lock into place, securing him. Once they've all clicked into where they are supposed to be, two long needles come out of the left and right sides of the armor and insert themselves into Midnight's arms. He winces slightly as they go in. The tubes leading up to them fill with his blood. From the guts of this machine, I can see his blood being drawn through various tubes toward the front, where it loops through the metaband via two small metal arms holding it in place.

The metaband emits a faint glow, and with a sudden burst of energy, the mechanized armor reconfigures and slams itself shut with Midnight inside. Suddenly, the eyes light up and the entire suit springs to life. It moves less like a robot and more like Midnight himself, albeit a much, much larger version of him.

"How the hell did you—" I begin before Midnight cuts me off.

"Get to Silver Island. Teleport inside, and get those people out. I'll do my best to hold off the Alphas," Midnight says.

There's more rumbling inside the station, and in a moment of confusion, it almost feels like a train is coming through the decommissioned tunnel. I look up and realize that the source of the rumbling is from the ceiling, which is opening to reveal the sky above. Before it's even fully open, two jets of fire roar out from the back of Midnight's armor, and he takes to the air, disappearing into the night sky in the blink of an eye.

I have to get to Silver Island.

THIRTY-TWO

"This is Omni, requesting teleportation coordinates for arrival," I yell into my communicator.

I'm high above Bay View City, looking at Silver Island off in the distance. Even without using my enhanced vision, I can see flashes of light and explosions from miles away. Midnight is already there, doing whatever he can to keep the Alphas out of the detention facility. My mind is still reeling at the fact that he's had a metaband all along. He knows more about how they work than anyone else I've ever heard of because he's been working with one all along. Somehow, that metaband was tied to his DNA; that's the only way to explain the need for his blood to be filtered through the band itself in order for it to provide power.

That's the easiest part to understand, though. It still doesn't explain how on Earth he was able to turn it on, let alone draw enough power from it in order to make whatever the hell he calls that thing he built work. It also explains at least some of the secrecy. If the wrong people knew what he had discovered and built, or knew that it was possible to tap the energy inside these bands like that, it would be World War III in no time. Imagine a bomb powered by that technology? As dangerous as some people think metas are, that would be a lot worse. That type of energy could destroy half the world.

Careful to keep a safe distance, I radio into Silver Island again requesting coordinates. This is the third time now, and still no response. On my way over, I called Sarah's phone only to be sent immediately to voicemail. I'm terrified that she's in there and not getting a response from inside the facility isn't putting my mind at ease.

I decide that I've waited long enough. I can't just hover miles away from the facility while Midnight fights alone and

Sarah's possibly in danger. It's time to go in whether I can teleport or not.

A few hundred feet from the facility, I have to quickly roll to my side to avoid a body flying through the air at high speed. I turn to look as it passes; it's Delta. I'm confused for a moment before I look back and see what it was that sent him flying: Midnight.

Midnight is a blur of motion, leaping back and forth hundreds of feet through the air from one side of the island to the other. He lands just long enough to smash a fist into a member of Alpha Team before turning to dropkick another behind him. Even with the bulky armor, he's moving with speed and fluidity, the likes of which I've never seen before.

Delta flies back and smashes into Midnight's abdomen, sending him reeling backward into a steel wall of the detention center. Midnight leaves a sizable dent, but isn't phased as he grabs Charlie, who is barreling toward him with a follow up attack, without even looking. In a blur, Midnight moves toward Delta and grabs him by the head, still holding Charlie. He takes both of them and smashes them into each other before winding up and throwing them as high into the sky as he can. Midnight realizes that he doesn't have a chance of beating all of them, but he can at least slow them down long enough to hopefully figure out another plan, or at the very least, get everyone else out of here.

Finally, there's a crackle over the radio inside my earpiece and a voice comes through.

"Request acknowledged, Omni. Teleportation coordinates are B-7," the voice says.

I immediately envision that place on the grid and concentrate on teleporting in.

"Wait! C-7!" I hear through the radio just as I jump.

It's too late; I've already landed in B-7 and can feel the ground moving swiftly beneath my feet. I'm high in the air and realize that the pillar is already moving into place to block out this coordinate. Within an instant, I'm already twenty feet higher, which means I'm just a few feet away from being crushed against the solid steel ceiling. There's no time to think, only to throw myself forward into the space now being vacated for C-7.

I hit the ground face first, but I'm alive, and most importantly, not a pancake. A moment later, a line of columns in front of me lowers, creating a pathway to the Receiving Area. A technician who I don't recognize comes running up to me, apologizing profusely. I tell him that it's okay and wave him off. There are much bigger problems to contend with right now, first and foremost being that the entire facility seems to have devolved into complete and utter chaos. There are Agency employees running everywhere as steel beams from the ceiling come crashing down to the concrete floor. Alarms and warning lights are everywhere, making it impossible to tell what specific problems they're meant to be warning anyone about.

But the worst part is in front of me. I can see through the bulletproof glass leading to the main detention center that the prisoners are out of their cells. A small group of guards fight against them, trying to keep them contained to the detention center part of the facility, but without help from any of the metas who routinely help out with guard duty, they're losing ground fast.

It's a full out sprint toward the glass wall, conserving my energy and only teleporting through it when I'm a stride away. I'm not sure yet what the rest of today is going to hold for me, or even for this city, but if I don't make it, I want to at least be sure it's not because I used up all the energy in my metabands before I needed it.

I launch into the air as I run toward the crowd of former metas attempting to fight their way past the woefully outnumbered guards. Besides conserving strength, I also need to be careful since these aren't metas; they're just humans. I need to make sure I don't accidentally kill anyone, so I quickly swipe my left band to bring it down to its lowest power setting.

Midnight's combat training comes in handy here. I have half the prisoners incapacitated and on the ground before the rest even realize what's happening. Unfortunately, I miss the one prisoner who *does* realize what's happening and manages to clock me in the back of the head with a fire extinguisher. This knocks my vision out of focus for a moment and the prisoners in front of me take advantage of the fact that I'm temporarily stunned to get a few more free shots in. Maybe I shouldn't have turned the bands down so far after all.

A fourth fist is just about to land a shot square on my face when I catch it with my hand, much to the surprise of the person behind it. A quick twist snaps his wrist, making sure he won't be trying that again any time soon. A front kick followed immediately by a back kick takes out two more. It was a lucky guess that *someone* had to be standing behind me.

Three more seconds and it's over. The prisoners are all lying on the ground, moaning and holding whatever part of their body happened to get in the way of my fist, foot, or head.

"Thanks for that," one of the guards says to me.

"No problem. We've still got to worry about getting everyone out of here, though," I say.

"There's an emergency access tunnel that goes under the bay and lets out in downtown. Most of the staff is in there already. The ones with half a brain anyway."

"Good. You four need to get down there too. There isn't much more you're going to be able to do here."

"Don't have to tell us twice. We'll get everyone out of here."

Most of the guards take off running, ushering all of the employees they can find toward the once-secret escape tunnel. A few grab the now incapacitated prisoners and drag them along. There isn't going to be very much time for them to get out of here before the Alphas bore through this place to get in. As it is, I can already hear them slamming into the roof above, shaking the entire building every time one of them makes an impact.

"Omni to Midnight. How's it going out there?" I ask.

There's a brief pause before I get my answer. "How the hell do you think it's going out here? I'm getting my ass kicked, but the suit's holding up. I'm able to distract these guys, but there's no way I'm going to be able to put them all down before they make their way inside. You gotta get everyone you can out of there, kid."

"What about the high security metas? How the hell am I supposed to get them out of here?"

"One thing at a time. We can't worry about them yet. They're a mile underground. Even if the Alphas get into the main facility, they're going to have a hell of a time getting down there as long as you and I are still here. You're going to need to ..." Midnight says, right before his transmission cuts out.

"Midnight? Midnight!" I yell into my receiver, but I don't hear an answer back.

My mind immediately jumps to thinking that the worst has happened before I'm jarred back into the present by a steel beam falling from the ceiling. It comes within feet of landing on evacuating staff before I just barely catch it above their heads. They quickly thank me before moving on their way toward the emergency exit, still in shock from what's happening.

If Sarah and her dad are here, I need to find them. I wouldn't be able to live with myself knowing that anything happened to them if there was even the slightest chance I could have prevented it. The first employee that I stop, a scientist of some sort, judging by her white lab coat, doesn't know who I'm talking about. While frustrated, I'm not entirely surprised.

Silver Island is a huge facility, and from what I've seen of it, they tend to keep departments as separate as possible. If it's not part of your job, you don't need to know about it or talk to anyone involved in it seems to be their motto.

The Receiving Area is the first place I think to look when I can't find either one of them. It's where Sarah works and where I've seen Halpern most often. So if they're anywhere inside the facility, that place would make the most sense. The Receiving Area is completely empty by the time I get back there, though. It's eerily quiet and the first time I've seen the place not bustling with some type of activity. Even when I've brought a bad guy or two in here at three a.m., there's always *someone* here.

It dawns on me that I should check underneath the desks up in the elevated computer den above the main Receiving Area to make sure that there's no one hiding under there or injured, especially since it looks like I might be the last one to check up here before the entire building is evacuated and sealed.

There's no relief in finding the area completely empty since that means I still don't know where Halpern and Sarah are. For all I know, they're not even here, and I'm risking my life and the lives of everyone here running around trying to find them. I'm about to leap off the tower and return to my search when one of the computer monitors catches my attention. The monitor is showing a camera that seems to be trained on an empty hallway somewhere in the facility. A hallway I've never seen before.

There is some*one* that I've seen before on the feed though: Iris.

It takes a moment of watching the grainy black and white footage before I'm sure it's her, and another moment to figure out what the hell she's doing. She's hunched over the floor, punching and clawing at it. The progress she's making looks to be slow, but she is managing to get through whatever this floor is made out of. It isn't until I look at the nameplate under the monitor that I put together *exactly* what she's doing. She's in the restricted high security section of Silver Island, and she's trying to dig down to where the high-risk prisoners are. The prisoners who refused to remove their depleted metabands. The prisoners' metabands have undoubtedly regained their charges and are just waiting for someone to come along to remove their restraints so they can reactivate their metabands and exact revenge on the people who put them down there in the first place.

Midnight put me in charge of clearing out this facility and getting everyone to safety, but if those metas get out, the entire city is in danger. I'm conflicted about what to do. I need to stop Iris, but I need to make sure Halpern and Sarah are safe.

After figuring this out, I'm off running again. The only problem is that I have no idea where I'm running. That part of the facility is beyond restricted, and the way down there is a closely guarded secret. I doubt many, if any, of the employees left here know how to get to it. I'm now moving at hypersonic speeds around the facility, careful not to run into anyone but ambivalent about using up my energy. If Sarah and Halpern are here, I need to find them now to get them out.

Three seconds into my run, I've covered the majority of the facility that isn't behind locked doors. The damage to the facility is deeply concerning. If anyone is going to make it out of here alive, they're going to have to do it soon. It's on the second pass through the facility that I finally find Halpern exiting one of the locked rooms that is inaccessible to me.

"Where's Sarah?" I yell at him. He's surprised and momentarily flustered.

"How do you know Sarah?" he asks.

"It doesn't matter. Where is she? Everyone needs to get out of here immediately. Iris is in the high security vault attempting to break out the prisoners located there."

"My God. I don't know where Sarah is. That's why I'm still here. We have to stop Iris or else there isn't going to be a city for anyone to go back to."

"How do I get down there?"

"Follow me."

Halpern leads me to a seemingly dead-end hallway where he presses his hand to a random section of the wall, revealing a hand scanner that authenticates his identity. I'm beginning to think that I'm the only one in this city that doesn't have a hand scanner and a secret compartment. No time to start feeling jealous, though.

The wall slides back and reveals a very, very long ladder leading straight down. It's so long that I can't even see where the bottom of it ends.

"This will lead you down there. The elevator down has been destroyed. I thought it was due to other destruction to the building, but it's obvious now that Iris must have done that to prevent anyone from following her. She must not have known about this backup ladder. It's the only other way in or out."

"Good. Find Sarah. Get everyone you can out of here. I'm going to do my best to stop Iris," I say before bringing my metabands up to full power and leaping down the ladder.

It's not worth the extra time it would take to climb down versus just falling. Another perk of being nearly invulnerable. Even with nothing but gravity standing in my way to the bottom, the fall seems to take an eternity. I'm not sure exactly how deep this hole is, but judging by how long I've been falling, it's *deep*. Most of the descent takes place in complete darkness before a pinhole of light below me grows rapidly before I fall through it and land on the steel floor below with a thud that echoes throughout the cavernous hall.

The first thing I notice is that, aside from the quickly dissipating echo of my fall, there is no other sound. It's too quiet. I look around, quickly trying to spot Iris. In front of me is another deep, but not nearly as uniformly dug, hole. It's the one Iris was digging. Approaching the hole, I cautiously peer over the side, expecting to see Iris still in there, digging away.

She's not down there, but before I have a chance to look around again, I'm falling in the hole thanks to a kick to the back. Before I have time to turn around, I'm already at the bottom of the hole being pummeled repeatedly in the spine. I manage to get onto my knees and launch into the air, throwing Iris off my back and getting out of the hole and back onto solid ground.

"What are you doing?" I scream at her while I regain my composure and prepare for her next assault. She stands opposite me on the other side of the hole, fists in front of her, ready to fight. "I don't want to fight you, Iris. You can't do this, though. These metas are dangerous!"

"These metas are people. You think they deserve to just be slaughtered down here when the Alphas break through the roof?"

"There has to be another way. We can stop them. Together. We can come up with something."

"No, we can't. All we can do is give these metas what anyone deserves: a fighting chance."

Before I have a chance to respond, Iris rushes into me with both fists in front of her. The force of the unexpected blow throws me hard into the wall behind me. I've never felt such a hard surface, at least as a meta. It must be made out of some type of metal alloy that's harder than anything else I've seen or heard of before. The perfect material to encase metas you want to keep away from the rest of the world.

Except Iris is still somehow digging through it as though it were sand.

Before I can stand back up, Iris is attacking me again. A flurry of fists and energy pulses from both her eyes and hands, battering me up against the wall. It's all I can do to summon the strength to block them momentarily in order to drop to the floor and sweep kick her legs out from under her, causing her to momentarily lose concentration and join me on the ground.

"You have to stop this, Iris. I don't want to fight you!"

"Too bad," Iris says as she levitates back into an upright position to continue her assault.

There's nowhere to hide and nothing I can do other than attack her back. I unleash a blast of pure energy from my eyes, sending her flying backward into the opposite wall. This only seems to faze her temporarily, and if anything, just makes her more determined. She doesn't seem mad, just set on taking me out. Not killing me, just incapacitating me in order to finish her job.

I don't want to kill her either, but I'm beginning to worry that this fight will escalate to the point where that's the only option other than to surrender, or if one of us kills the other accidentally. I need to do everything I can to get her to give up before we cross either of those bridges.

Iris stands up slowly and adjusts her neck. She begins running at me, and I don't back down. She's faster than she was before. I'm not sure if she was holding back earlier, or if something else happened. She throws a punch that I try to dodge, but it's no use. It feels like she's knocked my jaw clean off my face. The flurry of punches doesn't stop. Hundreds of them are coming at me at the speed of sound, pummeling my face and abdomen. There's no hope in blocking them, and it seems like she's not going to stop until I'm incapacitated.

There's a split second hesitation on her part, and I take

advantage of it, delivering a head-butt directly to her nose as hard as I possibly can. This sends her flying back across the hall. It's a dirty move, and I immediately regret it, but I need to stop her.

Before she can get back on her feet, I fly across the room and pivot behind her, putting my arms through hers and behind her head into a submission hold where she can't reach me.

"Iris, please. Just stop, we can figure this out, together. I don't want to do this," I plead.

There's no response from her, or at least not a verbal one. Instead, I'm answered with a swift blow from the back of her head right into my chin, causing me to let go of my hold over her.

That's when I notice her entire body beginning to glow and pulsate in a way I've never seen before. Not from her or any known meta. Suddenly, I feel very dizzy and disoriented. The walls look like they're melting. It's the last thing I see before I black out.

"Come on, wake up!" a voice says to me as I slowly regain consciousness.

I lift my head and try to focus through a gray haze of fogginess. Everything hurts as though I've been hit by a truck. My ears are ringing, but in front of me, I see Sarah's face yelling at me to get up.

"You have to get out of here!"

She's not actually here, though. Instead, I'm seeing her face through a monitor in the wall in-between two other monitors displaying emergency evacuation information in white text on a flashing red background.

"How?" I ask her, not necessarily about what she's telling me, but more of a general "how" in regard to everything that's happening right now.

"There's a hole in the facility's Faraday cage if you can still teleport," she says.

It's then that I notice a shaft of sunlight cutting through the concrete and steel dust in the air, hitting the ground in front of me. This must be the remnants of how Iris and the other metas were able to get out.

"What happened?" I ask as I struggle to get myself to my feet.

"That meta freed the high security captives. I was in the escape tunnel when I got the alert and saw you on the cameras. You have to get out of there; the entire facility is about to collapse."

"I have to talk to Midnight," I say as I reach for the communicator in my ear.

"Radio transmissions won't work down there. You have to leave, now!" Sarah yells.

I don't ask again and begin crawling on my stomach toward the light. My metabands are still in place, but extremely low on energy. There won't be enough power to repair my injuries and teleport out of here so I choose the latter for now; I can worry about fixing all these broken bones later. They're not going anywhere.

"Come on, hurry!" Sarah yells, her face shaking as she runs while holding the mobile phone she's using to patch into Silver Island's systems.

There're only a few more feet to go, but they feel like miles. I hear a low rumble from above, and more dust and rocks fall through the hole.

"The facility is collapsing, Omni. You have to get out of there now! Just teleport anywhere; it doesn't matter, but you need to leave now!"

"Okay, okay. I heard you the first time."

If almost getting killed wasn't bad enough, now I've got my ex screaming at me too. Today's lining up to be an all-time high. Only another foot to go. I struggle to reach my hand toward the beam of light that's slowly beginning to darken and shrink as the building collapses. All I need is a line of sight to get out of here, just enough of a connection with the outside world to teleport. My fingers are outstretched as far as they'll go; the low rumbling above me is getting louder and closer. Screaming in pain, I push down on my broken right foot and lean forward ever so slightly. It's enough to reach out and touch the sunlight and establish a connection.

I concentrate the last remaining bit of energy I have left on teleporting and think of the first and most familiar place I can: home.

THIRTY-THREE

When I thought about where I was going to teleport, I did what I always do: I imagine the area about five feet above where I actually want to land. This ensures that I don't wind up with my feet inside the floor or a toilet. Usually, this works really well for me. All of my limbs are still attached and none have ever found themselves stuck inside other matter occupying the same space, which is a sure recipe for an amputation.

The problem with teleporting this time is that it takes almost everything I have left. When I pop back into existence at home, five feet in the air of the living room, I'm neither upright nor am I able to hover in the air before gently easing myself down to the ground. Instead, I wind up crashing directly onto the coffee table. It shatters into a million pieces of glass and wood under the pressure of my full weight coming down on it. Normally, that wouldn't hurt when I'm wearing my metabands, but since they're almost completely dead, it hurts like hell.

I roll onto my back and off the larger shards of broken glass. I'm cut and bleeding, but the wounds seem to be mostly superficial. Thankfully, nothing is deep enough that I'll need stitches, because I'd have a hell of a time trying to explain what happened and why I'm wearing this suit to an emergency room doctor.

"Connor!" Derrick yells from the hallway inside the apartment as he rushes toward the sound of my fall.

I'm only able to groan in recognition. He's already on his way; no need to put too much effort into speaking right now.

"Oh my God, what happened to you?" he yells from the entryway once he's seen what I look like.

"Had a little accident," I reply, still trying to move my body into a position where it doesn't feel like every muscle is on fire.

"We have to get you help, Omni," Derrick says.

"No, I don't need any help. I just need to power back down, and I'll be okay. The bands need to charge before they can heal me, and they can't do that while I've got them active. Why are you calling me Omni?" I say, taking my arms up across my chest to bring my metabands together and deactivate them.

"Wait!" Derrick yells, but it's too late.

I've already turned off the bands. The deep red Omni suit retreats back into the bands, and I'm once again a sixteen year old. The wounds are still there, but already beginning to close up now that the metabands can direct their full attention and energy to just putting me back together again.

"Hi Connor," a voice says from the hallway Derrick just came from.

I don't recognize it at first, and I almost don't want to turn around to see who it is. The thought briefly enters my mind to just reactivate the bands and try to teleport back out of here to try to avoid exposing my identity. The thought only lasts an instant before I realize that whoever it is just saw everything anyway.

I turn my head to look and find Veronica leaning up against the entryway, her arms crossed in front of her, watching. She doesn't look nearly as surprised as she should, considering what she presumably just witnessed.

"I know what this looks like, but it's not. I can explain everything, Veronica," Derrick says, working his way from my side back to his feet.

He's already doing that stutter thing he does when he's nervous and frantically stalling for time, hoping that his brain will come up with the perfect elaborate lie to make this not look like a metahuman just teleported into the living room, and then changed into her boyfriend's brother.

"Yeah, Derrick will explain everything," I say, putting my

right hand down on the ground as leverage to lift myself onto my feet as well.

After what I've just been through, there's no way I'm in any kind of mental shape to come up with the kind of elaborate lie covering this up would take. Better to let Derrick try his hand at it instead.

"Derrick, it's okay. I already understand," Veronica calmly says to Derrick before he's able to make his way back across the living room toward her.

"No, no, no, no, no. I mean I'm sure you think you understand based on what this looks like, but it's not. It's just a joke. A trick. You see, Connor is friends with one of those metas and he, um, used his powers you see, to, um, make it look like Connor was a meta himself, but, um, really the whole time he was—"

"Derrick. Shhh. It's all right. You don't need to make up some story. I know what's happening. I know what Connor is. I've suspected it for a long time, and I need to be honest with you. Well, with both of you. My name isn't Veronica," she says.

"It isn't?" Derrick asks.

I've already flicked my wrists out and am ready to reactivate my bands. They may not have much juice left in them, but Veronica isn't who she said she was, and usually that's a bad start.

"My name is Michelle Hunt. I've suspected what Connor is for a long time, and it's the whole reason I'm here in the first place. We've been following you for a long time, Connor. Waiting to see with our own eyes if you are actually what we thought you were," the woman who up until two seconds ago I knew as Veronica says.

"How did you know?" I ask, stalling for time myself now.

If Michelle's intentions are bad, like I think, I could use all the time I can get for my bands to recharge before I take her on. Asking questions always seems to stall bad guys for just long enough in the movies, so it's worth a shot.

"School records, cell phone tracking data, social media usage. All of these things were flagged for signs of erratic behavior typically associated with leading dual identity lifestyles. Your brother's interest and knowledge of metahumans was also another gigantic red flag. From there, it was just a matter of tracking you long enough in order to confirm it. You're good. A lot better than most at hiding what you really are."

Just enough time. I feel my metabands hit the minimum level of recharge they need to reactivate, and without hesitation, I swing my arms together to activate them, except my wrists don't meet. Michelle has her hand in-between them, stopping them from touching.

"Connor, I'm not here to hurt you, take you in, or anything like that. I'm here to recruit you," Michelle says.

"Wait, so you were lying to me the whole time?" Derrick blurts out, finally joining the conversation.

"Shh. Quiet, Derrick. Recruit me for what?" I say. Derrick. Always interrupting.

"We're putting together a program. A kind of school, if you will. We were hoping to have more time, but the release of the high security metas at Silver Island today, along with the threat of the Alphas still being out there, has led us to move up our time frame."

"To when? For what?" I ask.

"To now. So I need to know, right now. Are you in?"

Thank you so much for taking the time read my book. If you enjoyed it and would like to leave a review about it on whatever Internet website you bought it from it would mean the absolute world to me and make sure that there's more. The whole reason this book even exists is due to the amazing readers who supported Meta with reviews and telling their friends, so thank you, thank you, thank you.

To stay in the loop on all things 'Meta' and otherwise with me, please sign up for my mailing list at tomreynolds.com/list. You'll get the first chapters of any new books before anyone else and other fun stuff early. No spam either, I promise.

You can find my online elsewhere at the following, or you can email me at tom@tomreynolds.com. Don't be a stranger!

Internet: tomreynolds.com
Twitter: @tomreynolds
Instagram: instagram.com/tomreynolds
Facebook: facebook.com/sometomreynolds
Podcast: tcgte.com

About the Author

Tom Reynolds lives in Brooklyn, NY with a dog named Ginger who despite being illiterate proved to be a really great late night writing partner. The Second Wave is, conveniently, his second book. He wrote this biography in the third person, unlike his books.

Also by Tom Reynolds

96906109R00173

Made in the USA
Lexington, KY
24 August 2018